Praise for Gardenias for Breakfast

"A good story touches us. The best stories change us. *Gardenias for Breakfast* captures the strange dance mothers and daughters do, morphs it into a rhythm our own hearts recognize, then lets it free. Robin Gunn's best story not only changes who we think we are, but through a mirror of hope, it changes who we think our mothers and daughters may become."

— Anne de Graaf, Christy Award-winning author and author of *Into the Nevernight*

"Robin Gunn's storytelling is a breath of fresh air. Sit back and let yourself be drawn into the world of *Gardenias for Breakfast.* You won't be sorry."

— Karen Kingsbury, bestselling author of *One Tuesday Morning, Oceans Apart,* and the Redemption Series

"Settle into your favorite chair and indulge yourself with *Gardenias for Breakfast,* a warm and gentle novel about grandmothers, mothers, and daughters. You'll be glad you did!"

— Robin Lee Hatcher, author of *Beyond the Shadows* and *The Victory Club*

Gardenias for Breakfast

Gardenias for Breakfast

Robin Jones Gunn

WestBow
Press
A Division of Thomas Nelson Publishers
Since 1798

Published by WestBow Press, a division of Thomas Nelson, Inc., P.O. Box 141000, Nashville, Tennessee, 37214.

Published in association with Janet Kobobel Grant, Books & Such Literary Agency, 4788 Carissa Ave., Santa Rosa, CA 95405.

WestBow Press books may be purchased in bulk for educational, business, fundraising, or sales promotional use. For information, please email SpecialMarkets@ThomasNelson.com.

Publisher's Note: This novel is a work of fiction. Names, characters, places, and incidents are either products of the author's imagination or are used fictitiously. All characters are fictional, and any similarity to people living or dead is purely coincidental.

ISBN 0-7394-4956-7

Printed in the United States of America

TO THE THREE
GARDENIA WOMEN IN MY LIFE.

In memory of my grandmother,
Great Lady Gertrude, who taught me how
to make my memories beautiful;

my mother, Barbara, who taught me how
to make my home beautiful;

and my daughter, Rachel,
who is teaching me how to make
my words beautiful.

Because of the three of you,
my story came and found me.

Jesus said, "Daughter, you took a risk trusting me, and now you're healed and whole. Live well, live blessed!"

—Luke 8:48

Prologue

Everybody has a story. You listen to their story, Honeygirl, and your story will come find you."

I was twelve the summer my grandmother gave me those words. She touched my flushed cheek with her small, soft hands and kissed the end of my freckled nose. We were sitting on her porch swing, listening to the lush Louisiana twilight being beckoned to our corner of the world by the crickets' persistent chitter-buzz.

I think I remember that moment so clearly not because of Grand Lady's words but because of her touch. For years she had given me words. Every year on my birthday she had sent me a book. Each Christmas she had sent me a handwritten poem along with a pair of pink slippers. But on this rare occasion when I sat beside Grand Lady and she gave me her soft touch along with her words, I felt blessed by some sort of beauty that was larger than life.

Last spring, my daughter turned twelve, and I had only one wish. I wanted Hannah to go to Louisiana, as

I had when I was her age. I wanted my ninety-two-year-old Grand Lady to touch Hannah's face and to give her the soft words that would go inside and bless her. I wanted Hannah to know the same mysterious beauty that had filled a solitary place in my spirit with hope.

No one, not even my husband, knew about my secret wish. If I had told Tom, he would have tried to scrape together the money, and I knew we didn't have it. We own a small business on a small island. The island of Maui. Yes, we are blessed to live there. We realize that. Visitors from around the world come to our shop to rent snorkel gear and tell us if they lived here they would never want to leave. I didn't want to leave for good. Only for a week or so.

Then an unexpected twist caused my wish to come true.

The day school ended for the summer, Hannah and I took off on our adventure. We drove hundreds of miles with Arizona sunsets in the rearview mirror and Texas thunderstorms through the windshield. We arrived in Louisiana on a sultry summer's eve, and I felt as if we had stepped into a dream. Everything was familiar: the Big House, the cemetery, the Piggly Wiggly, even the pew where we sat beside Grand Lady on Sunday morning and I slipped my grown hand into hers.

Hannah shucked corn at Mr. Joe's fruit stand and ventured into the attic where she discovered Aunt Peg's sixty-year-old mothballed gowns. My sweet girl gathered gardenias by the basketful and wore them in her hair the night she lit up the evening sky with sparklers. We drank Southern sweet tea like humming-birds and ate enough Louisiana black-eyed peas to last us for a good long while.

Then one afternoon, when I wasn't looking, Grand Lady touched my Hannah's face and gave her words that crushed her.

That was the day my story came and found me.

Chapter 1

May Day is Lei Day in Hawaii.

On the island of Oahu, the outstretched arms on the giant statue of King Kamehameha the Great are looped with hundreds of trailing leis made from delicate, golden *'ilima* flowers. These tiny blossoms resemble the feathers of the now-extinct *o'o* bird that once were collected and woven into elegant, long capes for the royalty of these islands.

Kamehameha the Great is remembered as a strong warrior who united the Hawaiian Islands. He and his descendants are still honored by the people of Hawaii. Whenever I see his statue draped with those fragrant flowers on May Day, I think of the great lady who stretched out her arms to me long ago, wearing a fragrant gardenia in her white hair. Her name is Charlotte Isabella Burroughs, and she is my grandmother. My Grand Lady.

I was thinking of Grand Lady on May Day this year as I arrived at the elementary school in Lahaina, where we live on the island of Maui. As a long-standing tradition, the students participate in a lei-making contest each May 1. In the eighteen years that I've volunteered as one of the judges, I've never seen a lei made from gardenias. I thought about how, if I were granted my wish for my daughter, Hannah, to go to Louisiana to meet Grand Lady, I would make a lei from the gardenias that exploded like popcorn on the huge bush by the Big House. I would drape my Grand Lady in fragrant flowers and let her know while she was still living that she was honored by her most enamored descendant.

Entering the cafeteria, I detected the faint scent of fried Spam and steamed white rice lingering in the air. *Must be Thursday. Spam and rice every Thursday. With teriyaki sauce.*

Two teacher's aides looked up and smiled when I entered. They were busy placing numbers in front of the leis on the long tables, so I hung back and waited next to the open windows while they completed their task. I was glad for a breath of fresh air. After nearly twenty years on this island, I still had not taken to Spam the way my son and daughter had after their weekly school lunches of the local favorite. I was thinking of corn on the cob dripping with butter and my Uncle Burt's hickory-smoked ribs smothered in barbecue sauce.

The gentle trade winds tumbled in from the ocean, treating the flattened window slats like welcome mats, wiping their wet feet quickly and asking the startled strands of my long brown hair if they wanted to dance. My hair, as usual, said, "Yes!"

I didn't try to stop the familiar tousled jazz routine but rather gazed out at the sparkling blue Pacific and felt a rising sense of wild-eyed restlessness. West Maui has to be one of the most beautiful places God ever made. I love it here. Yet sometimes I think I know every inch of this island. I wonder what it would be like to drive and drive and not know where I am. I dream of snow-capped mountains. If I start thinking about how small our island is or how we're surrounded by all that salt water—miles and miles of nothing but ocean—I can work myself into a respectable panic. I must confess this because, when I made my wish for Hannah to go to Louisiana, I think my rising bout of island fever factored into the wish.

Marilyn, the school principal, entered the cafeteria with several plumeria leis strung over her arm. She offered one to me with a friendly "aloha" and a brush of a kiss across my cheek. I received her greeting and flowers with a warm "*mahalo*," reminding myself why I loved to live here. The people, the sweet fragrance, the gentle aloha . . . yet what was it that was drawing me away from Maui to that place of my childhood memories?

Directing me to the first table by the door, Marilyn said, "The scoring sheets are on the clipboards. Remember, no conferring with the other judges until after you've completed your tally."

I had to smile at the way everyone took this lei contest so seriously. All expressions of art are taken seriously in Lahaina. Young artists have an assortment of talented mentors available to them as well as a variety of contests throughout the year designed to promote their talent. My own Hannah has won the annual Art Night in Lahaina for the best watercolor painting in her age group three years in a row.

Every year for the Lei Day contest Hannah would go over to her friend Pua's house where the two of them created their leis. That way I never saw Hannah's work ahead of time and couldn't be influenced when I did the judging. She takes her art contests seriously, especially when she's allowed to give her creativity free rein.

I scanned the scoring sheet and remembered the first time I had volunteered to do this. I stood in this same cafeteria and looked out at the ocean through these same slatted windows. That was the first time I saw a humpback whale breech. The beast shot out of the water, made a slight half-turn, and belly-flopped with a great, white splash. I gave a cry and pointed out the window. No one else had noticed the spectacle that day. It was the most amazing thing I'd ever seen, but I stood alone in the wonder and felt sure I would never grow tired of this amazing place.

Since then I've seen dozens of whales. Maybe hundreds. Tom and I often go sailing in the middle of January and watch the frolicking whales from only a hundred yards away. I have gone swimming with dolphins and sea turtles. I've seen more rainbows than I can count. I've slept in a hammock under the stars and sauntered through a bamboo forest. I dine regularly on fresh-picked pineapple and sweet papayas that drop from my neighbor's tree into my front yard. I've hiked through a volcano and kissed my husband behind a waterfall. I experience wonders in my daily routine that other women wait a lifetime to experience once.

In the wake of such daily abundance, was I crazy to long for the treasures of the mainland? Why did I crave the sight of fireflies, magnolia blossoms, or a forest thick with pine trees? Why did the thought of Cajun sausage sound so delicious at this moment?

The tall, lanky palm trees outside the cafeteria window rustled their shaggy manes, as if to scold me and to say, "The trees are always greener on the other side of the ocean, you know."

Yes, I know.

Focusing on the task before me, I examined the first three leis. They were all made from candy, a popular choice with the lower grades. Two were crafted from shells, and one was made from bones.

Chicken neck bones, I think.

I hope!

The budding artists seemed to get more creative each year.

About ten years ago, I was in agreement with the organizers when they decided that the students could use something other than flowers to make their leis. That year one student entered an octopus lei. The dead thing smelled so bad that even after we disposed of it, we had to move all the other entries outside to continue the contest.

No sea creatures this year, I noticed, moving on to the next table. I gave a score of "3" to a vegetable lei featuring radish roses spaced with black olives. The Ninja Turtle figurine lei fastened with rubber bands received a "2," and I debated over a "2" or a "3" for a lei made with colorful buttons.

My favorite was a lei made from lipstick tubes, bright pink crayons, and magenta bougainvillea. I don't know why I liked it so much. Perhaps it was the great balance of the bright colors or the added touch of the flowers. I gave that lei the highest score so far.

The final lei came with a clever tag: "U.S. of Lei." The designer, most likely a fifth-grader looking for extra credit in history, had drilled holes in puzzle pieces of the fifty states and had strung them together. All those states connected as one big whole.

Being dependent on boats and planes here on the

islands to go anywhere, I stood there, thinking of how people can travel from one state right into another state without even stepping out of their car.

Cautiously touching the dark-orange puzzle piece shaped like Louisiana, I thought of Grand Lady and whispered my secret wish once again. This time, my words sounded more like a prayer than a wish.

Running my finger up the jagged coastline of the California puzzle piece, I thought of my mother and wondered what it would feel like to be connected once again. Not with my mother. That would take a miracle. But what would it feel like to be connected with the rest of America? My America. I wanted to pick up that U.S. of Lei, drape it triumphantly around my neck, and see what it felt like to have all fifty states circling me.

My cell phone rang. My brother, Jon, who lived in Seattle, was calling.

"Hey, Abby. Glad I caught you. Listen, I have something to talk to you about. We're going to Europe again this summer. I have a meeting in Brussels, but then Patty and the girls and I are going to Paris and Rome. We're flying back to Atlanta and driving our new SUV up the East Coast and then home."

"Wow. Europe and half of the U.S. in one summer." I checked the tone of my voice.

"Yeah, well, you know. You gotta do it while you can."

I wanted to bite him the way I did when he was eight and had pulled off my favorite doll's head.

Handing over my clipboard to Marilyn with a nod that I'd completed my judging, I stepped outside and tried to sound gracious. "I hope you have a great time, Jon."

"I'm glad you feel that way, Abby, because our potential for having a great time might depend on you."

My brother missed his true calling. He may have made a small fortune working for a high-tech computer corporation for the past twenty years, but he should have been a vacuum cleaner salesman. He was good at shaking out all the dirt and making you stand there and watch him suck it back up.

"How would you and Tom and the kids like to drive our SUV from Seattle to Atlanta while we're in Europe?" Jon asked. "I'll pay for everything: airfare, gas, hotels, food. That's the only way we could think of to get our vehicle to Atlanta. What do you think?"

What do I think of a free trip across the U.S.? I couldn't respond.

"You don't have to answer right now," Jon said. "Talk it over with Tom and call us back tonight."

I managed to say "okay" and then returned to our beach gear rental store so stunned that, instead of enthusiastically telling my husband the good news, I accused him of contacting Jon and trying to set this up as a surprise.

"Abby, I'm telling you, I didn't talk to your brother." Tom lowered his voice so that the customer who was trying on sunglasses near the front door wouldn't hear us.

"Then how did Jon know?"

"Know what?" Tom asked.

"How did Jon know I wanted to go to Louisiana to see Grand Lady?"

Tom's jaw relaxed. "You do? When did you decide that?"

"On Hannah's birthday."

The customer left, and Tom and I were alone in the store so I told him about my secret wish and how Jon's phone call was just a little too perfect.

Tom nodded slowly, taking it all in.

"So, what do you think?" I asked. "Should we take Jon up on the offer? It would be our first vacation in a long time."

"Abby, who's going to run things if all of us leave for two weeks?"

"We can find someone."

"Who?"

"I don't know. What if we only went for a week? Ten days at the most. We could drive to Atlanta in a diagonal line. Through Colorado. You always wanted to go to Colorado, Tom. We could take turns driving. Doesn't the trip appeal to you?"

The squint lines around his eyes softened. My tall,

going-gray husband looked much younger than I felt at that moment.

"You need to get off island, don't you?" He sounded like a doctor making a diagnosis.

I nodded slowly and confessed to him all my island fever symptoms, concluding with the emotionally patriotic moment I had with the U.S. of Lei. "I wanted to put all those beautiful fifty states around my neck and see what it felt like to be connected with the mainland again."

One of the best things about Tom is that he doesn't laugh at me unless he knows for certain I'm trying to be funny.

True enough, he didn't laugh. Instead he said, "Well, then, why don't you go? You and the kids. I don't need to go with you."

"But Jon offered the trip to all of us. Don't you want to go?"

"Not particularly. Your wish was for Hannah to meet her great-grandmother; so there it is. Go and take Hannah. It sounds like an offer you can't refuse."

"Are you sure?"

"Yes, I'm sure."

For a moment, my husband and I stood in silence, gazing at each other.

"Do me a favor though, Abby. The next time you make a wish, try to include the words "Tom" and "sailboat," will you? Preferably a Hobie Cat." He winked.

I love it when Tom winks.

"Who's getting a Hobie Cat?" our eighteen-year-old son, Justin, asked, entering the store wearing three leis around his neck. Two were open-ended garlands made from flat maile leaves. The other was a short strand of dark, round kukui nuts. The leis were the type traditionally given to men who had a place of honor. My son obviously had several admirers at school this Lei Day.

"What are you doing out of school so early?" Tom asked.

"I decided to ditch."

Tom straightened his back and gave Justin a stern look. "What do you mean you decided to ditch? You have only a few more weeks of school before you graduate, and I'd advise you not to pull any stunts that could jeopardize your scholarship to Rancho Corona."

"Hey, I'm just messing with ya. Man! I thought you could take a joke. If I was ditching, do you think I'd come here?" Justin straightened a row of boogie boards that was leaning on the surfboards—the only two rental items in our store that our son treated with extra care.

Tom glanced at me. I was the one who always was telling him to give Justin the benefit of the doubt. We had a good son. I don't think Tom fully believed that yet.

"Did they dismiss the high school early for the Lei Day events?" I asked.

"Yeah, something like that. It was short schedule

today, that's all I know. So what were you guys talking about when I came in? Are we getting a Hobie Cat? To rent or for us?"

"No, we were talking about going to the mainland," I said with a smile. "You wanna come?"

"Maybe."

I gave Justin the details of my brother's call and watched my son's expression to see what he thought. Justin didn't jump at the chance to share the driving with me through miles and miles of southwest desert or to spend days and days in Louisiana with relatives he had never met.

"Would you rather stay here?" Tom asked quickly. "I can use your help."

"I guess." Justin shrugged and looked at me. "You're still going, aren't you, Mom?"

I looked at Tom, watching his expression, as I fumbled for an answer. "Maybe. Probably. I don't know. Hopefully. I guess."

"Mom!" Justin laughed. "Just pick one answer and go with it. Yes or no." He had not yet developed his father's good manners of only laughing at me when I was trying to be funny. A few weeks with me gone and Tom at the helm would be good for this man-child, who thought he was so cool with the girls.

"She's going," Tom said firmly. "Hannah, too."

Justin lifted one of his maile-leaf garlands and placed

it over my head, tapping my cheek with a kiss. "*No ka oi, momi.*"

Certain Hawaiian phrases have become as common as English in our corner of town. "*No ka oi*" was one of those phrases. It meant "the best." "*Momi*" is a pearl and had long been my son's nickname for me. In the way a ship is christened and named before being sent out to sea, I felt as if my man-child was christening me and, in his own way, was joining in with Tom's blessing to send me off island.

What my boy lacked in manners he managed to make up for in charm. I knew that attribute would be useful as Justin navigated his way through the white-water rapids ahead. He had splashed and crashed more than once on his passage from boyhood to manhood, but he had the feel of it now. I was confident that he would be more than ready for college in California by the end of this summer.

It was Hannah I was concerned about. She teetered on the edge of womanhood with a waterfall of transition waiting just ahead. This was her last year of elementary school. In the fall, Hannah would start at Lahaina Middle School. Last year two girls at Lahaina got pregnant and dropped out of eighth grade. Eighth grade! What would happen to my sweet Hannah once she was immersed in a sea of such preteens?

The rest of the afternoon I thought about my little girl.

This trip to Grand Lady's in Louisiana really was for Hannah. The timing was perfect. God-time. A God-gift. My daughter would find in Louisiana the same blessing I had found when I was her age. I could barely believe that I'd made a wish and that wish was coming true.

When Hannah arrived home that afternoon, her face was beaming. She has my eyes. Small, round, and cocoa brown with a dove's innocence. Her long, silky blond hair is her best feature, a gift from Tom's Scandinavian heritage.

She held her hands behind her back and gleamed. "Guess what, Mom?"

I gleamed right back. "You're going to the mainland."

"No. Guess again," she said.

I didn't want to spoil her surprise with my surprise so I said, "I give up."

"My lei won! First time ever. I got first place!"

Before Hannah pulled from behind her back the prize-winning lei, I knew which one she was holding. I also knew why I had liked it so much. Crayons to lipstick. Yes, that was my Hannah. Crayons to lipstick linked together by a string of bold, magenta-tinted bougainvillea as soft and colorful as a Louisiana garden full of ripe tomatoes.

Lei Day held for me the delicate promise of a wish about to come true. In a few short weeks my daughter and I would be greeted by the outstretched arms of Grand Lady herself.

Chapter 2

My brother sent a limousine to pick us up at the airport when Hannah and I arrived in Seattle on June 20.

Hannah couldn't stop smiling. She took to the leather seat of that ridiculously large vehicle like royalty. Twelve-year-olds must find it easier to embrace a princess frame of mind than a midlife mama who secretly harbors an inferiority complex whenever she's around her brother.

The driver wove through the early morning traffic while Hannah tried out a few buttons on the control panel next to her seat. With a click, a flat TV screen lowered from the ceiling, and Hannah was in cartoon heaven.

"Keep it turned low, will you, honey?" I didn't want to scold her for playing with the buttons, but I felt the compulsion to somehow correct or direct her.

I closed my eyes and wondered if I had any headache pills in my purse, or if I'd only packed them in my luggage. I was too tired to dig in my purse to find out.

We had taken a red-eye flight that left at 11:30 the night before and routed through San Francisco. Hannah slept some; I hadn't slept at all. Not a good way to start such a journey as the one that lay before us. It was almost eight in the morning, and I was a little confused over how this day would unfold.

For the last week and a half, Tom had been marking maps and making calls to relatives, asking if Hannah and I could stop by for a visit. I left a lot of the details to him because I was busy preparing meals to freeze for Tom and Justin, and packing for Hannah and me. According to my "organized" husband, everything I needed was in the binder he had prepared for me. Maps, schedules, phone numbers, recommended attractions. My husband, the armchair virtual vacationer, knew more about what I should expect from here on out than I did.

When Tom had taken Hannah and me to the airport last night, he said he felt as if he had been on the trek across the States already, due to all the planning he had done. He said, "I kept a map in the office so I can follow along. I'm going to pray for you every day. Have a great time and come home richer."

I felt like a '49er, off to strike gold. I imagined the gold flecks of pleasure I hoped to see in my Grand Lady's eyes when she saw my Hannah for the first time. That was the way I was going to get rich on this trip.

My brother, however, was rich in other ways, which

was evident when the limo pulled into his gated community and drove up a circular driveway to a grand, modern house. Wide steps like those found at the entrance to a luxury resort led to the front door, which was made of stained glass.

"I'll get your luggage, ma'am," the driver said, as Hannah and I stepped out. "You are expected, so please go on in."

Hannah tried the elaborate door handle, and we stepped inside the open, airy home decorated with black furniture with chrome accents. In the far left corner of the sunken living room was a waterfall integrated into a main wall that was made from river rock.

"Cool," Hannah said under her breath.

"Hello?" I called out timidly. "Jon? Patty?" My voice echoed in the openness. I felt as if I were in a nature display at a natural history museum. The recorded bird sounds should start any minute. I looked around for stuffed chipmunks.

"Maaa-omm!"

I jumped. So did Hannah. It wasn't birdcalls we were hearing through the overhead sound system but rather the universal call of a preadolescent daughter.

"Maaa-omm! Daaa-ad! They're here!"

We still couldn't see anyone. Hannah looked in the corners of the high ceiling and nudged me. "Over there," she said. "Do you see it?" She nodded at what looked like a lighting fixture to me.

"What is it?"

"A camera, Mom. How else would they know we're standing here?"

Jon came bounding in from a side room and grabbed me by the shoulders, kissing me on both cheeks, as if we were French and had been raised on caviar and cotillion dances at the country club.

"Abigail," he said in his best paternal voice. "Look at you. You look more like Mom than ever!"

That made me cringe. Not only because of his patronizing tone, but also because the last person in the world I wanted to resemble in any way was our mother.

"And this must be Hannah." He offered her a gentlemanly handshake. "How was your flight? Any problems?"

"No."

The limo driver came through the front door just then with our luggage.

"Is there more?" Jon asked.

"No, that's it."

"You two sure travel light! Good for you." He pulled from his pocket a tiny device that looked like a credit card and shot a thin beam of blue light at a box on the wall. "Patty, are you on your way down here? Girls?"

Patty's slightly flustered voice came through the elaborate intercom system. "I'll be down in a minute, Jon. I just stepped out of the shower."

Jon gave me a sideways smirk. "That means we have a minimum of half an hour to ourselves before she makes her appearance."

"I heard that!"

"We'll be in the kitchen, Pattycakes. Girls? Come to the kitchen and meet your cousin."

No response.

"They're on their way," Jon said confidently.

I wondered how he knew that. Did some other high-tech device make it possible for him to be the only one who could hear the voices? These had to be innovations from his company he was demonstrating for us. One of his personal achievements? I didn't ask, because I didn't know if I could absorb the truth if his answer was yes.

Jon led us to the left side of the house past a huge fireplace open on both sides. I looked over my shoulder and noticed that the limo driver had disappeared. Our battered luggage sat in the entry where he had deposited it.

The kitchen was a surprise to me, because I expected it to have an industrial look with lots of stainless steel appliances and countertops. Instead it was full of bright blues, yellows, and reds in French country style, complete with a stuffed hen perched on the counter. It didn't fit with the rest of the house, but somehow it fit with Jon's quirky tastes. Or perhaps this kitchen had emerged from Patty's preferences.

"Is that chicken real?" Hannah asked in quick surprise.

"Yep," said Jon. "It's a real, stuffed hen."

"Is it okay if I touch it?"

"Sure. Monsie? Are you here?"

When no one responded, Jon said, "I think Patty said she wasn't coming in until we get back from our trip. Looks like I'm your chef for the morning. What are you two hungry for?"

"We had a bagel at the airport in San Francisco," I said. "I'm okay. Hannah?"

She shrugged.

"Scrambled eggs," Jon announced. "I'll whip up a bunch for the gang. Have a seat. Hannah, you like orange juice? I'm sure we have some juice there in the fridge."

Hannah went over to the refrigerator and responsively pulled out a carton of orange juice. "Where do you keep your glasses, Uncle Jon?"

He stopped his search for the perfect, copper-bottom frying pan and gave Hannah a big smile. "Uncle Jon," he repeated. "I like hearing you say that, Hannah Banana."

Her expression turned to an instant grimace.

"Oh, sorry. You don't like that name, do you? What do you like to be called?"

"Hannah. Or Hana." She paused. "That's my Hawaiian name."

"Haa-naa," he repeated. "Okay. Like ha-ha. Ha-ha Hana. Easy enough. Glasses are in the cupboard on your right. Any food allergies I should know about? Dairy products? Peanuts?"

Hannah shook her head.

"Prepare to be dazzled." Jon cracked the first egg high above the bowl and then repeated the performance with the entire dozen. He added salt and pepper and his "secret" spice, which I recognized as basil, and kept Hannah entertained as he went after the concoction with a wire whisk.

I didn't know Jon cooked. Or at least he entered into the process of cooking as if he enjoyed it. Our mom didn't cook. Or bake. Her thin frame could live on air, like one of those little oxygen plants that needs neither food nor water to grow.

Jon and I grew up fending for ourselves in many ways, including meals. Maybe necessity was the mother of invention in our childhood development of cooking skills. Necessity was, in some ways, our only mother. At least in the kitchen.

The older of Jon's two daughters entered with her bare feet slapping against the polished, hardwood floor. She was wearing flannel pajama bottoms, a pink top covering very little, and a stocking cap over her head.

"Tiff, come meet your cousin, Ha-na." He over-emphasized the pronunciation, as if he had learned a foreign language overnight and was demonstrating his proficiency.

The two girls politely said hello. Tiffany was thirteen and seemed to have immediately sized up the situation and realized she had the advantage with her age. She covered her mouth as she yawned. "Did anybody call for me this morning?"

"Not that I know of." Jon sprinkled shredded cheese on top of the eggs.

Jasmine entered with a younger sister's expression of timidity. She and Hannah were only three months apart in age. Hannah was older.

Jon made complimentary introductions all around and then wisely put the three girls to work setting the table. None of them spoke, but all of them used their eyes like scanners to examine each other when they thought the observed party wasn't paying attention.

I was proud of Hannah. She had taken an all-night flight that left Maui only a few hours after her last day of school—the last day of elementary school, no less. This was her first time on the mainland since she was five and her first time to meet these two cousins. She did a good job all through breakfast of being polite and attentive.

When Tiffany and Jasmine finished picking at their

eggs and toast, Jon suggested they take Ha-na up to their room. Hannah willingly agreed, and I thought that she was made of sturdier stuff than I was when I was her age.

For my twelfth summer, I was shipped off to Grand Lady's big white house in Howell, Louisiana. Jon had graduated from high school a year early. Our father was ill. My mother didn't know what to do with me.

I spent my first two weeks of rural Louisiana life reading every book I could carry home from the musty-smelling Howell Public Library. With the door shut to the upstairs guest room of the Big House, I begged those novels to take me to faraway places, and every one of them obliged. Sometimes, when the temperature rose to sweltering in my room, I was forced to move out to the bench that circled the big magnolia tree. But that put me in plain view and frightened me.

Whenever any of my four boy cousins came near me, I wished I could put on a magic ring, like Frodo, and disappear. My cousins didn't read books. They went wading down at the creek where they caught frogs and snakes and sometimes spent the whole night sleeping outside in their pup tents. My brother, who spent his summer days in the garage building small robots, never had done those sorts of outdoor boy things. I didn't know what to make of my cousins.

"I am so, so sorry." Patty made a whooshing sort of

sound as she brushed past me, reconnecting my thoughts with the present. She lightly touched my shoulder before taking her place at the table in front of a plate of cold eggs.

I said, "That's okay. It's good to see you."

Patty was focusing on Jon, giving him an expression that silently pleaded for forgiveness, before turning her attention to me. "I do apologize, Abby. It's nice to see you, too. Sorry I haven't been very hospitable. It's this trip! I am not ready. I can't find anything! We have so much to do before we leave in the morning. Sorry I'm in such a state." Her frameless glasses looked crooked on her thin face. I hadn't seen her hair that deep shade of red before.

I smiled my benevolence. "It's okay, Patty. If I can do anything to help you get ready—"

"Oh, heavens, no! You've done more than enough just being willing to come all this way and drive our car to Atlanta. My parents still can't believe you agreed to do that. You saved the day with their anniversary party. Really."

"It's a . . ." I paused not knowing the right word. *Privilege? Honor? Treat?* I took a shortcut through the woods of pleasantries and came right out in the clearing.

"Listen." I leaned forward. "I really, really appreciate this. All of it: the chance to see so much of the States with Hannah, the chance to visit so many relatives. It's very generous of you to pay for everything. I want you to know how grateful I am."

Patty turned to Jon and said in a low voice, "You told her *we* were paying for everything?"

He nodded slowly.

"Gas? Hotels? Everything?"

Another nod.

Patty's mouth dropped open.

I stopped breathing.

A fleeting thought I'd had a week ago returned. My son was lamenting a surfboard trade he had made with a guy who worked at the pizza place next to our shop. Justin had ended up with the short end of the deal when it came to the value of the two boards, and vowed never again to agree to any deals without getting all the conditions in writing up front. I had wondered at that moment if I should call Jon and verify the details before activating his plane tickets and flying to Seattle. Sitting at his kitchen table now, I wished I had made the call.

"Jon, you and I should have talked about this more before you made such promises to your sister." Patty gave him a stern look.

I braced myself for the disastrous conversation that was sure to follow.

Patty glibly reached over and grabbed my sweating hand. She laughed loudly. "I had you going there, didn't I?"

I glanced at my grinning brother and back at his wife.

"Oh, Abby! You should see the look on your face!" Patty squealed. "You can stop worrying. Of course we're going to pay for everything!"

She laughed. Jon laughed. I remembered why these two were perfect for each other. I also remembered why it had been a long time since I had visited them.

Once the dishes were loaded in the supersonic, silent, garbage-disposal-included dishwasher, I asked again if I could do anything to help.

"Packing is pretty much a one-woman deal the way I do it," Patty said. "Aren't you tired after your all-night flight? I would be. Why don't you take a nap?"

"You haven't seen your room yet, have you?" Jon asked. "Man, we're lost around here without Monsie. Come on, I'll take your luggage up for you."

I willingly followed Jon through the labyrinth to a large, simple guest room with an inviting, queen-size bed covered in a white down comforter. The lull of the ocean surf was playing over the sound system.

"We thought the ocean sounds might help you feel at home." Jon was so proud of himself.

"It's very nice. Thank you."

"Sure. We're going to spend the day getting ready around here. I have to run over to the office for a few hours this afternoon, but make yourself homely."

I looked up at Jon with a start. Our dad used to say

that. It was his private little joke, and he used to mortify me with it when my friends came over.

"I can't believe you just said, 'Make yourself homely.'"

"No, I didn't. I said . . ." Jon looked at me with a strange shadow over his face. Was it fear? Remorse? Shock that I had caught him using that phrase?

"My point is, make yourself comfortable, and we can go over details about the SUV and the trip after your nap."

"Okay." I looked at him more closely. Jon even looked like Dad, now that his face had filled out and his hairline was receding from his broad forehead. I wouldn't tell Jon that I saw the resemblance. I was afraid he might turn on me, and I'd lose it. It was easier to keep up the long-standing tradition we had grown up with of pretending nothing was wrong. That's what we did as children. With Jon, I realized, I still felt like a child.

As an adult, in my relationships with Tom and others, I had always spoken the truth. And in so many ways, the truth had set me free, just like Christ had said it would. The truth was that our father dispersed his money to horses and greyhounds, begging them to run faster. But the ones he bet on never ran fast enough. He dissolved his liver by soaking it in a steady supply of gin. He disillusioned three people who were too quick to believe him every time he said this time it truly would be different. He died unexpectedly during Jon's first day of classes at MIT. For that, I think my brother never had forgiven him.

I was in Louisiana when our father died. My mom's brother, Uncle Burt, was the one who had told me. He came to Grand Lady's Big House in the middle of the day and asked me to sit with him in the living room. He took off his fishing hat, held my hand, and didn't say anything at first. I watched a big, fat tear bubble over the edge of his eyelid and squirm down his rugged cheek like a fishing worm trying to burrow back into the earth. I knew my father was gone.

Three days after we scattered my father's ashes in the Pacific Ocean, my brother packed up the last of his belongings and left for the East Coast. My mother and I moved a few weeks later to Lake Arrowhead in the San Bernardino Mountains. I started my seventh-grade year with a small class of close-knit students who called me a "flatlander" and had no spare envelopes in their stacks when they passed out birthday party invitations. Books were my only friends. The highlight of the year was winning an award for being the seventh-grader who turned in the most book reports during the second semester. One hundred and two reports. It was a school record.

I begged my mother to let me return to Louisiana that summer. But she was getting married to Stan in August and said she needed my help. In the midst of her giddiness over being pursued by a financially stable x-ray technician, I was a whisper in the hallway that could only be heard if someone was curious enough to come looking for me.

But my mother never came.

"Anything else you need?" Jon asked.

I shook my head, tossing off the long-forgotten misery and giving my big brother the warmest little-sister smile I could find in my scrapbook of memories. The past was long gone. No, I didn't need a thing.

"Hannah might," I said. "I'll check on her before I take a nap. She might be tired, too."

I found the three cousins in an entertainment room watching a movie on the largest television screen I had ever seen. I was glad to see it was a video I'd watched with Hannah before.

She looked over at me when I entered the great room. I motioned for her to come to me so I could talk to her. In a low voice I asked, "Are you okay?"

"Of course." She looked at me strangely.

"Do you feel comfortable enough staying here while I take a nap?"

"Sure."

"Now, Hannah, the same rules apply to the TV here as they do at home. If Tiffany and Jasmine want to watch something that's okay for them, but you know that Dad and I wouldn't let you watch it at home, then you have to be the one to get up and find something else to do."

"Mom, I know. It's okay. Don't worry. I know the rules." Her voice elevated on the last few sentences, and I was pretty sure Tiffany and Jasmine heard what we were talking about or at least figured it out.

I stroked Hannah's silky, blond hair and brushed a crumb of toast from her top lip.

"I'll be down the hall in the guest room if you need me," I whispered.

"Okay, Mom."

I left with a glance over my shoulder. I was sure that Tiffany and Jasmine were two fine young ladies, but I felt no warmth toward them and no sense of trust. I knew that was a terrible thing for an aunt to think. They were draped over the leather couches looking like the lifeless *akule* fish that Sam catches in Kahana Bay and splays over the mounds of shaved ice at Saturday market in Honokowai. I wondered if I should be keeping Hannah away from those two less-than-holy mackerels.

Finding my way back to the guest room with the piped-in ocean sounds, I kicked off my sandals and lowered myself onto the bed. I instantly was enveloped in poofiness. The soft ocean sounds really did make me feel relaxed, and I fell asleep effortlessly.

The worst thing that happened that day was that I slept for almost nine hours.

The best thing that happened that day was that I slept for almost nine hours.

My body received the replenishment it needed for the long trip ahead, but I missed out on a full day with my brother and his family. That part didn't seem like a loss to me at the time. It took many hours of thinking along many miles of desolate highways between Seattle and Howell before a simple thought whispered down the hallway of my mind. I had only one brother. And I had never been curious enough to go find him.

Chapter 3

Late that night, after my nap and a dinner of Chinese food that was delivered to the front door, Jon led me to their five-car garage and went over the features in his customized vehicle. He kept saying, "But it's not as big as a motor home," and "It's not as convenient as a motor home." I finally took the bait and asked why he hadn't bought a motor home instead.

He looked appalled. "To conserve gasoline, of course."

I wanted to laugh. But I didn't.

My brother lived in opulence, yet sounded sincere when it came to doing his part to preserve the environment. I wondered if extravagantly wealthy people lived in a different sort of reality.

At least his reality included an interest in organization. The SUV was packed with necessities he, Patty, and the girls thought they would need for their drive up the East Coast and back to Seattle via Chicago. Their

Eddie Bauer canvas bags fit under the shelf bed that took up the back third of the van. It looked like our not-so-brawny luggage would fit nicely beside theirs.

Jon had printed out detailed maps from one of his software programs. For my part of the trip, the directions were "suggestions" of travel routes. For his part of the trip, each day was planned down to the rest stops and the arrival time at each five-star hotel where he had made reservations. He even had information on which major highways were undergoing construction or repair and the alternate routes he could take. Between Jon's information and all that my husband had compiled, all I would have to do was start the engine and follow their directions.

"What time should we plan to leave tomorrow?" I asked, as Jon concluded the tour of the garage.

"Our flight leaves at 7:30 in the morning, so we're taking the limo to the airport at five. You and Ha-na are free to leave whenever you want."

My brother's household was a flurry of packing pandemonium until deep into the night. They burst out the door close to 5:30 with a lot of yelling and scrambling around. Hannah and I stood in the frame of the stained glass front door and waved good-bye. It felt strange to be standing there, knowing that Jon's kingdom was at our disposal. Yet all I wanted to do was get out of there before I broke something or set off an alarm. I had the creepy feeling that his voice might come over the intercom system from some device he had invented and had taken with him to Belgium. It was all I could do not to check the vehicle for cameras or special speakers. For all I knew, a satellite might be tracking every mile of our trip.

Determining that I would not become paranoid, I asked Hannah if she was ready to leave.

She decided to shower. I decided to take my brother up on an earlier offer to pack some food and make use of the small built-in refrigerator in the SUV.

We didn't leave until close to eight o'clock. I locked everything, using the directions Jon had left for me to set the security codes. I stored the keys inside the safe-deposit box hidden in the side of van and backed the luxury liner out of the dock, ready to launch her on her maiden voyage.

Halfway around the circular drive I stopped.

"What's wrong?" Hannah asked.

"I think we should pray," I said.

"About our trip?"

"Yes. For our trip and for Uncle Jon and his family, too."

"Okay," Hannah said. "Mind if I pray first?"

"Sure. Go ahead."

"Dear Lord, please be with Uncle Jon and my cousins on their trip. And all I ask for us is that we have fun. Amen."

I prayed for all the important things Hannah had left out, like safety and protection and wisdom and direction. I think a pinch of paranoia remained in my thoughts, because I found myself praying for Jon and his family as if he could hear me and would evaluate my prayer.

It should have been clear to me then that Hannah and I had two different views of what this trip was all about. But I didn't see it because I was nervous. Nervous about somehow damaging Jon's super SUV or messing up the programmed direction-finding system with the blinking monitor staring at me from under the center air-conditioning vent. I was nervous about getting lost. Nervous about being run off the road by a logging truck. For all my grandiose daydreams about the freedom of the open road, I now found myself cowering in the reality that lay stretched out before us.

Jon's computer program analyzed the route I would most likely take and printed out the following details: "Seattle to Atlanta—3,445.4 miles; 7 days, 55 minutes; 2 time zone changes."

Such reports can dampen one's sense of romance about an endeavor.

"Can I sit in the back and watch a DVD now?" Hannah asked when we reached the end of the street.

"No."

"When can I watch one?"

"Later. When it's dark, and there's nothing to see outside the windows."

She waited until I found my way to the freeway, and then she said, "What if I kept the headset on so the sound doesn't bother you? Then could I watch a DVD before it's dark?"

"No, Hannah. This trip isn't for watching DVDs. It's for seeing the world outside and appreciating the beauty."

Twenty minutes later, when it was evident she was more bored than any girl her age had ever been since the beginning of road trips, Hannah pulled out a handheld video game from the drawer under the passenger's seat.

"Tiffany brought this for her part of the trip." Hannah held out the device like an offering in her palm. It was as if she wanted me to see how tame and harmless the little creature was. "Tiffany said I could use it any time I wanted as long as I didn't break it or waste all the batteries."

"I'd prefer you save it for another part of the trip when you're looking for something to do."

"But I'm looking for something to do now," she said.

"Look out the window."

"I have been looking out the window."

"Aren't the trees beautiful? Everything here is so green and lush, don't you think?"

"It's like Kipahulu," she said, referring to the backside

of Maui where the annual rainfall is four times the amount we see in Lahaina.

"They don't have trees like this in Kipahulu," I said.

"No, but they have a lot of green."

She obviously isn't impressed. Wait till we get to the snow when we drive over Mount Hood. That will get her attention.

"Mom, Jasmine gave me something."

"She did?"

"Yes, but I didn't know if you would let me keep it."

"What is it?"

"A Discman. She got a new MP3, and she said I could have the Discman because she was going to throw it away."

I was about to say, "That was nice of her," but I wasn't sure if Jasmine's gesture was born of niceness or apathy born of her abundance.

"Jasmine also gave me a bunch of CDs and likes a lot of the things I like, and I don't think any of the songs will be ones I shouldn't listen to. So, may I at least listen to this if I can't play video games? I don't have anything else to do."

"Hannah," I said firmly, "I do not want you to spend the whole summer with your nose in a book. Do you understand me?"

"My nose in a book?" Hannah repeated.

I felt my heart do a flip.

That sounded exactly like my mother! Where did that come from?

"I'm sorry, Hannah." I felt shaken. "It's okay. You can listen to the music on Jasmine's CD player."

I could tell she was staring, waiting for me to add a final caveat before releasing her to so much freedom. But I had no such warning or condition. I felt the familiar return of a tension headache rising from the back of my neck and making its way to my shame-soaked brain.

"Mom?"

"Yes?"

"Why did you say 'book'? You said I shouldn't keep my nose in a book."

"It's nothing." I summoned a smile. "I mixed up my words, that's all."

Hiding behind my right as a mother to be vague, I drove down I-5 with my eyes straight ahead. Hannah put on the headphones cautiously, like a scientist placing her stethoscope just right before examining a previously unknown life force.

It didn't feel this difficult to be Hannah's mother at home. There, all the boundaries were in place. Here, on the road, in the wild, so to speak, we had to start all over to define the parameters.

Why hadn't I been honest and explained to her why I said she shouldn't keep her nose in a book? When will Hannah be old enough to hear about my childhood?

This didn't seem like the right time. My memories stayed deep inside yet played themselves out with such vividness that it seemed as if they had just happened. The memory started with a phone conversation I had with my mother when I was twelve. I had been in Louisiana for a week. She called to see how I was getting along. I told her about my new friend, Josephine, who worked at the Howell Public Library.

"Josephine introduced me to Charles Dickenson and Walter Scott," I announced. I wanted her to know that my reading ability had skyrocketed.

"Who?" my mother had asked.

"Charles Dickenson and Walter Scott. You know, *Great Expectations*? *Ivanhoe*?"

"Oh, Dickens," she corrected me. "Not Dickenson. You mean Charles Dickens and Sir Walter Scott." Then she delivered the line I had just placed on Hannah. "I do not want you to spend the whole summer with your nose in a book. Do you understand me?"

I got the distinct impression my mother would have been pleased with me if Charles and Walter had been two living, breathing boys who were teaching me how to catch crawdads at the local fishing hole. She wanted me to "experience" nature and reminded me that, when she was growing up in Howell, she interacted with the outdoors by sketching the frogs and painting with watercolors whenever they went to the lake. Her only use for books had been to stack them high to press wildflowers on waxed paper.

I pulled out of that sharp remembrance by focusing on the magnificent trees and patches of purple and blue wildflowers that lined the freeway. Washington was a beautiful state. Drawing in a deep breath, I released it slowly and told myself to relax and to stop being so paranoid and nervous. I wasn't my mother. Just because I slipped and made a statement similar to one she had made to me so many years ago didn't mean that I was about to morph into her.

Hannah and I were the next generation. All things were new. Weren't they?

As we entered Oregon, Mount Hood could easily be seen out my side window.

"Look, Hannah. Isn't that incredible?"

In the distance, clear blue sky formed the backdrop for the pyramid-shaped mountain covered in dazzling snow. Flowing under the elevated freeway was the mighty Columbia River, reflecting the deep blue of the sky. A speckling of white sailboats raced across the wide waterway, and several jet skiers headed for an island thick with towering evergreens that was in the middle of the river.

"What a view! Isn't this gorgeous?"

Hannah nodded.

"We're in another state now," I said. "Wouldn't it

be fun if we had to use passports so we could get a stamp showing each state we've been through? I think Washington slipped under our tires too quickly. We have to stop and see more of the countryside the rest of this trip."

Hannah nodded.

"Are you listening to what I'm saying?"

She nodded again.

"Hannah." I raised my voice. "Hannah!"

"What?" She pulled out one of the earplugs.

"We're in Oregon."

"Oh."

"Did you hear anything I was saying?"

"Some of it."

"Why don't you put away the music for a while? We need to stop for gas."

She reluctantly tucked the Discman under the seat, and I pulled off the freeway. Hannah looked out the window at the convenience store next to the gas station and asked, "Can I go in and get something to drink?"

"I brought drinks. They're in the little fridge."

"Did you bring any candy?"

"No."

"Then could I buy some candy?"

"No."

She slunk down in the seat and looked dejectedly out the window.

"I don't know if it's safe for you to go wandering into stores by yourself here," I said. "This isn't like walking over to the Whaler's General Store the way you and your friends do at home."

"I know."

I let her sulk and pulled out the map and schedule my hubby had prepared for us. I saw that, instead of staying on the freeway, we needed to head east to drive over Mount Hood. It didn't look too complicated. I guessed we would arrive at Tom's brother's house in central Oregon before dark. That was one of the nice parts of being so far north. I had noticed last night that it stayed light until nearly ten o'clock. It's never light that late in the tropics.

The drive up to Mount Hood was a little confusing, but once we left behind the populated area and started heading up the mountain, I felt invigorated. The temperature cooled. I opened the windows and breathed deeply. I could taste the greens of the moss and the fir trees.

"It's cold." Hannah reached for her sweatshirt in the backseat.

"Do you smell that?"

She sniffed. "What?"

"The green."

She sniffed again and nodded. "Smells like one of those candles you burn at Christmastime."

"Evergreen," I said. "But this is the real thing." I noticed she had unplugged herself from the Discman.

"How would you like to get out once we reach the snow?" I asked.

"Sure."

We both were in shorts and sandals, so when we drove up to the snow level and got out, the coldness stunned us.

"This is colder than it was that time we went up Haleakala for New Year's!" Hannah pulled her sweatshirt close.

A ten-thousand-foot-high crater on Maui, Haleakala has a paved road that winds around the mountain's side. Along the way there is a clearing where my husband loves to go on special occasions. Tom likes to watch the sun rise from the clearing because the view is spectacular. One year when we went up on New Year's morning, the clouds that often wreathed the great volcano were heavy with sleet. Shrill winds filled their quivers with jagged bits of ice and took turns trying to hit us with them. We got cold and wet and thoroughly slushed.

But it wasn't the same as snow. Mount Hood had real snow. In June. Amazing. A thin dome of ice crusted over the snow, but underneath that slick coating lay several inches of pristine snow.

I packed a small snowball with my bare hands and threw it at Hannah. She laughed and retaliated. My feet tingled from the cold. We had tennis shoes in our luggage but no desire to pull them out and put them on.

Our free-for-all snow war lasted a grand total of about four minutes before I thought to pull out the camera.

"Smile!"

Hannah struck a pose, shivering and looking as if she were about to toss a snowball at me. I took another picture of her scooping up an armful of the white stuff. Then I tried to line up one of the trees in the viewfinder. I leaned my head back. All I could capture was the top of the enormous evergreen and my breath as it came out in airy little clouds.

I snapped the picture and knew it was going to be one of those photos that, when I show it to others, everyone would say, "Did you accidentally take this one?"

I would say "no" with a contented smile, and no one but me would understand a slightly clouded picture of the top of a tree was a happy thing.

"Are you ready to go?" I asked Hannah.

"Not yet. I want to eat some snow. Is that okay?"

"If it's in a clean area, sure."

Hannah looked around. She picked her "clean" spot and stepped into the ankle-deep snow in her sandals the way she stepped into the shallow water at Kapalua Bay.

"Isn't it cold?" I asked.

"Freezing," she said with great composure. She cleared a small patch and scooped out a handful of snowflakes. I snapped a picture.

"It's like shaved ice," she said. "Without the flavors."

I noted the way she had been describing each new experience in terms of what she knew from home. And why shouldn't she? Island life was the only life she had known.

"Are you getting cold?"

"Yes." She stomped her feet on the road and jumped back into the SUV. "Can we put on the heater?"

"Good idea." I started the engine and turned the temperature control system to seventy-two degrees. "If I did this right, I started warmers for the car seats. Does that feel warm to you?"

"A little."

We pulled out from the side of the road, continuing our drive over the mountain and down into the dry, flat desert. The contrast in only a few miles was stunning. The heater and the seat warmers were turned off quickly as we opened the windows to let in the warm air. By the time we drove into Madras, I had turned on the air conditioner.

"I liked the snow," Hannah said all of a sudden. "Thanks, Mom."

"You're welcome."

"Thanks for bringing me on this trip. I always wanted to see snow."

"I always wanted you to see snow, too," I told her with a broad grin.

My confidence soared. We had made it through Washington without my doing any damage to my brother's vehicle. Hannah had seen and touched real snow, and she was happy about it. She was talking to me instead of begging to watch a DVD. This trip was going to work out okay.

"Where are we staying tonight?" Hannah asked.

"Uncle Nate's."

"Is that Dad's brother?"

"Yes."

"Does he know we're staying with him?"

"I think so. Dad said he called him. But I'm glad you said something, because I should give Uncle Nate a call to let him know we're going to be there in about an hour or two."

I used my cell phone, even though I had to pay a roaming charge out there in the barren, rugged terrain of central Oregon. No one answered, so I left a message telling Nate that we would be there a little after five o'clock, if my calculations were correct.

"Is Uncle Nate the one who got married a couple of years ago?"

"Yes."

"We gave them the ice cream maker, didn't we?"

"That's right. How did you remember that?"

Hannah shrugged.

"I'm surprised you remember. That was two years ago."

"I remember because you asked Dad what his brother liked, and he said, 'Ice cream.' So you bought an ice cream maker, and then you and Dad got in a fight about it because he said you should have just sent money, and you cried and told him the next time his brother got married, Dad could be in charge of buying the present."

Her accuracy on the details caught me off guard.

"It all turned out fine." I tried to appear cheerful. "Do you remember the thank-you note we received from Su Ling?"

"Is that Uncle Nate's wife?"

"Yes."

"Was it the note in the shape of a bird with the tissue paper over the top?"

"Yes, that's the one. Su Ling made the cards herself. She said they liked the ice cream maker and had used it to make frozen yogurt. So it all turned out fine in the end."

I spotted a gas station and put on my blinker. This tanker certainly was guzzling the gas. Maybe Jon had a point when he decided against a motor home.

"Mom?"

"Yes?"

"How many times has Uncle Nate been married?"

I hesitated and then decided that with her keen attention to detail, she probably already knew.

"Three times. Su Ling is his third wife."

"Did you like the other two wives?"

"I only met the first one briefly. I didn't really know her."

"But did you like her?"

"Yes, I liked her." I pulled into the gas station and turned off the motor.

"Mom?"

"Yes?"

"Do you think Uncle Nate is going to stay married to this wife?"

"I hope so."

"Me too," Hannah said quietly. "I think it's better when a man and woman stay married all the way to the end of their lives."

"I do, too. But, you know, sometimes it doesn't work out that way."

"I know. But I think it's better."

I handed the gas-station attendant the credit card Jon had given me to use on the trip and felt strange sitting in the car while having the tank filled. I wondered if Oregon was the only state left that didn't allow customers to pump their own gas.

"Mom?"

"Yes?"

"Do you plan to stay married to Dad until the end of your life?"

"Yes, of course. Your dad and I are very committed to each other."

As we left the gas station and began the last thirty-seven miles to Nate and Su Ling's house, Hannah let out a little sigh. "Pua's parents are getting a divorce. Pua is moving back to Samoa with her mom."

"Oh, Hannah, I didn't know that. When did you find out?"

"Two days ago. She might be gone when we get back from this trip."

"I'm so sorry. I'm really, really sad for you and for Pua and for her parents."

"I know. Me too."

Hannah reached over and touched my hand. I looped my fingers through hers. We drove in silence, holding hands.

Chapter 4

Hannah was asleep when we arrived at Nate's house. Or maybe I should say Nate's mini-ranch. When Nate married Su Ling, she brought four llamas into the marriage but no children. The climate apparently was good for raising these stately creatures, because I noticed several other ranchers in the same region kept llamas in their fenced yards. As we turned off into the driveway to Nate and Su Ling's place, two llamas with their camel-like poker faces and long eyelashes stood nearby, casually observing us.

"Hannah, we're here, honey. Wake up. Look at the llamas."

She opened her eyes and peered out the window. "Those are llamas?"

"Yes."

"They're cute. Do they like to be petted?"

"I have no idea. I'm sure we'll find out."

Hannah and I got out of the car and stretched before

walking up to the front of the simple, cabin-style house. Clay pots with friendly red geraniums lined the walkway that led to a raised wooden deck. Two large chairs made from bent willow branches sat like sentinels on the deck. A dog barked from inside the house.

"Hello!" I called out before we knocked.

"Do you think anyone's here?" Hannah whispered.

"I hope so."

"Are you sure we're in the right place, Mom?"

"Pretty sure."

"Hello?" I called out again, trying to see through the screen door. I realized I'd never actually talked to Nate or Su Ling. Tom had contacted his brother and set this up, but I didn't know any of the details.

I was trying to remember how far back along the road I had noticed a respectable-looking motel where we could stay if we had to.

"They might not know we were coming," I said, lowering my voice. "Let's go back to the car. I'll try calling them on my cell phone."

We had just walked behind the SUV when a truck pulled into the driveway behind us. A tall man wearing cowboy boots and hat hopped out and rushed past us with a cell phone to his ear.

"Was that Uncle Nate?"

"No, I don't think so. I didn't see his face very well, but Nate isn't that tall."

"Look, Mom. The paniolo is going into that building behind the trees."

I was caught off guard when she said *paniolo.* It's the Hawaiian name for the Portuguese horsemen who immigrated to Maui generations ago and still run cattle ranches upcountry. Hannah didn't think to call this guy a cowboy. All she knew was the Hawaiian version, the paniolo.

"That must be their barn. Let's see what's going on." I sounded braver than I felt. For all I knew we could have driven into the wrong driveway and some illegal cockfight was going on.

Taking one courageous step after another, Hannah and I approached the barn and heard a woman's voice saying, "This is it. You got here just in time."

"Hello?" I called out in a cracked voice, as we cautiously entered the dimly lit building.

In the corner of a dusty stall we saw the frame of a small woman and the face of an indignant looking llama as it turned to us and let out a terrible bray. The woman didn't turn our way, but the cowboy did. He looked at my timid expression and then at Hannah.

With a finger to his lips to silence us, he motioned with his other hand for us to come closer. Hannah took him up on the offer. I hung back because my guess was this involved something in the veterinary field, and I didn't do well with blood of any sort, not even llama blood.

Undaunted, Hannah peeked around the corner of the stall and turned to me, her eyes wide, and mouthed the word "Baby!"

I nodded and stayed where I was, feeling a little clammy. I could hear another car pulling into the driveway and footsteps rapidly approaching. My brother-in-law, Nate, skimmed past me without seeing me in the corner. He entered the stall, dropping down on one knee in the straw.

"I just got the message," Nate said. "How's she doing?"

"Good, now," the woman responded. "I thought she was in distress for a while. The cria seemed to be stuck in the birth canal, so when I couldn't get a hold of you, I called Jason. But I've been keeping her calm, and by the time Jason got here, she seemed to be okay."

"Hey, Jason."

The cowboy tipped his hat.

Nate looked over his shoulder at Hannah. She was standing to the side with her arms folded across her middle.

"Hey," Nate said to her.

"Hi."

I should have said something then. I should have stepped out of the shadows and let Nate know that we had arrived. But just then Su Ling let out a "Whoa, okay!" and seemed to go into action.

"Hold on," she said. "Don't start spitting at me, now. You're okay. That's a girl. You're doing fine. You're doing fine. That's right. Here, Nate, right here. That's it. Okay. That's it!"

I heard the most peculiar sloshing sound followed by an intense snort from the mama llama, and my imagination filled in all the details that my queasy eyes had not been willing to take in.

Hannah turned and looked at me. I have never seen such an expression on my daughter's face. It was a blending of raw shock eclipsed by ecstatic wonder. She drew closer to the miracle in the straw while I, unfortunately, had to leave the building.

I wish I had the stomach for such marvels, but I never have. Hurrying through the trees, back to the driveway, I went over to the SUV and leaned against the side, breathing hard.

In the west, a range of mountains rose, sharp and commanding, dressed in lily-white snow. By focusing on the grandeur of those steady peaks, I tried to regain my equilibrium.

"Okay," I said, half in prayer and half as a pep talk. "This is all normal, right? Happens every day. It's okay. I'm okay. Don't think about the blood."

Staring at the mountains, I realized I was in Oregon. Up until that moment, everything had clicked along, and I hadn't fully made the connection. This wasn't a three-dimensional dream. I wasn't in the middle of some surround-sound cinema. I was in Oregon, and my daughter had just watched a baby llama make a sloshing entrance into the world.

"Abby?" Nate called to me, hustling my direction from the barn.

"Hi." I drew in a fortifying breath and tried to stand up straight.

"Abby! When did you get here?"

"Just a few minutes ago. We—"

"I just met your daughter. I thought she came with Jason. When she spoke up, we all looked at her, and none of us knew who she was."

"I'm sorry, Nate. I should have—"

"No, it's fine. She introduced herself. She said you came out here. Are you okay?"

"Yes, I'm fine. Weak stomach," I added with an apologetic shrug.

"I see. Well, hey! I'm glad you made it. We could have done a better job of welcoming you. Do you want to come back in and see the cria? It's a female."

I hesitated, pressing my lips together.

"Or you can go on in the house, if you'd like."

"Thanks."

"Can I get your luggage for you?"

We pulled our bags from the back of the van, and I noticed that Nate had aged a lot since the last time I had seen him. He wasn't as heavy as he had been in the past, and his hair was now more gray above the ears, but his expression seemed the least oppressed I'd ever seen it. The few times I'd been around Nate in the past, he had looked as if he were contemplating something with far too much intensity. Even at happy occasions, like weddings, Nate always seemed as if he were about to implode. But now he looked as if his spirit was one hundred pounds lighter.

"This way." He led me through the front door, as the dog barked from some closed-off room. Nate called out, "It's okay, Bailey. Calm down. It's only me."

Bailey quieted down.

The decor was simple but light and airy with an open-beam ceiling. A brightly colored Indian rug hung on the wall behind the couch, and an assortment of candles lined the top of an antique buffet.

Nate led me to a room with a king-size bed covered with what looked like a handmade quilt. On the end of the bed were two sets of folded towels. A quick look at the pictures and the personal items on the tall dresser gave me the impression this was Nate and Su Ling's bedroom.

"This okay for you two?"

"It's great, but isn't this your room?"

He nodded.

"Where are you and Su Ling sleeping?"

"Don't worry about us. We have it all figured out," he said. "We wanted you and Hannah to feel at home and to be comfortable."

I could picture my brother-in-law and his wife sleeping on an air mattress in the living room or on the couch, and I wished we had stayed at a motel instead.

"Before you protest, let me tell you this is my wife's idea. Her insistence, actually. She's really something, isn't she?"

"We didn't actually meet yet, but yes, she is something." The woman had just assisted in the delivery of a baby llama. I was pretty sure there wasn't anything she couldn't do.

"How about something to drink?" Nate offered.

Again, I hesitated. Memories of a family picnic when Tom and I were first dating came back to me. Nate had gotten so drunk that Tom had to drive him home. I didn't know exactly what Nate was offering me to drink.

"I know that Su Ling made some lemonade this morning. We have some organic apricot juice. And water, of course."

"Water would be great. Thanks."

I followed Nate back into the cheerfully decorated kitchen and fumbled to start a conversation, as he poured a glass of water. "How long have you guys lived here?"

"Two years. We bought the place right after we got married. I sure wish you and Tom could have come to our wedding. It was great."

I nodded, sipping the water.

"The Lord has been blessin' us in so many ways."

I nearly spewed the water out of my mouth. I had never heard Nate talk about the Lord. Nate had been labeled the black sheep of the family years ago. Tom and I dropped out of communication with him after his first wife left him. When we received the invitation to his wedding to Su Ling, we didn't consider going because of finances. Even when Tom contacted Nate to see if Hannah and I could stay with them, I had protested, saying I'd rather stay at a motel. But Tom said it would mean a lot to him if I'd make the effort to see his only brother just for one night. Tom said it might turn out to be a good visit.

He could be right.

An hour later, over bowls of ginger-carrot soup, made from carrots grown in their organic garden, and Indian flat bread, Su Ling sang a blessing over our food and then Nate prayed. The two of them told us how they had met at a singles' retreat. Nate said it was the first church event he had ever gone to, and Su Ling was the first person he met there.

"I was trying to make him feel welcome," Su Ling said, her petite, round face glowing as she looked over at Nate. "We ended up talking for hours that first night and—"

"And she hasn't stopped talking since," Nate said with a wink. It was the same wink my husband used in his best teasing moments. Left eye only, never the right. With both Tom and Nate the left corner of the mouth drew up as they winked and a barely perceptible dimple appeared under the left cheekbone. It was an extraordinary experience to see that same wink on the face of someone other than Tom.

Su Ling seemed to adore the teasing and the wink, because she beamed a little love note back to him with her deep-set eyes. "And Nate hasn't complained about my outgoing personality even once." She looked at Hannah. "There's more soup. Are you still hungry? Would you like some more?"

"Yes, please."

"It's hard work helping to clean up afterbirth, isn't it?" Su Ling went to the stove to fetch the kettle of soup.

Hannah asked, "What did Jake do with that sack thing that came out at the end?"

"He buried it. We have to take the afterbirth away from the barn and bury it deep enough so the coyotes don't dig it up."

I quietly excused myself from the table and headed for the bathroom.

"I'm sorry, Mom," Hannah called out. "I forgot. She doesn't do well with blood and stuff."

"I'll be back in a minute." I wished I could grow out of this squeamishness.

When I returned, with my composure back in place, Su Ling was telling Hannah that she could name the cria.

"The what?" Hannah asked.

"The cria. A baby llama is called a cria. What do you think we should call this one? Have you thought of a name?"

I was beginning to notice that whenever Su Ling asked a question, she asked it twice, phrasing it differently each time. It was charming in a way.

"I'd like to name her Pua."

"Pua?"

"It's the Hawaiian word for flower. My best friend, Pua, is moving to Samoa. When I get back from this trip, she might be gone already."

"Oh!" Su Ling hopped out of her seat, went to Hannah, and wrapped her slender arm around my daughter's shoulders. "What sad, sad news. Of course we will name her Pua. As soon as we're done eating, we'll go tell Pua her name, okay? Would you like that?"

Hannah nodded.

Su Ling planted a kiss as gentle as a raindrop on Hannah's brow and brought us cherries, grapes, and sliced kiwi topped with a scoop of frozen yogurt. Su

Ling said she made the yogurt with the ice cream maker we gave her.

Hannah caught my eye and tried to wink, but both her eyes closed. She definitely had my facial coordination and not her dad's.

"These are good," Hannah said. "We don't have this kind of fruit very often at home."

"It's expensive," I explained. "And by the time it arrives at our stores, it's not very fresh."

"What's Tom up to these days?" Nate asked. "How's business going?"

I gave a brief summary of how we do best with snorkel and scuba-diving equipment rental during the high tourist seasons. "We're starting to see more rentals on the surfboards, and we do a lot of booking for chartered boats and sailing excursions, too. We're doing okay. Not great."

I learned a long time ago it does no good to complain to anyone about the financial challenge that comes with life on Maui. No one ever feels genuinely sorry for us.

"I sure want Tom to meet Su Ling," Nate said. "Maybe we need to get over to Maui sometime."

"My dad would be so happy to see you," Hannah said.

"Yes," I agreed. "Please come anytime."

"When you guys come, you can stay in my brother's room. He's going away to college. His room is smaller than mine, but he has a bigger window."

"That settles it." Nate winked at Hannah. She kept her gaze fixed on his face. I guessed that she had noticed the familiar wink, too.

"Our house is really small," Hannah said. "Just so you don't expect too much. And it's not very close to beach. You have to walk about seven blocks to get there."

Su Ling chuckled. "All of seven blocks? You poor thing!"

"I guess it's not that bad. It's just that where we live they built all these vacation condos along da bes' property makai and all da ka'amainas gotta live mauka."

When Hannah starts talking fast, she takes on a twinge of the local pidgin slang that a lot of her classmates used. That, with a few true Hawaiian words thrown in, makes it hard even for me to follow her sometimes. Su Ling and Nate both turned to me for translation.

"Most of the long-time residents who live and work in our area have to live inland, closer to the mountains, since it's too expensive to live near the ocean. We actually are in a pretty nice location since we bought our house so long ago. If we tried to buy anything now, we wouldn't be able to afford it."

"Still sounds pretty nice to me." Su Ling rose and cleared the dishes.

Hannah jumped up and carried the ceramic bowls to the sink, chattering about how she would take Su Ling to her favorite place to snorkel and to the best place to buy shell necklaces.

"You know, Abby, you haven't changed much," Nate said. "You look younger even."

These were welcome words after my brother's evaluation of how much I now resembled my mother.

"Must be the island living," I said.

"No, I think it's the clean living. You and Tom, you both got your souls infused with God early in the game. It makes a difference. You're reaping what you sowed, and so am I." He turned over his left palm and pointed to a straight, two-inch scar across his wrist.

It took me a moment to realize how a scar like that would have been made and for what intended purpose. I forced myself not to let a visual image form and was glad Hannah wasn't still at the table.

"I had to go all the way to the bottom before I'd call out for a Savior. You and Tom . . . you both got a good, clean head start on what really matters in life."

"Nate, I didn't realize things were that bad for you. I'm sorry we didn't do a better job of staying in touch."

He shook his head. "Naw, you guys didn't do anything wrong. I wouldn't have taken your calls or your help back then anyhow. It was God himself who had to hold out his hand to me. His is the only one strong enough to lift someone like me out of the cow pie I'd fallen into."

Hannah and Su Ling returned to the table, and Su Ling said, "We're going to check on Pua and tell her what we named her." She linked her arm through Hannah's. They were the same size and could probably wear the same clothes. "Anyone else want to come?"

"Sure," Nate said. "You up for a second round, Abby? It'll be easier to stomach this time."

"Okay." I pushed back from the table.

"She fainted one time when we were camping at Waianapanapa," Hannah confided to Su Ling, as we strolled through the cool evening out to the barn. "My brother found a dead mongoose with its head bitten off, and he left it on the picnic table. My mom came out of the tent, and when she saw it, she just went plop."

"Are you telling stories about me?"

"Yes." Hannah shot a mischievous grin over her shoulder. She looked so happy. Her long, blond ponytail had a definite swish to it that hadn't been there earlier.

Apparently Auntie Su Ling, the mama llama midwife, was the answer to the prayer Hannah had offered in Jon's driveway that our trip be fun.

Hannah was having fun. And I was trying to. I really was.

Chapter 5

The sun had not yet risen when Hannah and I hit the road the next morning. I knew we needed an early start for the long stretch down the spine of the great Golden State; so I roused my sleeping beauty at four AM and shuffled her out to the car.

Hannah grumbled for the first hour we drove in the dark, saying she wished we could have stayed another day with Su Ling and baby Pua. Eventually her complaining leveled off, and she cuddled up under the gorgeous, hand-knit blanket Su Ling had given her the night before. The blanket was made from yarn Su Ling handspun from her llamas. Hannah thought it was "the most amazingest, softest blanket in the world," and I agreed.

Su Ling's hospitality had been so generous. Here I was the one who had told Tom I'd rather stay in a hotel than stop to visit his brother. We would have missed out on so much.

As I drove, I thought about something Su Ling had

asked when she helped me load up the car that morning. I had been standing there in the chill of the new day, rattling off how many miles I needed to cover to reach my mother's house in southern California that evening, when Su Ling asked if I was eager to see my mother.

The truthful answer was too complex to address in such a short time, so I summarized by saying, "I'm sure it'll be okay."

"How long are you staying with her?" Su Ling asked.

"Just one night. We have a lot of miles to cover before we reach Louisiana."

"When was the last time you saw your mom?" Su Ling asked.

I stopped and thought. "It's been about six years. Hannah was in kindergarten."

Hannah leaned over the seat and entered into the conversation Su Ling and I were having at the open back of the car. "Was that the time we went to Disneyland?"

"Yes."

"I remember that trip," Hannah said. "Justin got carsick when we were driving up the mountain to Grandma Celeste's house, and I helped to put out the birdseed for the squirrels. Oh, and I remember Disneyland and the hat Dad bought me after we went on the Dumbo ride."

I closed up the back of the SUV and felt relieved that Hannah had good memories of that trip. All I remembered was the tension between my mother and me. Either

Hannah didn't recall walking in on us in the middle of our icy moments or else she was hiding that memory the same way I had buried so many of mine.

Walking me around to the driver's side of the vehicle, Su Ling said, "So you're looking forward to seeing your mother, then?"

I wasn't sure why she was asking again, looking at me with such tenderness.

"It will be fine," I said. "It's only for one night."

Su Ling tilted her head. "It's funny about love, isn't it?"

"What do you mean?"

"It's funny whom we end up choosing to love and who ends up choosing to love us. It's rarely the people we think it should be."

I nodded, as if I knew what she was trying to say.

"Love never gives up, you know. Love believes all things, endures all things, hopes all things." Then she hugged me good-bye and smiled, as if she knew a special secret.

I thought about Su Ling's words now, as I drove through southern Oregon. I wondered if her choice to love my husband's wayward brother, along with God's outstretched hand, had been the cure for Nate's long list of moral failings. Certainly something had happened to that man, and the change was nothing short of miraculous. Was it God? Su Ling? Or both?

I thought of how Su Ling assumed that love is a

choice. *But is it?* I wondered. It seemed to me that if it was, my mother had chosen long ago not to love me. Had it been a choice on both sides?

Squirming uncomfortably in the deluxe driver's seat, I reminded myself that I had a beautiful collection of people in my life that I chose to love. My mother didn't need to move onto that list. We were polite to each other, and that was enough.

For the next few hours I listened to a radio talk show and thought how the people who were calling in had much worse problems than I did. It boosted my spirits in a smug sort of way.

The morning sun was stretching out its golden rays over magnificent, snow-capped Mount Shasta when I stopped for gas. If Mount Hood hadn't satisfied my need for mountain majesty, Shasta filled in the tiny, missing gaps with her freshly scrubbed appearance in the brilliant first light of day.

"Hannah, look. Isn't that a glorious sight?"

She squinted out the window. "Another mountain?"

"Yes, another mountain. Mount Shasta. Are you hungry?"

"No. Can I sleep some more?"

Hannah slept through most of the day. She had stayed in the barn with Pua until nearly two in the morning. I had fallen into bed at ten o'clock and hadn't expected her to stay up so late. My Hannah would rather help with the llamas all night, knowing she could sleep the next day in the car.

I didn't mind. Hannah was content and cozy under her luxurious llama blanket, and I was swallowing the antidote for island fever by the spoonful. Steering the smooth-riding SUV over miles and miles of uncluttered highway, I filled my mind with images of immense beauty. I loved the variety of colors. The browns, tans, and soft gold shades in the landscape were rich and refreshing after living so long in a land of lush greens and blues.

When we breezed through the Sacramento freeway system, I enjoyed the sight of each tall building, and since we didn't have billboards at home, I read every billboard we passed as if it carried an important message. Some of them made me chuckle.

My power food for the day consisted of gas station fare: sunflower seeds, beef jerky, bottled water, Scottish shortbread, and an extra-large slushy cherry drink. I felt like a kid who had run away from home, the way I had dreamed of doing after I read about Tom Sawyer and Huckleberry Finn. I remember making a list of all the supplies I would put in a bandanna, tie them to a fishing pole, and sling them over my shoulder. Sunflower seeds and Scottish shortbread were on the original childhood list.

My cell phone had great reception as I cruised through the belly of California. I called Tom to give him an update on our trip. Hannah sat up and took the phone so she could tell her dad about the baby llama.

"It was the coolest thing in the world, Dad. You shoulda been there. I wish we lived where we could raise llamas."

I smiled thinking of how many twelve-year-old-girls who lived on Oregon ranches were wishing they could live in Hawaii and see a dolphin or sea turtle any day of the week.

Trucks loaded with bright red tomatoes kept passing us. I told Tom about the extensive orchards we were driving by and how they were lined with elegantly shaped almond trees.

So much open space. So much produce.

"Sounds like you're enjoying your time in the land of plenty," Tom said.

"More than I can ever express. Thanks for all your support on this trip, Tom."

"I think this is turning out to be a good thing for all of us. Did I tell you Justin and I went sailing yesterday?"

We talked for another ten minutes before Tom said he had to go.

Feeling buoyant, I called my mother when we were about an hour north of Bakersfield. She wanted to know a specific time when we would arrive. I wasn't sure how to estimate the time or distance without consulting Tom's or my brother's schedule.

"No matter," my mother said. "If Stan and I get too tired waiting, we'll go to bed and leave the back door unlocked for you."

"Thanks," I mumbled and hung up.

A scowl settled on my forehead, and Hannah noticed.

"You okay, Mom?"

"I'm getting tired."

"You've been driving a long time. You want me to drive for a while?" she teased.

I smiled at my well-rested pixie. "Yes, as a matter of fact, I'd love it if you could drive for a while."

"Could we stop to eat something?" Hannah asked.

Taking the next off-ramp, we parked at a fast-food restaurant. My legs felt stiff as I walked into the crowded hot spot. After placing our order for burgers, shakes, and fries, Hannah followed me outside so I could walk around some more and stretch my legs.

"I wish we could stay at that hotel down the road." I glanced at my watch. "I'd fall on the bed and sleep straight through until morning."

"Why don't we?" Hannah asked. "They have a pool!"

"No, I told my mom we would get to their house tonight."

"How many more hours is it?" Hannah asked.

"I don't know. At least three hours. Maybe four."

It turned out to be nearly six hours to Lake Arrowhead because of the traffic we hit in Los Angeles and because

I had to stop several times to walk around so I could stay awake.

We parked the SUV along the side road behind my mother's mountain home and entered quietly through the back door. It was after midnight, and I knew my mother wouldn't wait up for me. I motioned to Hannah not to make any noise as we tried to find our way to the guest room without a hall light or nightlight to illuminate our narrow path.

The double bed was a bit challenging for Hannah and me. She fell asleep immediately and stretched out, taking up more than her side of the bed. I curled up and found I was too tired to sleep. Staring into the darkened room, I tried to count. First I counted the number of beverages I'd had that day that contained caffeine. Six. No wonder I couldn't sleep. I counted the number of times we had stopped for gas since we left Seattle. Eight. I fell asleep somewhere in the middle of counting the number of days we had to drive before we got to Grand Lady's.

My stepfather's pet terrier, Mulligan, woke both of us at seven o'clock with his persistent yipping at the closed guest room door. Mulligan apparently knew strangers were in the house, and he wasn't going to let that fact go unnoticed.

Hannah flailed around under the sheets and went back to sleep. I slipped out of bed and opened the door, quietly scolding Mulligan for making so much noise. The white-haired burglar alarm wasn't threatened by me and barked all the more for the thrill of finding his suspicions confirmed with a living, breathing intruder.

"Some guard dog you are," I muttered, going into the bathroom and closing the door before Mulligan could follow me inside. "Where were you last night when we came in through the back door?"

Not that I would have minded your greeting then, since you would have been our only welcoming party.

The shower helped wash off some of the stickiness I'd felt after our long day on the road. It also helped to wash off some of my sour attitude. I knew I needed to make the most of this visit. We would only be here for eight or nine hours. I didn't want to leave with any regrets, as I had after the last visit. Turning off the shower, I turned on the cordial, attentive daughter attitude and stepped into the hall, dressed and ready.

Mulligan lay like a corpse by the door. Apparently the old boy had worn himself out barking while I was in the shower. Unnoticed, I stepped over him and went into the kitchen with a pleasant expression on my face.

My stepfather, Stan, was sitting at the large kitchen table using only a small corner of it for his bowl of Raisin Bran and the morning paper. The rest of the antique walnut table was spread with strategic selections of my mom's art.

"Good morning!" I said.

Stan looked up. "Well, there you are. Sleep well?"

A familiar sadness floated into the room. Stan didn't move a muscle to greet me. He rarely hugged me, and despite his not having seen me in more than six years, this was not going to be one of those hugging moments.

"Yes," I answered routinely, walking over to the coffeemaker and asking if I could have a cup of coffee.

"Help yourself. I think there's some left."

I poured the coffee into a familiar cup. My mom had kept the same set of dishes with the trailing grapevine around the rim since I was a child.

"Where's my mother?"

"Out for her morning walk. She hoped you would go with her, but you were sleeping in, so she went ahead."

The pattern was old and deep. My mother "hoped" I'd walk with her, even though she never had expressed her expectation to me. I should feel guilty for "sleeping in," regardless of being exhausted and then roused at seven o'clock by their yipping dog.

Pulling out the chair across from Stan, I was careful not to touch the watercolor paintings.

"So, how are you?" I asked.

He looked up from the paper. "Fine. How's the trip so far?"

"It's been good. I think Hannah is enjoying it. She's still sleeping, though."

"Um-hmmm."

"You'll be surprised to see how grown up she is."

He nodded.

"I was surprised to see Mulligan," I said, fishing for a topic that would interest him.

"Surprised? Why?"

"Because he has so much energy for such an old dog. How long have you had him?"

"Sixteen years," Stan said. "He's a tough old coot. Keeps your mother and me company. It would be pretty quiet around here without him."

Nodding and sipping the weak coffee, I glanced around at everything. So little had changed. So very, very little.

The windows were open, letting in the crisp morning air, and that was pleasant. Familiar tinges of fir-tree fragrance laced the air with a dusty hint of ponderosa pine needles drying in the sun. A pinecone fell to the ground beside the bird feeder and startled a blue jay that didn't waste a second before squawking his shrill scolding to the inconsiderate pinecone.

A tenacious squirrel hopped up on the platform feeder. I'd seen a lot of squirrels while growing up in this house. Their fluffy, silver-gray tails seemed to form a question mark behind them as they perched on the rim of the platform feeder and examined the feast before them.

My mother had invested in huge bags of sunflower

seeds and expensive nuts for the squirrels over the years. Every morning she filled their feeder, and they would come with their beautiful tails punctuating the daily question: What shall I choose first from this smorgasbord of seed and nuts?

Often I would sit alone at this long kitchen table that was really my mother's worktable, pouring a bowl of cold cereal and wondering what it would be like to have a mother who made French toast or scrambled eggs for breakfast.

Sometimes I would sit here and wish I were a squirrel. My mother adored them. She made sure they always had something good to eat. She gave them nicknames and paid attention to all their comings and goings and spent hours painting pictures of them.

Stan would sometimes say to my mother, "Why do you love those squirrels so much? Take off those bushy tails and they're just rats."

My mom would say, "Oh, Stan, you don't know a thing about art or nature, do you?"

Then Stan would say, "No, I guess I don't." And he would leave the room.

I never said anything good or bad about the squirrels. In that way I always thought I was smarter than Stan.

And I never had anything but cold cereal for breakfast until the summer I was shipped off to Louisiana. My first morning there, Grand Lady made flapjacks for me, and I couldn't stop eating them. I ate until I was nearly sick.

The next morning Grand Lady made me corn fritters and eggs Benedict. In one week I sampled such scrumptious breakfast foods as hot grits, soft-boiled eggs with croissants, hot oatmeal with brown sugar and raisins, my first Denver omelet, and my favorite: Swedish sour cream crepes dotted with raspberries. I was in breakfast paradise!

My most memorable breakfast in Louisiana was my last morning there. The day before, Uncle Burt told me my dad had "departed this earth." Aunt Peg arranged for me to fly home in time for the funeral, and everyone made a fuss over saying good-bye. Every one of them told me to come again, real soon.

I was all packed and waiting for Uncle Burt to drive me to Shreveport that final morning when Grand Lady came downstairs and pulled her chair up next to mine at the kitchen table.

"Have you had anything to eat, Honeygirl?" she asked.

I stared at the four perfectly white gardenias floating in a ceramic bowl at the center of the dining room table. Their rich, heavy sweetness came through my nostrils and filled the emptiest part of me. Without looking up I said, "I'm not hungry."

Grand Lady put her arm around me. I snuggled up

close, tucking the tip of my small nose under her jawline and resting my cheek against the curve of her soft neck. I fit perfectly. I didn't ever want to leave.

"Then we shall sit here, you and me," Grand Lady said. "And the two of us shall have ourselves some gardenias for breakfast."

Chapter 6

I was lost in the memory of Grand Lady and the gardenias we shared for breakfast when Stan mumbled something about Techlos.

"Pardon me," I said.

"Techlos stock is up again."

"Techlos?"

"Your brother's company. Jon told me I should buy some stock last summer, and now I wish I would have listened to him."

"I know. He told us to invest, too."

"Did you?"

"No." I wanted to say "Invest with what?" but Stan didn't understand our financial limitations, and I didn't feel compelled to confide any details to him.

"Looks like we both missed the boat on that one." Stan turned the page and studied the paper, as if scanning all the ads for local garage sales was more interesting than a conversation with me.

I sat in silence for a few moments, considering going outside to meet up with my mother on her walk. She always walked the same route, so I knew if I started at the end and went toward her, we would meet somewhere along the way.

But something in my rebellious spirit whispered a wicked truth. I didn't want to meet my mother. Not even halfway.

Sitting at my mother's large, unwelcoming table with nothing more than a cup of weak coffee I had poured for myself, I felt resigned to the way things were. It would be unrealistic to keep hoping things would change. I might as well see what I could find to feed myself for breakfast.

I checked inside the refrigerator for some milk. If Hannah and I were going to eat cereal, I wanted to make sure there was enough milk. Otherwise I'd go to the country store and buy some for us.

"Your mother has plans for those eggs," Stan stated without looking up from his newspaper.

"What are you talking about, Stan?" My mother surprised us, entering through the living room instead of the back door near where we sat. She stepped over to the table, her thin arms folded across her middle, sharp chin pointed toward her husband. Her long, salt-and-pepper hair was pulled up in a loose knot held in place by two bright red chopsticks. The going-gray-naturally process seemed to lend credibility to her aura of being an artist.

"I'm talking to your daughter," Stan said.

"Hi, Mom." I stepped out from behind the refrigerator door and moved into plain view.

"Abby. I didn't think you were up yet."

I shrugged like a shy five-year-old and struggled to remind myself that I had not just been caught with my hand in the cookie jar. I was an adult. A guest. Her daughter. I wasn't an intruder. This had once been my home, too.

"I'm up. How was your walk?" I managed to ask.

"Nice. It's a nice day. How was your long drive?"

"Good. Long. Hannah is still sleeping."

Just then we heard a loud wail from down the hall. "Maaa-omm!"

"Is that Hannah?" my mother said with a start. "She sounds like Jon's girls."

"Mom, come here, quick!"

I could tell Hannah wasn't practicing her preadolescent squall. She sounded panicked. I took off running and found Hannah kneeling beside Mulligan by the bathroom door.

"He's not moving!" Hannah cried when she saw me.

"Mulligan," I called out, clapping my hands. "Mulligan!"

"What's the matter?" my mother asked. Stan was right behind her.

"Mulligan!" Stan bellowed. He bent over and rubbed the dog's belly. "Mulligan!"

"I think he's dead," Hannah said in a faint voice. "Is he dead, Mom?"

I instinctively reached for my daughter and drew her into my arms. "He was an old dog," I whispered into her tousled hair.

My usual queasiness eluded me. All that mattered was how Hannah felt at this moment.

"Come on." I led her away from Mulligan so Stan could have space.

"What are you doing, Mulligan?" Stan roughed up the dog's fur one more time. "Come on. Wake up, you old mutt." Stan looked up. His expression revealed the truth we had suspected.

I shuttled Hannah out of the way, thinking we should go in the other room. I didn't want Hannah to mention that Mulligan had woken us up with his vigorous yipping. He had seemed fine then.

Hannah pulled away from me and placed her hand on Stan's shoulder. "I'm sorry, Grandpa," she said. "I remember Mulligan from when I was here a long time ago. He was a nice dog. I'm sorry he's dead."

My stepfather's expression softened. He looked up at Hannah and placed his big hand over hers where it rested on his shoulder. "I appreciate your saying that." He reached up and patted her cheek, using his rough finger to brush away her tears. "He was a good ole dog."

As I watched, my mother stepped in and placed her long, slender fingers around Hannah's shoulders and softly said, "Come, Hannah. Let's go in the other room."

I followed, surprised at my mother's tenderness toward my daughter and at the same time pleased, because every young girl should be treated with such gentle esteem by her grandparents.

We went into the kitchen where my mother wrapped her arms around Hannah and held her, stroking her long ponytail. I doubted if Hannah's hair had been combed at all the day before. Her mane looked like a squirrel's tail that was sufficiently fluffy but had not yet learned to stand up and form a question mark.

"This is a terrible way for you to begin your visit," my mother said. She went over to the sink and turned on the water. "Your grandpa touched your hands after he touched Mulligan. You should wash with soap."

Hannah obeyed, and with a sniff she said, "Yesterday I watched a baby llama being born. And now I saw a dead dog."

Mom looked over at me, stunned.

"At Nate and Su Ling's ranch in Oregon," I explained. "We arrived just as the llama was giving birth."

"And you watched?" Mom asked.

"Not me," I said. "Hannah did."

"And I got to name the cria. That's what they call a baby llama. A cria. I named her Pua."

"You did?" My mom dipped her head and gazed at Hannah, all eyes and ears for my little girl. It was the strangest thing to observe. My mother was acting like a grandma. A sweet, tender grandma. I looked at her and thought, *Who are you? Where were you when I was growing up?*

Hannah dried her hands and took the center stage being offered. She went into animated detail about the birth of Pua and our time with Su Ling. Mom leaned against the counter and took in Hannah's stories.

"And what about your time with your cousins in Seattle?" My mom's slight Louisiana twang on the last part of the sentence gave a hint that her guard was down, and she was sounding like the down-home girl she had once been. "Did you enjoy being with Tiffany and Jasmine?"

"Yes. They have a big house," Hannah said.

"Yes, they do. I've been there," my mother said.

"Did you know that Tiffany and Jasmine have their own TV? It takes up a whole wall in the entertainment room."

"Yes, I've seen it. Did you go out in the boat on the lake behind their house?"

"No. We saw the lake, but we didn't go down there. I like the picture Jasmine has in her bedroom. The one of her. She said you painted it. I think it's really good."

My mother appeared deeply touched. "Why, thank you, Hannah."

"I like to paint, too," Hannah said.

"Yes, I know. Your mother has sent me some of your work."

"Has she sent you anything lately? Any of the ones I entered in the contest for Art Night in Lahaina?"

My mom looked to me for the answer.

I shook my head, no. The pictures I'd sent her were "extras," meaning that Hannah would most likely have thrown them away if I hadn't confiscated them.

"Are those some of your pictures?" Hannah walked toward the table.

"Yes."

I watched my slender, artistic daughter standing beside her slender, artistic grandmother, and both of them automatically shifted their weight to their right foot. They both tilted their heads to the right and drew their left hand up to their mouth where they curled their hand under their chin and tapped their full lips with their thumbs.

Neither of them noticed the mimicry. I couldn't look at the pictures. The two of them were a more fascinating work of genetic mastery.

Before Hannah had thoroughly gazed at each picture, Stan came around to the back door with a shovel in his hand.

"I'm ready," was all he said.

My mom seemed to understand. She pulled several carnations from the bouquet in the blue vase on the kitchen counter and handed one to Hannah and one to me. It felt as if this was a ritual they performed every day rather than something she was making up as we went along.

We followed Stan outside, past the bird feeder and concrete bench, and down a neglected trail I used to walk along as a young teen. I would take this trail into the forest with a book in my hand, pretending I was Anne and this was the path that led to Green Gables.

Today I was only Abby, and this was the path that led to Mulligan's freshly filled grave.

"I'll make a sign or something later," Stan said. "I suppose we could say a few words."

I hadn't thought this morning could become any more surreal, but here I was, standing in the clearing where the ageless sun broke through the towering trees and warmed the pine-needle-covered patch of earth where I had spent hours with an old army blanket and all my favorite books.

Hannah stepped forward and placed her carnation on the mound. "You were a good dog, Mulligan."

My mom silently placed her carnation beside Hannah's.

Stan's lower lip jutted out. He bowed his head and said nothing.

They were all taking this so seriously and seemed to be waiting for me. I stared at the plot of freshly turned earth where the sun beamed through the shadows. A few words from one of my old literature classics came to mind. I cleared my throat and quoted, "His lamp shines upon my head, and by his light I walk through darkness. In this light Christian came to the end of the valley. Then he sang."

I could feel the gaze of the others now turned on me, waiting for an explanation.

"*Pilgrim's Progress*," I said a little apologetically. "You know, the book. By John Bunyan. It's all that came to mind at the moment."

"Oh," Stan said.

"We should sing," Hannah said. "Like you just said, Mom, 'He came to the end of the valley and then he sang.'"

"Okay."

No one else moved. I flipped through the song files in my brain, trying to come up with something appropriate for the funeral of a dog I'd never liked.

Hannah sang in her feathery, clear voice. "*Ke Akua pu a hui hou ka kou.*"

The song was "God Be with You till We Meet Again."

It was the closing hymn we sang at the end of every service at the church we went to when Hannah was younger. She grew up singing it each week and seemed to think that was the appropriate benediction for Mulligan's memorial.

I joined her on the chorus.

"Hui hou—hui hou, ma ko Iesu mau wawae."

(Till we meet—till we meet, at Jesus' feet.)

Hannah's voice, so pure and celestial, gave this moment a sacred significance. On the last line, I looked at my mother, and she was crying.

"Amen," Stan said, his voice cracking.

"Amen," Hannah echoed.

Our peculiar little party broke up, and we returned to the house down the overgrown trail. Past and present collided as I hung back, saying good-bye, not to Mulligan, but to a sweet and tender part of my childhood I had forgotten. It seemed I'd never sung a benediction over that season of my life.

It was here, in this enchanting forest, that I had spent innumerable hours with my blanket and my books. This had been my magic kingdom, and it had been filled with all my favorite characters. Never had my stomach turned queasy during the imaginary thrill rides I took on flying carpets, treasure-laden ships, or galloping horses.

For all the things I thought my childhood lacked, I had been rich in books. Stories shaped my life, and many of the books I read in this forest had been gifts from Grand Lady.

Returning to the house, I entered the kitchen and heard my mom say to Hannah, "Are you sure? It wouldn't be a problem."

"No, that's okay," Hannah said. "You don't have to make anything for me to eat. I like cereal."

Hannah girl, you just succeeded in winning my mother's heart.

"What about you, Abby?" my mom asked. "What would you like to eat?"

I paused only a flicker of a moment before saying, "Cereal is fine."

We ate at the table, listening to my mom finish her discussion of her artwork. She concluded by asking Hannah which of the pictures she would like to have.

Hannah crunched her cereal and contemplated each picture again. Several of them were of squirrels, two were of the birdbath at the front of the house, one was of a tall hollyhock bush with soft pink blossoms. I thought Hannah might select that one. It was the only one that would sort of fit in with the island decor of our house.

"Well," Hannah said, drawing out her final answer, as if she were a contestant on a TV game show, about to win a million dollars. "Actually, if you don't mind, I'd like one that isn't here on the table."

"Which one is that?"

"Well, it's one you don't have yet."

I couldn't begin to guess where my daughter was going with this.

"What do you mean?" my mother asked.

Hannah's disheveled ponytail looked like something that belonged on the backside of a wild and skittish squirrel. "Actually, Grandma, what I'd like is for you to paint a picture of me the way you painted one of Jasmine. That's the picture I'd like to have. I'd like you to paint my portrait."

My mom was flabbergasted. It was an expression I didn't recognize on her.

"We have so little time," she said, shooting a look at me that carried a definite hint of displeasure. "If you were staying a few days I could do that, but . . ."

"What if we sent you some photos?" I suggested quickly.

"You know I can only paint from life. I've never been able to copy one-dimensional art."

I didn't know that. But then, I didn't know a lot about my mom's hobby. The only way I had acquired any insight or appreciation of painting had been through the wonderful programs Hannah and Justin had been exposed to in Lahaina.

"We have to stay on schedule," I said. "It's a long way to Louisiana. Then we have to go on to Atlanta, you know, to meet Jon and Patty when they fly in."

"I see."

My mom appeared to be silently counting the number of days we would be in Louisiana. I could tell because her lips were moving ever so slightly. She scratched her right eyebrow, and I knew she had figured it out. If all went well, we would have three or four days at Grand Lady's in comparison to barely a day at her house. The inequity of the two visits was evident.

"Maybe you can come another time," my mother said with an edge to her voice. "Another time when you can stay longer. If that wouldn't be a problem."

"Would it be okay if I took a shower?" Hannah jumped up and placed her empty cereal bowl in the sink. I guessed that her internal sensors had lit up, letting her know she had inadvertently ignited a slow-burning fuse.

Women of all ages know what that feels like. It's not something any of us has to be taught. At twelve years of age, Hannah knew when to clear out of the area before the explosion.

What Hannah didn't know was that my mom had a long fuse. She burns at an inordinately slow pace. The waiting is torture. I remember crying over a very civil argument my mother and I had one night during my sophomore year of high school. I yelled through my closed bedroom door, "Why don't you scream at me and get it over with?"

My mom didn't scream. She grew quieter as the smoldering fuse got closer to her explosive emotions. Then somewhere in the silence, almost in slow motion, the shrapnel would fly, and I would walk right into the spray when least expecting it. I would then limp around for as long as I wanted to believe I was a victim.

Of course, by that point my mother would feel all the pressure released, and she would go on as if nothing had happened. We never resolved anything.

Hannah left the kitchen, and I tried a new tactic. Instead of standing back, watching the flicker in my mom's eyes from the slow-burning fuse, I decided to take a sledgehammer to the bomb and set it off myself.

"I know you're upset that we're not staying here longer, but this is the way the trip has been planned, and I'm sticking to the plan." I lifted my round chin up into the air. That statement would have had so much more punch if only I'd inherited my mother's angular chin instead of my father's pudgy one.

"I'm not upset," she said. Her voice was low and steady.

I wanted to say, "Yes, you are." But I curtailed my crusade for truth and simply held my ground. "This is the way things are set, and I don't think it would be a good idea to make changes now. Maybe next time we can stay here longer."

Now I was the one who was lying. When would there be a next time? My stomach began to grumble loudly.

"I understand," my mom said quietly.

We stood there, only a few feet apart, neither of us willing to be the one to make the first move either forward or backward. It was all so familiar.

Outside, a sleek tabby cat jumped up on the feeder tray, ousting the curly-tailed squirrel and scattering the walnuts, hazelnuts, and pistachios to the ground.

"Hey!" my mother yelled, marching toward the back door. She shrieked at the neighborhood prowler, inflicting on him the anger I knew was meant for me. "Get out of there! Right now! You hear me? Shoo! Scat! We don't want you around here!"

When my mom turned around, I was already down the hall. If there was one thing I had learned growing up in this household, it was how to scat.

Chapter 7

Our drive through the California desert into Arizona didn't seem as lonely and desolate as I had imagined it would feel. It could be that I already was dry and depleted in my spirit after the visit at my mother's. In comparison to how our short visit had affected me, the landscape seemed refreshing. All that open space. All those muted shades of silence. The world around us sighed with a lonely sort of peace. The barrenness appeared uncomplicated, and right now that was very appealing.

"We're going too slow," Hannah said. "All those trucks keep passing us."

I looked at my speedometer. We were going the speed limit. *Why is everyone in such a hurry?*

At home the visitors often complained about the locals being on "Maui time," meaning we did things slower in Hawaii than in the rest of the world. Things got done when they got done. If the surf was up at

Fleming Beach, well then, whatever it was that needed getting done would just take a few more days.

"Mom, when can we go back to see Grandma Celeste again?"

I wasn't prepared for her question. "I don't know."

"I was thinking, what if I went there sometime by myself?"

"Why would you want to do that?"

Hannah gave an incredulous squeak. "Because!" Then she added, "Didn't you go to see your grandmother all by yourself when you were my age?"

"Yes, but that was different."

"Why?"

"It just was, Hannah."

She waited a minute before adding, "If I went, I could help Grandpa pick out a new dog, and Grandma Celeste would have time to paint my portrait. What's wrong with that?"

"Nothing is wrong with that, Hannah. It's just not a good idea. It's not . . . practical."

Hannah turned and looked out the side window.

"The purpose of this trip is to get Uncle Jon's car to Atlanta and spend some time with Grand Lady in Louisiana. This trip wasn't supposed to be about spending a lot of time with your grandmother."

"I know. But couldn't I go see Grandma Celeste another time?"

"I don't know. Maybe. We'll see."

"That means no," Hannah said dejectedly.

"No, that means we'll see."

"It's usually the same thing. 'We'll see' really means 'no' when you say it the way you just did."

"Hannah," I stated firmly, "I want this to be a good trip for both of us. You'll see what I mean when we get to Grand Lady's. There will be lots to do at her house. You can go swimming every day in Uncle Burt and Aunt Peg's pool. It'll be fun."

A long pause was followed by Hannah saying, "Well, no duh!"

"What?"

"That sign. Did you read that sign?"

"No, what did it say?"

"It said, 'State Prison Next Exit: Do Not Pick Up Hitchhikers.' That's why I said, no duh! Like they have to tell people not to pick up hitchhikers."

"That was a strange sign," I agreed.

The tension broken and with the topic of my mother diffused, Hannah tried a new request, one that would be easier for me to agree to. "Could I sit in the backseat now and watch one of the DVDs? We've been looking at the same thing outside for a really long time."

"No," I said, still trying to hold on to my position as the decision-maker. "Why don't you read for a while?"

Hannah sighed. "It's getting too dark. Would it be okay if I at least listened to the radio?"

It seemed she was determined to find something that I would say yes to.

"Okay," I finally said.

With the slightest air of victory, Hannah turned on the radio and fiddled with the buttons.

Behind us the sun was setting. A flock of Joshua trees clumped together and settled in for the night like oversized flamingos, standing on one leg and casting a thin pink shadow over the sparse terrain. The road ahead stretched out like a long footbridge across an endless ocean of sand. I felt small and powerless on so many levels.

As the last bit of sunlight faded, darkness covered us as thoroughly as a winter night at sea. Headlights from the oncoming cars kept flashing in our faces before switching to a lower beam. I did the same clicking between high and low for many miles. It was as if we were ocean-going vessels adrift in the vastness, blinking out our ship-to-ship greetings.

Hannah tuned in to a radio station that belted out a contemporary song, and she began to sing along.

"You have a beautiful voice," I told her as the song ended. "I loved it when you sang in the forest this morning."

"You mean for Mulligan's funeral?"

"Yes. I forgot that you knew that hymn."

"Do you really think I have a beautiful voice?"

"Yes. You have a very beautiful voice. I love listening to you sing. That was the perfect song for the moment."

Hannah seemed to let the compliment soak in.

"Mom?"

"Yes?"

"Did your mom love listening to you sing when you were my age?"

I hesitated. "I don't have an especially good singing voice."

"But did she ever listen to you and say it was beautiful?"

"No. I don't think so. If she did, I don't remember it."

"Mom?" Hannah leaned over and turned off the radio. "Why do you hate your mother?"

"I don't hate my mother." My words were evenly paced and delivered in a low, steady voice that sounded just like my mother's. I felt a fist forming in my stomach.

"Okay, then why don't you *like* your mother?"

"I like her, Hannah. In fact, I love her."

"Not the way you love me."

Whack! The fist punched me in the gut.

"You don't like to be close to your mother or touch her. You don't like the things she does or says. And she doesn't like you. How come?"

I didn't answer Hannah. I couldn't. The punch had knocked all the words out of me.

Finally I managed to offer what felt like an apology. "I need to try harder," I said in a small voice.

"Is that how it works?" Hannah asked, as we ventured deeper into the dark void of silent desert.

"Is that how what works?"

"When you love someone, do you have to work hard at it?"

"Sometimes."

"Do you have to work hard at loving me?"

"No," I said quickly, finding a sweetness returning with my words. "Not at all. Loving you isn't hard at all."

"But it's hard with Grandma Celeste."

I paused. "Yes, I guess it is."

"Why?"

"I don't know."

To my relief, Hannah stopped the interrogation. She leaned her head back, and I thought she might fall asleep. But then softly, with a tender shyness, she began to sing. For the next half hour my little songbird filled the air with music in Hawaiian and English. The fist in my gut unclenched.

The last fifty miles into Phoenix were the longest. Hannah had fallen asleep, and I was fighting fatigue by listening to the radio and opening the window so that the cooling night air could fill my lungs. The desert smelled old, dusty, and void of any hint of dampness. Like invisible bandits, the night winds came through my open window and pillaged all the moisture they could snare from my lips, eyes, and even from my throat.

I was ready to be done with the desert and out of the darkness. This was not a soothing or comfortable place for me. Loss of moisture felt like loss of energy. I preferred humidity and looked forward even more to the dampness that would replenish me in Louisiana.

Arriving at the hotel, I bought four large bottles of water from the vending machine in the hallway and coaxed my sleepy Hannah to drink a little before we climbed into bed. With the thick drapes shutting off all light and the air temperature at a comfortable level, Hannah and I were lulled to sleep by the hum of the air conditioner.

According to our schedule, we were supposed to be on the road again by 8:00 the next morning. My organized husband had marked it clearly on the agenda. Wednesday, depart Phoenix at 8:00 a.m., stay that night in Albuquerque, New Mexico. Thursday we were scheduled to drive from Albuquerque, through Amarillo and drop down into Dallas. From Dallas it was only a five- or six-hour drive to Grand Lady's in Howell, Louisiana.

However, Hannah and I didn't leave Phoenix at 8:00 AM. We didn't even wake up until noon.

In a scramble, we threw on some clothes, checked out of the hotel, tossed our things into the back of the SUV, and took off as if we were late for the start of a race.

The car had been sitting in the direct sun and was unbearable. We rolled down the windows and cranked up the air-conditioning at the same time.

"My legs are getting burned on this seat!" Hannah cried.

"Can you find a sweatshirt or something to sit on?" I was ready to pull out of the hotel parking lot, when I looked into the rearview mirror and found we had no rearview mirror. It had fallen off and was on the floor. I drove to the first car repair place I found.

"Happens all the time," the service manager said. "It's the heat, you know. You can leave it here for us to fix."

"How long will it take?"

"We're pretty backed up today. We could have it to you by closing time."

My expression must have tipped him off that closing time wasn't the answer I'd hoped for because he looked over his shoulder and then in a lower voice said, "Or you can go to Rod's Auto Parts and buy your own repair kit and do it yourself."

"What kind of repair kit?"

"It's basically a tube of super-strength glue," the service manager said. "Comes in a package with directions. Ask Rod. He'll fix you up."

"Where is Rod's located?"

"Over on Juarez and Third. Are you from out of town?"

I nodded. I almost told him I was from Hawaii, but I didn't want to get stuck standing there hearing all about whose cousin went to Waikiki on their honeymoon and how overpriced everything was and how this guy always wanted to come visit and could I recommend any good places to stay. I merely nodded, and he drew a map to Rod's Auto Parts Store.

"Can we get something to eat now?" Hannah asked, when we reentered the roasting car.

"I need to get the mirror fixed first," I said. "See if we have anything left in the little fridge. And make sure you drink some water."

"Nothing," Hannah said after peering into the fridge. "We need to buy some snacks."

I added snacks to my growing list: find Rod's Auto Repair Store, fix mirror, eat, go shopping for snacks, and get on the road. We couldn't possibly make it to Albuquerque by nightfall.

Fortunately, Rod's Auto Repair was easy to find, and Rod was having a slow day. When I explained what I needed, he came out to the car and helped me line up the mirror on the windshield just right. The mirror had to be held in place for a full two minutes after the glue was applied to keep it from slipping.

"I noticed your plates are from Washington," Rod said.

"Excuse me?"

"Your license plates. What part of Washington are you from?"

"It's not our car," Hannah said. "We're just using it to get to Atlanta."

Rod looked at me as if I were a criminal kidnapping this young girl and whisking her across the country in a stolen vehicle.

"It's my brother's car," I explained, with a calm, patronizing sound to my voice. "We're driving it to Atlanta for him. As a favor."

"Long drive," Rod said.

"Yes, yes it is."

I looked at the digital sign at the bank across the street. One hundred two degrees. And here we stood in the full sun with the parking lot asphalt, like hot lava, threatening to melt our shoes. We waited for this nice man to let go of the rearview mirror so we could be on our way.

"We live on Maui," Hannah said, freely entering into the conversation.

"Maui?" Rod's expression brightened. "You live on Maui? That must be nice. My wife always wanted to go to Maui."

"Is the mirror set now?" I asked impatiently.

"Should be." Rod let go, and the mirror held in place perfectly.

"Thanks," I said. "Thanks very much."

"No problem-o. Sure hope the rest of your trip goes well. Are you going south, through El Paso? Because if you are, you know, you should go to Carlsbad Caverns. One of the greatest wonders of the world, in my opinion."

"Carlsbad Caverns?" Hannah said. "We saw a movie about Carlsbad Caverns at school when we were studying bats."

"Did they show you how all the bats come flying out of the cave at night?" Rod asked.

Hannah nodded enthusiastically. "It was really cool the way they came out like a big black cloud. Are we going there, Mom?"

"No, we're going north, through Albuquerque."

"Why?" Hannah asked.

I gave Hannah a stern look that let her know we could have the rest of this discussion without Rod the Auto Repairman standing there listening in the 102-degree heat. I knew that my husband thought Albuquerque would be cooler than the route through El Paso, but I wasn't going to have this discussion with Hannah in public.

"If you don't mind my saying so," Rod said. "You could go the southern route, take in a tour of Carlsbad Caverns, and still make a straight shot for Dallas. You know, you have to take into consideration when you might pass this way again. If this turns out to be your only chance to see the caverns, well, it would be a shame to pass them by. Awful shame."

I don't think my response to Rod the Auto Repairman was very cordial. I don't remember exactly what I said, but I do remember feeling irritated beyond my ability to think straight. With the mirror back in place, Hannah and I headed for the main road.

"Why are we in such a hurry?" Hannah asked right after I had to slam on my brakes to avoid hitting the police car in front of me. I was willing to make a dash through the yellow light, but obviously he wasn't.

"Because we're off schedule," I snapped. "The way things are going, we'll be driving until after midnight, and I don't like being under so much pressure."

"Mom, whose vacation is this?"

"What do you mean whose vacation is this?"

"Well, is it Uncle Jon's car's vacation? I mean, I know we're supposed to get his car to him, but are we just part of Uncle Jon's vacation, or are we supposed to be having our own vacation?"

It took me several minutes to calm down before I could say, "This is our vacation. We're supposed to have fun."

"That's what I thought, too." Hannah said.

I spotted an International House of Pancakes and asked, "How about some pancakes for breakfast?"

"Don't you mean lunch instead of breakfast?"

"Okay, then how about some pancakes for lunch? I'll bring in the map, and you and I can decide what we want to do for the rest of our vacation."

It just so happened that our waitress had been to Carlsbad Caverns last summer, and she had all kinds of advice on the best way to get there, the best place to stay, and the best time to take the tour.

As Hannah's finger traced the route on the map now covering our table, I realized this was the first time she had been invited to enter into this trip in a tangible way. She could see the distance we already had come. She could touch the words *Phoenix* and *Dallas* and *Atlanta* on the map. She always had been a tactile learner. Why hadn't I offered her a map to touch earlier?

Fortified with lots of carbohydrates and a fresh camaraderie for the altered journey ahead, Hannah and I left the restaurant and searched out the nearest bookstore to buy a better map of the Arizona/New Mexico area we were going to be driving through. Along with the map we also bought two books on CD. One of them was a modern version of *Pilgrim's Progress*, the book from which I'd so randomly extracted the quote at poor Mulligan's memorial. I wanted Hannah to be exposed to more of the classics, and since she wasn't a reader the way I had been, this seemed like a good alternative.

We stopped at a grocery store to stock up on a blend of Aunt Su Ling–type organic snacks as well as several candy bars for Hannah and some Scottish shortbread for me.

At the checkout stand Hannah told the clerk, "My mom and I are on vacation."

In Hannah's voice I heard a hint of excitement, as if she felt invested in this journey for the first time.

Heading south, Hannah opened the detailed map on her lap, ready to navigate all the way. She informed me that we were going to take Highway 180 through El Paso, go around or over the Guadalupe Mountains, which contained the highest elevation in all of Texas, and then head north, back into New Mexico.

"So, actually, Mom, we'll be in Texas today for a short while, and then we'll go back into New Mexico on our way to Carlsbad." Hannah was clearly enjoying the power her new access to details allotted her.

I realized how a different sort of power balance had been in play on this trip. It seemed Hannah was eager to assert herself and her opinions while I was determined to subdue her. I knew how to be in control. I didn't know how to be my daughter's travel companion and friend. My praise of her singing seemed to be a positive step forward. The way I relaxed and adjusted the travel plans had to be fairly commendable as well.

But we had a long way to go. And I was still the mother and ultimate decision-maker in this adventure.

Hannah popped in the CD of *Pilgrim's Progress,* and for the rest of the simmering hot afternoon we drove in air-conditioned comfort, a couple of cushy pilgrims making progress in our emerging relationship as mother and growing-up daughter.

Chapter 8

We didn't arrive in Carlsbad early enough in the evening to watch the bats swarm from the caverns' opening. Hannah said that was okay because she had seen the bats on the movie at school. I was curious and a little disappointed, but not too much.

Remembering the advice of the waitress at the IHOP, we made sure to start our drive to Carlsbad Caverns early the next morning. The road was long and winding. At exactly 8:00 we pulled into a nearly empty parking lot and were among the first to pay for our admission and take the elevator down into the earth's depths.

The first thing that hit us as we entered the caverns was how the temperature had lowered dramatically. We were told that the caverns remained a constant 56 degrees. Pulling on our sweatshirts, Hannah and I made a mutual decision to first stop and have breakfast at the underground café, because it's not every day you can eat bagels and hot chocolate hundreds of feet below the earth's surface.

"This is colder than the snow on Mount Hood." Hannah stomped her feet under the table. "Look, I can see my breath."

"It's the steam from the hot chocolate. Come on. Let's walk. That will warm us up."

We took the self-guided tour, using the headphones to listen to our "tour guide," as we followed the smooth, roped-off trail through the part of the cavern called "The Big Room." This section of the cavern was immense and full of variations. Hannah loved the stalactites that hung from the ceiling in one area, which was referred to as "The Chandelier."

"Look at all those colors," she said.

I nearly said, "What colors?" but then I stopped and looked more closely. The chandelier had, indeed, as Hannah said, "been painted by God." It displayed desert colors: soft peach, taupe, sand, and gray. The colors were so subtle that I would never have noticed them if it weren't for my little artist and her sharp eye.

Hannah led the way into the "Temple of the Sun Room" where a Lilliputian-sized village of rock formations spread out at our feet and seemed to pay homage to a unique, spiral formation.

"Don't you think this is cool?" Hannah asked.

I smiled and nodded.

"Can't you just see a whole bunch of miniature-sized creatures turning these rocks into homes?" Hannah asked. "That would be the one I'd live in." She pointed to a formation that came to a point at the top with a slight twist, like a soft-serve ice cream cone. "I'd paint the roof white and put a little flag on top," she added.

We moved on, united in the experience and engaging our imaginations with each new part of the caverns we explored.

My favorite section was "The Rock of Ages." A tall, solid formation, the rock had stood unaffected by the thousands of visitors who had viewed it for more than a hundred years.

Standing alone before the massive rock, Hannah and I listened to the recorded tour information and learned a sixteen-year-old named Jim White first started an extensive exploration of the caverns in 1898. He offered private tours two years later and continued the tours for almost twenty-five years. At this spot in front of "The Rock of Ages," the tour guides would stop and conduct a ceremony that included singing the old hymn, "Rock of Ages."

Hannah and I looked at each other when the recording ended, and I said, "Should we sing?"

"I don't know that hymn."

I sang softly in my less-than-stellar voice, "Rock of Ages, cleft for me, let me hide myself in Thee. Let the . . . la, la, la, la, la . . ."

"Sounds like you don't know it either." Hannah

giggled. "My feet are cold. How much farther before we get back to the elevators?"

Our self-guided tour wound down quickly, and we returned to the earth's surface where the warm air thawed us by the time we reached our parked car. Aside from missing out on the sight of hundreds of thousands of what we learned were "Mexican free-tailed bats" that whirled counter-clockwise each night when departing the natural entrance of the cave, our tour was exceptional. I told Hannah I had to agree with Rod the Auto Repairman. We just had toured a small portion of one of the wonders of the world.

"You know what I think was the best part?" Hannah asked, as we drove back down the winding road.

"What?"

"The art."

"What do you mean the art?"

"All that natural art. God put all that art down there under the earth. It was like he hid his artwork in a secret vault, and nobody even knew about it for thousands of years. Then that teenage guy went in there and discovered all that treasure."

Hannah's insight hit me as profoundly mature.

"I was thinking how scary it must have been for that guy," Hannah went on. "Because the first time he went in, he probably didn't know if he would come out alive."

"You're right."

Who is this young woman in the passenger's seat? When did my little girl start having such deep insights?

We drove for several hours before Hannah said she had to go to the bathroom. I wished I had thought to stop sooner, because the SUV was coasting on empty when we finally found a gas station. Hannah hurried to the restroom. I stood by the pump, filling the tank and watching her until she was safely inside.

The vastness of this part of the country continued to astound me. Everything around us felt wide open. I could picture a modern-day cowboy riding off in any direction and not seeing another human for days, if he wanted to. He would see lots of antelope, such as the ones we saw yesterday while driving through a slice of Texas. The first antelope thrilled us. The second, third, and fourth were pretty exciting. By the sixth one we had decided we must have been driving through an antelope convention.

After I filled the gas tank and pulled the receipt from the machine, I went to work trying to wash all the smashed, iridescent bugs off the windshield. I thought of the bats, and what a great feast they could have had on the dead insects I'd managed to pick up along the road out of Carlsbad.

The car was ready, but Hannah was still in the restroom. I locked the vehicle, went over to the door on the side of the run-down gas station, and knocked.

"You okay, Hannah?"

"Mom?"

"Yes, Hannah. It's me. Are you okay?"

The door unlocked and opened an inch. "Mom, come in quick."

I slipped inside as Hannah locked the door behind me. She held a wad of toilet paper up to her nose. In a low, muffled voice she said, "Mom, I'm bleeding."

"Oh, did you get a bloody nose? That's understandable. It's been so dry, and the change in temperature and pressure from the caverns—"

"No, Mom." She removed the tissue to show that her nose was fine. She seemed to be trying to screen out the disgusting bathroom's odor. I could tell she had been crying.

"Hannah, what is it?"

"I'm blee-ding," she stated slowly with an exaggerated expression of apprehension.

I got the message. "Oh, Hannah," I said in my softest voice. "Did you just start your period?"

She nodded, her expression a mixture of timidity and discomfort.

"Come here."

I wrapped my arms around her in that scuzzy, stiflingly hot gas station restroom and held her so close I could feel her heart racing.

"Honey, it's okay. This is a good thing, really. It means

your body is doing what it's supposed to do. Right on schedule."

"I know."

A stream of perspiration drizzled down my back as I kissed Hannah on the top of her head. We held each other and stood there sweating and swaying as if cradled together in some ancient strength that is too translucent to describe. Nothing tangible and solid like words can express the deep mystery of how it feels to be entrusted by God with life-giving power.

Whatever this holy essence was, I felt it now. I was the rose opening into full bloom. Hannah was the dew-kissed rosebud about to curl back her first tender petals. And we were together, holding each other close for this advent.

"Hannah," I whispered, "this really is a wonderful thing. You're becoming a young woman. This is a gift to you from God."

Hannah pulled back, looking at me with an expression that said, "Yeah, great, thanks a lot."

I realized my best wishes might be a bit hasty. Change of any sort takes time to adjust to.

"Will you be okay if I go to the car and get a few things for you?"

She nodded.

"I'll be right back."

I slipped out into the heat. For several years I had speculated about when Hannah would start her period.

At nine years old Hannah started to ask questions based on things she had heard the older kids say at school. We had a conversation that day, and I think I provided enough information to satisfy her curiosity without dipping into graphic detail of how babies came into the world.

When she was ten, a few more complex questions started to come, so I planned a special evening for just the two of us. I went to the Portuguese bakery and bought her favorite, chocolate-covered coconut macaroons. I made sure we had the house to ourselves that night. I put on soft music, pulled out my china plates, made a pot of tea with lots of cream and sugar, and presented her with a fresh, white gardenia.

We sat in the cleaned-up living room and had a private talk about our womanly bodies and how hers soon would be changing. I wanted to guide Hannah gracefully into womanhood and make this transition a gentle passage for her.

I found it ironic that after all the lovely preparation for this event, here we were, sweltering in a smelly gas station, in the middle of Nowheresville, Texas.

A strange perception struck me. I wondered if Mary might have had the same sort of feelings so long ago in Bethlehem. All those prophecies and preparations for the Messiah who was coming to be the Savior of the world, and when the moment finally arrived, it happened in the middle of a smelly stable. The most ancient of shrouded mysteries came into this world through the body of a young woman who had once embarked on the same journey my Hannah was now beginning. Eve's curse turned into Mary's blessing.

Once we pulled back onto the road, I turned the air conditioning on high. Hannah crawled into the backseat, stretched out, and wrapped the elegant llama blanket around her bare legs.

"I love this blanket," she said. "I'm going to write a thank-you note to Su Ling. Could I send her one of those postcards we bought at Carlsbad Caverns?"

"Good idea."

Hannah nestled in, and I put the car on cruise control, thinking about Su Ling and her extravagant expressions of love. In the short time we had been with her, there had never been an awkward moment or a heaviness of any sort. I thought of how her love lifted and lightened those around her rather than burdened them with regret and shame.

That's what I feel around my mom. Shame. I don't want Hannah to feel that. I want a blessing for her, not a curse. With my mom I always feel as if I should be apologizing for something, like not getting up in time to go for a walk with her or not allowing enough time for a longer visit or . . .

I knew this was ridiculous, but I thought it anyway.

Or for getting Mulligan so riled up that he barked himself to death.

"Was it my fault Mulligan died?" I mumbled to myself.

No, of course not. I wish Hannah hadn't found him the way she did, but I couldn't have predicted that, either. I can't shield Hannah from death any more than I can shield her from life. She watched a baby llama being born, for goodness' sake! I can't stop her from growing up. She's turned a corner. She's a young woman now.

I cried softly. Hannah wasn't my baby anymore. Even her body was being transformed before my eyes. When my body went through its adolescent metamorphosis, my mother had provided information, but she wasn't personally involved in my transformation. I was certain she never had cried tears over me the way I was now weeping over Hannah. What I remembered most clearly from her was the phrase "the female curse is on you."

I felt so much shame. *Shame on you for being a female! Shame on you for having cramps and wanting to stay home from school! Shame on you for letting Mulligan die!*

"You know what? It wasn't my fault! None of it. I didn't do anything wrong. Not with Mulligan or with—"

"Mom?"

I looked in the rearview mirror, startled to see Hannah sitting up, looking at me with her head tilted.

"Mom, who were you talking to?"

I looked straight ahead and slowly said, "Myself."

"I think you were answering yourself, too, Mom. Just, you know. FYI."

"Thank you, Hannah."

"What were you talking to yourself about?"

"Nothing, really. Sorry if I woke you." I blinked away the final tears.

"You didn't wake me. I've been looking at these DVD covers and wondering if I could watch one of them now. I haven't watched any this whole trip."

"Yes, I know. Which one do you want to watch?"

Hannah held up one of the movies so I could spot the title in the rearview mirror.

"Not that one," I said. "It's too grown up."

She held up another one. I was familiar with that DVD and thought it was more appropriate, so I agreed she could watch it as long as she kept the volume on and didn't use the headphones.

Taking the car out of cruise control and becoming more attentive to my driving, I looked out the windshield at the huge, puffy white clouds that had gathered in the eastern sky. I had been so caught up in my thoughts while driving on the straight, unspecific highway that for many miles I hadn't paid attention to what was around me. Turning off the air-conditioning, I rolled down the window, hoping the fresh air would bring an additional slap of reality.

Instead of a slap, it felt more like a *fwap* from a wet towel. The Texas afternoon boldly pushed its heavy humidity into the car and bragged about the big storm waiting for me up ahead. Even though I preferred humidity to desert-dry air, this moist air came in the window like a bully. I had never made a soft spot in my heart for bullies of any sort, so I rolled up the window and whooped that braggart with my little finger by pushing the air-conditioning button.

Two and a half DVDs later, we pulled into the Dallas-Fort Worth area in the middle of a deluge. I saw rain all the time in Hawaii, but not like this. The raindrops were, like everything else in Texas, twice as big as any raindrop I'd ever seen. The great pellets of water seemed angry as they came at the windshield like liquid bombers on a suicide mission.

It was dark. A dark and stormy night. Tall tales that turn into legends were written on such nights. I had grown up reading those tall tales and loving every word. Now that I was in the midst of such a setting, I didn't want stories of any sort. All I wanted was to find our hotel and treat my gas-pedal leg to a long soak in a tall tub.

Jon had urged me to stay at as many five-star hotels as I could find on our trip. But when Tom helped with the plans, I had asked him to make reservations at the more moderate-priced motels so I wouldn't feel as if I were presuming on Jon's generosity. So far, we had stayed at moderately priced motels. All of them were clean and basic and felt safe.

However, when it came to making the reservation for Dallas, my dear husband selected an exceptional, high-rise hotel downtown. He said it was close to the original Neiman Marcus department store, and we might want to do some shopping.

Shopping was not at the top of our list.

We arrived at the hotel close to nine o'clock, tired, sweaty, hungry, and in the middle of another cloudburst punctuated by thunder so loud I could feel it reverberating in my chest. I was thrilled to have the uniformed attendant park the car for me while another tall Texan took care of our luggage.

"Can we order room service, Mom?"

"Sure. What are you hungry for?"

"Pizza. Do you think they have pizza here?"

"I imagine they do."

"What kind do you think they have?"

"Probably something really big."

Our room was spacious and oh-so-inviting after the long drive. I ordered the "Texas special" pizza while Hannah took a shower. When the larger-than-average pizza arrived, I grabbed a few slices and carried them into the bathroom where I ate pizza in the tub. I had never done such a thing in my life and was proud of myself for acting like I was on vacation.

The storm hung around most of the night, but by morning, we opened the curtains to let the strong sunshine fill the room. Hannah and I stood in the light, and I braided her blond hair into a single braid. I was amazed all over again at how thick her hair was. My sleek, coffee-colored hair had never been that thick or that long. Hannah's mane was like spun honey in the morning radiance.

"Aren't you tired of driving, Mom?"

"Yes, but this is our last day on the road for a while. When we get to Grand Lady's today, we can really relax."

"Except I can't go swimming," Hannah said.

"Oh, that's right." My mind processed the options available to her.

Before I launched that discussion, she said, "I thought about it, and I just want to stay with you at Grand Lady's when we get there. I don't want to go over to your aunt and uncle's and have them all asking me if I want to go in their swimming pool."

"Actually, Uncle Burt and Aunt Peg live in the Big House on the same property as Grand Lady's little cottage. The pool is between the two houses."

"Oh. Well, can we just not make a big deal about it?"

"Of course."

"Why doesn't Grand Lady live in the Big House?"

"She used to."

"Why did Uncle Burt kick his mother out of her own house?"

"He didn't kick her out. After Grandpa died, Grand Lady lived in the Big House all by herself for a long time. Then it got to be too much house for her to keep up. Instead of selling it, Grand Lady gave the Big House to Uncle Burt and Aunt Peg, and she moved into the cottage where she lives now."

"Does her cottage have a picket fence and shutters and window boxes with lots of pink flowers?"

"I don't think so. I don't know. I've never seen pictures of it."

"So, she could live in a shoe, for all you know." Hannah grinned. "She could be the old woman who lives in a shoe and has so many children she doesn't know what to do."

"Very clever, Hannah, but I'm certain she doesn't live in a shoe."

"She might. Whenever you talk about her, it sounds like a nursery rhyme. You make Louisiana sound like a fairy-tale place."

At that moment, with the light on Hannah's slim silhouette and her hair trailing down her back, she looked like a fairy-tale princess.

"It *was* a fairy-tale place for me, when I was twelve. I hope you like it, too."

"I probably won't."

I snapped the elastic tie in place at the end of the braid and gave Hannah a firm look. "Why would you say such a thing?"

"Because you and I don't always like the same things."

I stared at Hannah, trying to decide if she was being sassy or innocently honest. It was hard to tell. I reminded myself that her hormones might be doing the talking for her at the moment. This tug-of-war had pulled me back and forth with Hannah over the miles. Sometimes I thought everything between us was perfect. Then, at moments like this, I felt as if I were two inches from watching our relationship disintegrate. A power struggle definitely was taking place that had never been in existence before.

"Come on." I tossed her brush in the nearly packed luggage. "Let's hit the road."

Moving forward seemed the best response to all that I was feeling. Moving closer to Louisiana and to Grand Lady. Hannah was right. I had turned Howell into a fairy-tale sort of Promised Land. I didn't want to evaluate now if that was a good thing or a bad thing. Being so close to our destination I knew—just knew—that I wouldn't be disappointed once we arrived.

Chapter 9

My good intentions of limiting Hannah's viewing of DVDs in the car waned that morning when we got back on the road. Hannah lasted about ten minutes out of Dallas before she started promoting all the DVDs she hadn't watched yet and how her stomach was grumbly. I gave in without any debate to her video-fest on the mother-approved titles.

"There's a pottery shop up here off the road," I said, checking the gas gauge. "I have to pull off here anyway, so I thought it might be fun to check out the pottery."

Hannah's groan reminded me that my idea of fun wasn't her idea of fun. Certainly the short break would do us both some good.

We strolled up and down the aisles of the large pottery shop while I alone admired the plates and mugs. When we came to the pitchers, I stopped and smiled. Grand Lady had three pitchers made from this glazed pottery. I knew because of the distinctive way all the smooth, round pots had a single blue stripe around their bellies. The moment I saw them, I thought of cold milk, warm syrup, and fresh-squeezed juice, because that's what had filled these pitchers at Grand Lady's. She kept hers lined up in a row in her windowsill. Whenever she was ready to serve liquid of any sort, she would select the right size pitcher and place it on the table on top of a dessert-sized plate that was made of the same thick pottery and painted with Texas bluebells.

"Mom, do they have anything to drink here? I'm really thirsty."

We found some water, and I debated over how many pieces of pottery I should buy. I'd never seen this exact same thick, gray pottery anywhere. I loved all the sweet memories attached to these pieces.

"What do you think?" I asked Hannah. "Which ones should I buy?"

"Get 'em all, Mom. You always say later that you should have bought something after you walk away from it. Just get it. I mean, like, will you ever be here again?"

I bought three pitchers of varying sizes, four of the Texas bluebell plates, and one bowl exactly like the one Grand Lady had used on her kitchen table years ago. It was the bowl in which she floated her fragrant gardenias.

"That was your first souvenir, wasn't it, Mom?" Hannah asked when we climbed back in the car.

"Yes, I guess it was."

"Well, it's about time!"

"Do you wish you had bought more souvenirs along the way, Hannah?"

"No. It's not like we were in a lot of places that had the kinds of things I'd want to buy."

"Grand Lady is going to want to buy you something when we get to Howell. When I first called her and told her we were coming, she said one of our days with her would be a shopping day, and she would buy you something special."

"Where will we go shopping? I thought you said she lived in a small town."

"Howell is very small, but they have a little gift shop next to the Piggly Wiggly."

"The what?"

"Piggly Wiggly. That's their grocery store."

Hannah giggled and kept repeating the name. "Piggly Wiggly. Piggly Wiggly. You're making that up, Mom. They don't really have a grocery store called Piggly Wiggly."

"Yes, they do!"

"I'll believe it when I see it. So what else do they have in Howell? Besides a Piggly Wiggly?" She laughed again.

"They have a park, a creek, a cemetery, and a couple of churches. That's why Uncle Burt put in the swimming pool when they moved into the Big House. He and Aunt Peg wanted my cousins to have a place to hang out with all their friends. The summer I stayed at Grand Lady's there wasn't a pool; so we had to run in the sprinklers to cool off, or drive to the lake."

"Did you run in the sprinklers, Mom?"

"Yep."

"Did you really?"

"Yes, I really did. Is that so hard to believe?"

"I can't picture you running in the sprinklers."

"Well, I did. Several times. And I caught a frog at the creek and kept it in a bucket for two days before Grand Lady found it and made me let it go."

Hannah looked at me with a hint of admiration. "You actually picked up a frog. I never pictured you doing anything squishy when you were a girl."

"Anything squishy?"

"Yeah, the way you get so queasy around blood and everything, I didn't picture you ever getting close to animals."

"The little creatures I can handle. But blood, well," I shivered involuntarily. "I don't do well around blood."

"Why?"

"I don't know."

Hannah looked out the window for about a mile before she said, "There has to be a reason."

"A reason for what?"

"A reason for everything. There has to be a reason you hate blood so much. Something must have happened.

Maybe you blocked it out, Mom. Like on that movie I watched last night. When the girl fell off her horse at the competition, she woke up and said she didn't know how to ride horses. But then her grandfather took her out to his ranch, and she liked this one horse. When it got locked in the barn during the storm, she remembered she knew how to ride, and she saved the horse."

I gave Hannah a playful scowl.

"Well, you should at least think about it, Mom. You should think about a lot of things, because there has to be a reason for everything, you know."

"I should think about lot of things, huh?"

"Yeah. A lot of things."

I was the one with the driver's license, steering the vehicle in a straight line, as we lapped up the final stretch of Texas highway and headed for Louisiana. But Hannah's thoughtful admonition made me feel as if she was the adult and I the child. Hannah crawled in the back of the SUV and resumed her video marathon.

I kept my eyes on the road and thought. I didn't want to think about my mother, because that relationship exhausted me. I definitely didn't want to think about why I hated blood. So I thought about my brother and how I had really never pursued knowing him. Why was that? How could I have spent the first half of my life with someone every single day and yet barely know him?

In a deep, not often visited corner of my soul, I felt a strange sadness over not being close to my brother. I couldn't go back and change my childhood.

How much of love is a choice? How much of it is a mutual commitment? It was one thing for me to feel sorry for myself because I didn't feel sufficiently loved while growing up, but how many people had slipped through my life unpursued? Unloved?

I felt tired. Too much thinking.

"Hannah?"

"Yes?"

"How about if you drive for a while, and I'll take a little nap."

"Very funny, Mom. Are we almost there?"

It was the first time the whole trip Hannah had asked that question.

"Yes, we're almost there." Somehow, as I said it, I felt deep down that I wanted to be almost "there," too, wherever "there" was in my timid spirit. I didn't expect solutions to any of my complicated feelings. But if any helpful insights landed on the appropriate runway, I'd direct them to the right gate and see to it that they had a chance to enter the terminal of my heart. I wanted to be at peace.

Shreveport traffic was heavy due to road construction. I called Aunt Peg on my cell phone to let her know where we were.

"Well, isn't that good news, Sweet Abby!" my Aunt

Peg said. "Grand Lady has been as busy as a honeybee readying her little cottage for your visit. We have supper in the works, so y'all just drive safe and get here when you get here."

I drove through Minton, keeping to the right of the traffic circle by the courthouse, just as Aunt Peg had instructed me.

"Mom, who's that?" Hannah had returned to the passenger's seat and was taking in the sights of this small town, pointing at a large statue in the center of the traffic circle.

"I think he was an officer in the Civil War. I don't remember. Uncle Burt can tell you. He knows all the history of this area."

"Is Howell smaller than this town?"

"Yes, it's smaller than Minton."

Minton ended abruptly after the video rental store, and what followed was twelve miles of country road with slender trees gathered in wooded clumps on both sides. Every so often a rusted mailbox would appear at the roadside, leaning on a splintered post with the front panel unlatched.

"Hannah, look at those mailboxes. Don't they look like weary hound dogs with their tongues hanging out?"

Hannah turned to watch the mailboxes zoom by. Except for those occasional posts, this stretch of road appeared uninhabited.

"I wonder what sort of houses those hound-dog mailboxes are guarding," I said.

"Mom, every now and then you say things that I don't expect."

"You mean like about the mailboxes?"

"Yeah. How do you think up those things?"

"I don't know."

"It's like you make a picture with your words."

I took in Hannah's compliment and held it close. Perhaps that was her way of returning the praise I'd given her over her beautiful singing voice.

"Let's see how hot it is," I rolled down my window.

Hannah pointed to the internal temperature and directional gauge on the front console. "It says eighty-two," she reported. "That's not very hot."

I stuck my hand out the window. Hannah did the same. The late afternoon air slid through my fingers, feeling much hotter than eighty-two degrees felt on Maui. I rubbed my fingers together to see if I could feel the moisture that hung in the air. A smile crept across my lips.

We're really here!

"Are those daisies?" Hannah pointed to the patches of bright yellow flowers with dark centers that lined the ditches alongside the two-way road.

"Grand Lady calls them black-eyed Susans," I said. "They sure are growing in abundance around here."

"Hey, where's he going?"

We sped past a large, broad-shouldered man wearing long pants and a long-sleeved shirt with the sleeves rolled up. A baseball cap covered his head. I studied him in the rearview mirror. He didn't seem to be in a hurry, wherever he was going.

Looking back at the road ahead, I let out a squawk and slammed on the brakes. In front of us a wooden crate had split open in the middle of the road. Two flustered white hens flapped about, scurrying this way and that.

"Hold on, Hannah!"

I swerved to the right, opting to risk hitting one of the befuddled chickens rather than hit the broken crate. I missed the hens but must have run over part of the crate, because a terrible clanking sound rattled on the car's back left side.

The SUV obeyed my steering commands and stayed in a straight line as we teetered on the edge of the road. I realized I was flattening a whole row of black-eyed Susans that rose from the red dirt in the ditch. We came to a halt a few inches from a chair, a beat-up, old, straight-backed wooden chair sitting on the edge of the road as if it had sprung up there naturally like the yellow wildflowers.

"You okay?" I asked Hannah.

"Yeah. What happened? Did we hit that box?"

"I think so." I glanced in the rearview mirror.

"What is that chair doing there?"

"I have no idea. At least we didn't hit one of the chickens."

"Or the chair," Hannah said.

"I hope we don't have a flat tire. You stay in the car. I'll check it out."

"I want to come with you."

I turned to Hannah and what I read on her face was more of an expression of adventure than fear of being left alone.

"All right. But be careful. You have your shoes on, don't you?"

"I'm putting them on right now."

"Not your flip-flops. Your tennis shoes."

"My tennis shoes? They're in the back. I'll be fine in my slippers."

For years I'd argued with Hannah about wearing "proper" shoes to school. In Lahaina, most of the kids wore only thin flip-flop sandals all year round. About half of those kids kicked off their "slippers," as the Hawaiians called them, and left them under their desks for the rest of the day. Of all the local customs my kids had adopted in Hawaii, this was the only one I couldn't stand.

"Mom, these slippers are fine, see? I'll be okay."

I jumped out and slammed the door, not willing to

argue with her over shoes when I had bigger concerns over the car.

Hannah hotfooted her way around the front of the vehicle and had a look at what was left of the abandoned chair. I squatted to see what had caused the noise. The wheel well didn't appear to be damaged, which was a relief. The tire looked fine. I didn't want to tell my brother that I had smashed up his beautiful new SUV.

"It looks like everything is okay," I told Hannah, as she joined me at the back of the car. "I guess it was part of the crate that made the noise. But it didn't hurt the car. What a relief!"

"Look, Mom," Hannah said, facing the direction we had just come.

The man in the baseball cap was sauntering our way with the two protesting chickens, one under each arm. He didn't appear to be walking any faster than he had when we passed him. Hannah took on her art critic pose, tilting her head and shifting her weight to her right foot.

"Mom, can I take a picture?"

Her question seemed so random that I snapped at her, saying, "A picture of what?"

"Of that."

I turned, trying to see what Hannah saw. She was staring at the large man, the long, flat road with the broken crate now kicked to the side, out of harm's way for the next driver. On either side rose the tall, spindly trees lining the road as far as the eye could follow.

For a flicker of a second, I saw what Hannah saw. The late afternoon sun was pressing daylight out of the woods like a juicer pressing all the sweet juice from an orange and letting chunks of pulp glide through the filter. In the same way that the pulp makes the juice thick, the languid bits of woodland "pulp" that came floating through the light made the air thick and golden.

As the ambling man moved through the orange light, the scene looked like a study in contrasts: the fluffed-up white feathers of the hens against the molasses-black skin on his bare arms, the pale blue of his shirt against the early summer green of the tree leaves. He continued to move toward us at the same pace as the airy light pulp that floated out of the woods. The whole world seemed to move in slow motion, or underwater.

It was an extraordinary scene. I felt the same way Hannah did about taking a picture. I wanted to describe to someone what I saw.

But deeper inside me was a primal sense that I should protect my daughter.

"Hannah, come on. Let's get back in the car. We need to be on our way. You can take a picture from inside the car."

I tried the door, but it was locked. I tried it again.

"Hannah?"

She was around by the passenger's door now, and I could hear her tugging on the handle.

"Hannah, did you lock the car?"

She paused and then flapped around to my side with a contrite look on her face. "I thought you had the keys."

"No, the keys are still inside, Hannah. Along with the cell phone, my purse, and everything else!"

"I didn't know. I'm sorry. I'm really sorry, Mom."

I clenched my teeth and tried to keep all my angry words inside.

"What are we going to do, Mom?"

"I don't know, Hannah. Let me think."

With a glance over my shoulder, I saw the man with the chickens was almost upon us. The thick, filtered light was still illuminating him.

"Hannah, stay close to me," I said in a low voice.

"I am."

I put my arm around her shoulder and turned to face the approaching man.

He looked me in the eye. "Evenin', ma'am."

I nodded and offered a cold stare. He was even larger up close.

"You two fixin' to go into town?"

I looked away and didn't answer.

Hannah jumped in. "Yeah, we're going to see my mom's aunt and uncle and her grandma, but I accidentally locked the keys in the car."

I pressed my fingers into her shoulder. Why did she have to be so innocent and friendly?

The man bobbed his head in a sympathetic gesture toward our predicament. For some reason, I noticed that the chickens were unusually quiet and settled in his arms.

"Y'all have about a half mile 'fore you hit town. Nice enuf evenin' for a walk."

"Yes, it is," I said brusquely. "Thank you." I hoped he would take my staccato words as a dismissal.

But he didn't. He stood comfortably still, as if waiting for us. I stood uncomfortably still, waiting for him to leave.

"Mom, are we going to start walking?"

I faced Hannah and tried to keep my voice low and calm. "No, we'll wait here until another car comes by."

"But we haven't seen another car since we left Minton. Why don't we walk? It's only half a mile."

I looked up the vacant road, over my shoulder toward town, then down at my hands. Optimistically, I breathed a silent prayer and tried the driver's door just in case an angel had appeared and released the lock for me from the inside.

It was still locked. I looked at Hannah.

"We can walk," she said. "I don't mind walking."

Stalling for time, I wished the chicken man would grow weary of my indecision and hit the road. He didn't move. Hannah didn't move. I didn't move. The only thing moving was a fleet of perspiration trickles making their way down the front of me and collecting at the already damp waistband of my jeans.

The floating sunlight pulp no longer was visible. It would be dark soon.

"Okay." I grabbed Hannah's hand, as if she were three years old. "Come on. We'll walk." I took off with long-legged strides toward Howell and the safety of the Big House.

Hannah and I walked about four yards down the road before I glanced over my shoulder.

He was following us.

Hannah turned to look, and as she did, she stumbled in her flimsy flip-flops and took a dive onto the pavement. She let out a wail that frightened the chickens and set them off clucking and fluffing up their feathers.

"Hannah, are you okay?" I bent down to help her up, and the first thing I saw was a puddle of blood coming from her bare foot. Her knee and shin both were scraped and peppered with gravel.

Hannah cried. I braced myself against the wave of queasiness. When our kids were little, Tom was the one they went to with their bumps and bruises. This time it was up to me. Oh, how I missed my husband at that moment.

"Hannah, let me see." I knelt down beside her and bravely looked at the wound. A piece of glass had sliced the tender outside edge of her right foot near the top. Part of the glass was still sticking out.

"Hold still, honey. Let me see if I can get that out."

"What is it?" Hannah sobbed.

"It looks like a piece of glass."

"It hurts, Mom."

"I know."

That's when I realized I *did* know. I knew it would hurt to pull out the glass. Like a flash of light, a vivid memory came back from when I was seven and broke a drinking glass while washing the dishes. I stuck my hand into the soapy water, and the sharp edge of the broken piece went into my palm. My hand bled like crazy into the dishwater, turning it red and frightening me. I couldn't stop crying. My father stormed into the kitchen and looked at me holding up my hand, with the blood dripping everywhere and the piece of glass sticking out.

My father cursed at me. "You're making a mess! Clean it up!"

It was the first time I remembered seeing him in a drunken rage. I felt the room growing smaller, as I crumpled on the kitchen floor.

"It's okay," I said softly to Hannah. I knew I wouldn't

faint this time. Everything was becoming clear. A strange settledness replaced years of queasiness born of my fear of being abandoned in a moment of crisis.

"It's going to be all right," I told her. "I'm right here for you. I'm right here. It's okay." With a steady hand, I pulled out the shard. Blood continued to flow from the open wound. I had nothing to use to wrap her foot.

I looked up at our uninvited guest. It seemed unlikely he had a bandage of any sort with him, but I had to ask.

"By any chance . . ." I had a hard time asking help from anyone. I did so much better when I was self-sufficient and had planned things ahead of time so that I could take care of my own needs. But the disturbing truth was I didn't have what I needed to heal my daughter's wound.

"Ma'am?"

I blurted out my request. "Do you have anything I could use to wrap her foot?"

"Would a handkerchief do? I have one right here in my pocket. You mind holding on to these hens for a spell?"

I stood and let the stranger hand me the two nervous chickens. Then I watched him extract a perfectly clean white handkerchief from his back pocket and wrap it around Hannah's foot with tenderness and expertise.

She stopped crying.

"Thank you." I offered the chickens back to the man. "I appreciate your help. We can manage from here."

"How?" Hannah asked.

"I'll carry you," I said without thinking.

"You can't carry me."

"Then we'll wait here for a car to come by."

"But, Mom," Hannah started to cry again. "It's getting dark."

The man stood silently. The chickens were waiting patiently as well. I didn't think I could bring myself to ask this stranger to carry my daughter half a mile to town, but I was running out of alternatives. He didn't offer to carry her. He waited. I knew he was waiting for me to ask.

A thousand dreadful thoughts ran through my mind. This was so hard for me. I prayed and sighed and said, "Sir, would you mind helping us?"

He nodded and stepped closer, giving me the chickens again. I couldn't believe this was happening.

Hannah willingly let him scoop her up with one of his thick arms around her back and the other under her bent knees. With steady, even steps we began our twilight march toward Howell, looking like a tattered remnant of Dixie soldiers finding our way home. I led the way with a chicken under each arm.

Chapter 10

The darkness of the Louisiana twilight slowly came over us like a pewter candlesnuffer smothering a flame. Around us the air remained thick and moist, almost smoky, still holding in the day's heat. I hoped for a breeze; a breeze not only to cool us but also to blow away the childhood memories that had cluttered my thoughts in the midst of Hannah's emergency.

Now I knew why I didn't handle the sight of blood. Hannah was right; there was a reason. However, awakening the memory had not healed me. It had only brought a glimmer of understanding.

Glancing at Hannah, I noticed that the handkerchief bandage was starting to show the red of her blood. It was a good thing she was being carried. I couldn't have done it. Not this far.

"Thank you for helping us out," I said to our silent companion.

"No bother. I was goin' this way."

As we approached the first few houses on the outskirts of Howell, I realized I didn't know how to get to Uncle Burt and Aunt Peg's house. My directions were in the car.

"Do you happen to know where Burt and Peg Burroughs live?" I asked.

"Yes, ma'am. We take a right here on MacDonald. Their place is four houses down on the left side."

"That's right." I adjusted the chickens under my arms and walked a little faster. "I remember this street corner."

"Is that it?" Hannah asked, as soon as the Big House came into view.

"Yes, that's it! The Big House."

I was stunned to see that it wasn't big at all. In my imagination, the Big House had grown over the years to only a few pillars short of a true plantation. In reality, it was average. Old and common and worn. Two thousand square feet in size, at most.

The big front porch looked to me like a wide-mouthed grin. The old house was grinning at me. On the right side the memorable porch swing hung like the one faithful bicuspid remaining in the weathered smile of an ancient Cajun storyteller.

Our kind escort walked us right up the steps of the Big House. He placed Hannah on the padded seat of the porch swing and took the chickens from me.

"Thank you," I said, pressing the doorbell. "Everything should be fine now."

"I do believe it is so," he said.

Just then the front door opened, letting out a swish of cooled air and my Aunt Peg, who was all arms and squeals. "We were just about to start worrying about you two. Where's Hannah? Oh! Why, mercy sakes, what happened to your foot, Miss Hannah?"

Aunt Peg looked exactly as I had remembered her, creamy complexion with strawberry-blond hair cut so that the short, feathery strands skimmed her jawline. Only now her hair was completely white, and her creamy complexion was creased with character lines.

I launched into an abbreviated explanation of what had happened to us and why I had white chicken feathers stuck to my sweaty arms. I turned to motion toward our roadside assistant, but he was gone. Vanished. I looked in both directions and was stunned that he had slipped away so quickly and without a sound.

"Did you see a man standing here with two chickens under his arms when you opened the door?" I asked.

"No, Sweet Abby, but I think we best get Hannah here over to Doc Norton's. Burt? Oh, where is that man? I told him I heard the doorbell."

Aunt Peg called out, "Burt, honey! We have an emergency goin' on here!"

Uncle Burt came around the side of the house, hustling

like an old football coach and calling out his happy greetings. His thick head of hair had gone from brown sugar colored to white sugar with a few specks of brown-sugar showing on the sides. He looked more distinguished than ever.

Peg quickly apprised him of the situation, and he jumped into action, saying he would pull the car around.

"What about Grand Lady?" I asked.

"We told her we would give her a call over at her cottage as soon as y'all arrived, but I think we best be gettin' Hannah over to the doctor's first, don't you?" Aunt Peg looked flustered.

"Yes, of course," I agreed. "I didn't want Grand Lady to be concerned, that's all."

"What the dear woman doesn't know won't hurt her. Let's be on our way."

Peg and I helped Hannah down the steps, and the four of us loaded into Uncle Burt's Lincoln Continental. It wasn't a new model, but it was spacious and in excellent condition. Uncle Burt drove it through town as if his passengers were the masters of ceremony for a small, local version of the Thanksgiving Day Parade.

"Don't you think you should drive a little faster?" Aunt Peg coaxed her husband. "The dear child could be bleeding to death."

"I'm okay," Hannah said. "It doesn't even hurt that much anymore."

"You dear thing, you!" Aunt Peg said. "You just keep thinking those good thoughts, and your Uncle Burt will get you right to the doctor. Won't you, sweetheart?"

Burt picked up his speed and drove us to a large house with an arched trellis covered with pink roses at the front walkway. I somehow had pictured that we would be driving to the local clinic. I hadn't realized we would pay a visit to the family doctor at his home.

Dr. Norton received us graciously and examined Hannah's foot in a side room that was set up for minor emergencies. He gave her a mild painkiller, cleaned the wound, and told me to hold her hand "real tight" while he put her back together with four tidy sutures. She was so brave.

He offered her a lollipop, and to my surprise, Hannah accepted. At home she would have said she was too old for lollipops at the doctor's office.

"You're going to need to take it easy on this foot for the next few days," the doctor told her.

Hannah nodded.

He administered a few twists of white gauze and then expertly wrapped her foot with a stretchy sports bandage. "Make sure you keep your foot covered."

Hannah shot me a glance. How many times had she heard me say those exact words?

"Keep a sock on the next few days and wear a shoe that covers your whole foot," the doctor told Hannah.

"I want you to keep that area clean and dry. That means no going in the pool at least for the next couple of days."

I knew that would be a relief to Hannah. No one would be asking why she wasn't going in the pool now. Her foot would provide a great decoy while her blossoming body completed its first cycle.

We were about to leave when I realized I couldn't pay the doctor. "My purse is in the car."

"No need to worry about paying me," Dr. Norton said. "I'll get Burt to do me a favor sometime, and we'll be all evened up."

"Are you sure?" I asked.

"Course I'm sure. If you have any problems at all, you come back and see me. Any swelling, any redness or pain, you come back, all right?"

"Okay. Thank you," I said.

"Yeah, thanks," Hannah chimed in.

"Y'all take care," the doctor said.

"All fixed up?" Burt asked Hannah, coming alongside to offer his assistance.

Hannah nodded. "It doesn't hurt when I walk on it."

"Don't be using up all your strength, now. Let me help you to the car." Uncle Burt took Hannah under his wing and ushered her out the door.

"I've been thinking about our car problem," I said, following behind Burt and Hannah. "I think the best thing would be for me to call the Automobile Club and have them send out a locksmith."

"No need to do that," Aunt Peg said. "We'll just give Sneaky Pete a call."

"Sneaky Pete?"

"You remember him, don't you?" Uncle Burt asked. "Pete Smitherman down at the gas station. When you were here last time, Abby, Pete used to take you fishin'."

"He did? I don't remember going fishing."

"It was frogs," Aunt Peggy said. "Don't you remember, Burt? Pete and the boys used to always go down to the creek for frogs, and they would take Abby with them."

"That's right. It was frogs that summer, wasn't it?"

I still didn't remember anyone named Sneaky Pete in relation to fish or frogs.

"Sneaky Pete can break into any locked car or house," Aunt Peg explained, as we climbed into the backseat. "Sweetheart, why don't you give him a call on your cell phone?"

Uncle Burt pulled the car over to the side of the road as he dialed Sneaky Pete. He put his phone on speaker so all of us could hear. As soon as Pete answered, Uncle Burt raised his voice several levels and shouted his greeting. "And guess who we have here in the car with us, Pete? It's Sweet Abby. You remember my niece? The one who came here a few summers ago? You two went frog catchin' together at the creek."

"Burt, honey," Aunt Peg weighed in, "that wasn't a few summers ago. It was more like twenty. Back when the boys were all still in elementary school."

It had been twenty-eight years, and not all Burt and Peg's sons were in elementary school yet. Their oldest, Burt Jr., "BJ," was nine and a half that summer. The youngest of their four boys was barely five. When I finally put down my library books and went wading in the creek with my cousins and all their pals, I became the "Wendy Darling" to a whole tribe of lost boys. It's no surprise that Pete was one of the tribe, and no surprise that I didn't remember him distinctly. BJ was definitely the Peter Pan of the bunch.

"Hallo there, Miss Abby," Sneaky Pete said over the speaker. "How are you?"

"Fine." I leaned forward and spoke into the air.

"She's not exactly fine," Burt still was shouting, even though it seemed like Pete should be able to hear him if he spoke in a normal voice. "Abby's locked herself out of her car about half a mile this side of town from Minton. Any chance you can meet us out there and see about opening things up?"

"Don't see why not. I'll bring my equipment and meet y'all out there."

Uncle Burt hung up looking pleased. "Good ole Sneaky Pete. You can always count on him to come through in a crisis. Peggy, you remember that time the dogs locked themselves in the cellar?" He looked at me in the rearview mirror. "I was ready to break through the cellar door with a hatchet, but Peggy told me to call Sneaky Pete. He came right over and opened that door lickety-split."

"I hope he can open the door without damaging the car." I thought about how I didn't want to have to contact my brother with any bad news about his new SUV.

"Don't worry. Sneaky Pete will take care of everything," Aunt Peg said.

Uncle Burt drove toward my waiting vehicle.

"What about Grand Lady?" I asked. "Shouldn't we call her as well?"

"We could call her now," Burt said, as he stopped at a stop sign. He reached for his cell phone.

"Don't you think it would be better if we waited until after we have the situation squared away with your car?" Peg asked.

Letting the car sit at a stop sign only a few blocks from their house, Burt and Peg launched into a complicated discussion about what to do.

"She gets confused easily," Aunt Peg said, turning to me. "She does real well for a woman her age, but I'm afraid you'll be a mite surprised to see her in such a state."

"What state?" I asked cautiously.

"Old age, Sweet Abby. She's ninety-two, you know."

"Yes, I know. We don't need to call her, if you think it would confuse her too much."

"Should we drive on to the car, then?" Burt still held his foot on the brake at the stop sign.

I wanted to holler, "Yes! Go! Drive! Please!" I knew that Uncle Burt and Aunt Peg were not as quick as they used to be. But in the time it took us to discuss our course of action, we could have been to Grand Lady's cottage, explained the whole situation to her, and still arrived at the abandoned SUV before Sneaky Pete. And I thought life moved at a slow pace on Maui!

Burt eased his foot onto the gas pedal and drove through the intersection nice and slow. He didn't take the car above thirty miles per hour the whole way, even though we were on a main highway, and he could have gone twice as fast.

"Now when we get there," Aunt Peg said, "I think it would be best if I stayed in the car with Miss Hannah."

"You doing okay, Hannah?" I asked.

She nodded. "My foot is a little sore now."

"Well, you just rest yourself," Uncle Burt said in a voice as soothing as honey. "We'll get ourselves back to our house in no time at all."

We spotted the truck from the service station before we saw my brother's SUV, because the truck was sitting in front of the SUV at a peculiar angle. It looked as if the truck was lined up so Pete could jump-start the battery on the SUV. Burt parked a few yards behind the service station truck and left the lights on to help light our way on the now dark and desolate road.

"Hey, Sneaky Pete. How's it going?"

"It's going better now," the slender man replied. His back was to us as I approached with Uncle Burt. Before Pete turned around, I saw a glint of light shine off the large crowbar he held in his right hand, and then I saw the driver's window, smashed to bits with fragments of glass scattered over the highway.

"What did you do?!" I shrieked at the startled mechanic. "Did you break the window to get inside? I could have broken the window! This is my brother's car! What were you thinking?"

"I didn't break the window." He turned to face me. "When I pulled up, a couple of hoodlums were breaking into your car. I jumped out of my truck with this crowbar, and the two of them hightailed it out of here."

"Oh."

"I was having a look inside to see if they got away with anything," Pete said. "Looks like your handbag is still there. I don't think they had time to grab anything."

I approached the broken window cautiously, feeling the shards of glass crunch beneath my shoes. My purse was still there. The keys were still in the ignition. It looked as if Sneaky Pete had arrived at the right moment.

"I'm so sorry I yelled at you." Facing Pete, I could feel my hands shaking. "Thank you."

"Sure. No bother at all. Sorry about your window. A place over in Chester can fix that right up for you so you won't even know it was broken."

"Right," Uncle Burt said. "I know the place. Right next to Wal-Mart. We can take Abby's car over on Monday. What do you say you help me clean this up, Pete? Abby, you just step back for the time being."

I moved aside as the two of them unlocked the door and scraped pieces of glass off the front seat.

"What happened?" Aunt Peg called from her rolled-down window in Uncle Burt's car.

I trotted back to Peg and Hannah to tell them the whole story.

"Mercy sakes! What if you two were still waiting by the car when those rascals came by? I don't want to think about what might have happened to you. These are dangerous times we live in."

In a small voice Hannah added, "Our guardian angel made sure we got to your house okay."

Peg looked at Hannah with a peculiar expression. "Your guardian angel?"

Hannah nodded.

"Oh, you mean the man who walked into Howell with you. Didn't he tell you his name?"

"No."

"Was he young or old?"

"Kind of in the middle," Hannah said.

"Did he say where he lived?"

"No. He was just out walking, and then he picked up the chickens and came walking up to us. He waited for us to go into town with him. But my mom didn't want to go with him."

"Well, of course she didn't," Aunt Peg said. "Did the man give any indication that he was from the Celestial Emergency Roadside Service? Of course he didn't. Your mother was trying to protect you. You understand that, don't you? Like I said, these are uncertain times."

"I just think he was an angel," Hannah said quietly. "Because he smelled so good."

"He smelled good?" Aunt Peg turned to me. "What did he smell like?"

I tried to remember. He didn't smell like chickens, even though he had been holding them. I smelled like chickens now, but he didn't smell like chickens. He didn't smell like sweat, even though he obviously had been walking in the mucky heat for some time. He didn't smell smoky or dusty. The truth was, he didn't have a smell of any sort that I remembered.

"He smelled like a cloud," Hannah said.

Peg and I met each other's gaze. Neither of us blinked.

He smelled like a cloud. What does a cloud smell like? What should I say?

"Abby," my uncle called from a few yards away in his booming voice. "We're all ready for you over here.

Come on. Let's get you and Miss Hannah home for some supper."

I turned to go, relieved that I didn't have to come up with a response about my daughter's impression of the man who smelled like a cloud.

Aunt Peg slipped in her final comment, though, when she called, "You drive careful and watch out for low-flying angels, now, Sweet Abby!"

I followed my uncle into Howell, driving a puttering thirty miles per hour with Sneaky Pete following behind me. Pete lasted about twenty yards before he pulled up beside me, honked, and waved, and then sped past my uncle at a blazingly normal forty-five miles per hour. That didn't bother Uncle Burt. Our drive back to town continued at funeral-procession pace.

The sultry night air that entered freely through my open window carried the scent of mowed grass and burnt trash. I tried to imagine what a cloud smelled like.

As we pulled up in front of the Big House, Uncle Burt motioned for me to go around him and park on the grass in the side yard. I gathered a few of our things from the front seat and automatically locked the car, even though it was pointless. Hannah hobbled up to the back door with the assistance of both my aunt and uncle.

We stepped into the brightly lit kitchen and there, at the head of the large oak table, sat Grand Lady with her hands folded on the blue-checkered tablecloth. She was wearing a pink blouse with matching pink bauble earrings. Her spongy white hair was gathered up in a loose bun on top of her head. On the right side of the bun was a carefully balanced, perfectly positioned, big fat gardenia.

Chapter 11

As the clock on the wall behind Grand Lady chimed nine times, she smiled at me.

"Mother, what are you still doing up?" Uncle Burt scolded. "We told you we would give you a call when they arrived."

"However," Grand Lady paused. "You did not call me, now, did you?" She could still deliver her lines with all the sugary airs of refined sass that only a woman like her could get away with. I had almost forgotten the way she would enter a conversation by throwing out the first word in a low voice, then pause, as if to make sure she had everyone's attention before finishing her sentence.

"They had some terrible problems . . ."

Before my aunt could finish her thought, I brushed past her and flew into my grandmother's arms, kissing her cold-cream-preserved cheeks and drinking in the scent of the gardenia.

"We're here, Grand Lady." I leaned back and let her look at me through her trifocal glasses. "We're here at last. We finally made it."

"Indeed, you did, Honeygirl. Oh my, how you have changed. Just look at you."

"Well, look at you!" I said. "You haven't changed at all. You're as gorgeous as ever."

Grand Lady let a twittering chuckle escape her carefully painted pink lips. I noticed her dentures were spotted with the same pink as her lipstick, but I wasn't going to be the one to point that out to her.

"How very sweet of you to say such a thing. However, you know as well as anyone in this room that I am just an old lady."

"No, you're just a *Grand* Lady." I kissed her on the temple and sniffed the heady gardenia. "And *this* is my Hannah."

I turned and held out my hand for Hannah to come forward and approach my beloved matriarch without apprehension.

"Hello." Hannah hopped on one foot and gave Grand Lady an awkward hug.

"What happened to you, child?" Grand Lady asked.

"Oh, it's not that big a deal. I cut my foot on a piece of glass, and I had to get some stitches."

"What did she say?" Grand Lady asked, turning to me.

"She cut her foot," I said slowly and raising my

voice slightly. "We had to take her to the doctor's. To get stitches."

"I know. I heard the part about the stitches. I didn't hear the part about how it happened."

"It's Miss Hannah's accent," Aunt Peg said to me. "We have a hard time understanding some of the things y'all say."

Hannah looked as if she were about to laugh at the thought of us being the ones with the accents. Hannah did tend to talk fast and slur her words. I made a point to slow down my speech and speak loud enough for Grand Lady to hear me clearly.

"Well, a broken chicken crate was in the road, and then our keys got locked in the car and . . . it's kind of a long story."

"Go ahead." Aunt Peg busied herself in the kitchen. "Go ahead and tell her the whole story. She likes to hear the whole story."

Aunt Peg pulled food from the refrigerator and set it on the counter. Uncle Burt had seated himself at the other end of the table and was leaning back, taking it all in.

I pulled up a chair for Hannah and then took a seat next to Grand Lady and tried to abbreviate the events of the past few hours. I spoke slowly and louder than normal. Grand Lady listened with great interest, her eyes locked on me.

About halfway into my retelling, Aunt Peg interrupted.

"Hannah, why don't you tell Grand Lady the part about the angel?"

"Angel?" Uncle Burt said. "I didn't hear about an angel."

"Hannah said the man who helped them find our house was her guardian angel," Peg said. "Isn't that sweet?"

Grand Lady turned her gaze to Hannah. "You say you saw an angel then, did you, child?"

Hannah nodded.

"Tell Grand Lady how he smelled," Peg said.

I couldn't tell if my aunt was making fun of my daughter's assessment or trying to gather support for Hannah's theory.

"He smelled like a cloud," Hannah said plainly.

Grand Lady's expression didn't change. She didn't blink. It almost seemed as if she had fallen asleep with her eyes open.

"What do you think of that?" Aunt Peg asked.

Grand Lady drew in a deep breath so that her dentures gave a faint whistle. "What color was your angel?" Grand Lady asked.

Hannah looked at me.

"Well, he was white, of course," Aunt Peg said.

"Actually," I spoke up, "he wasn't white."

Hannah seemed confused. We lived in a place with a wide ethnic mix. She hadn't grown up with a daily emphasis on the shade of a person's skin, the way I had.

As a matter of fact, when Hannah was in first grade, she was one of three Caucasian students in her whole class, and the only one with blond hair. In that respect, Hannah was the minority student. But no one drew attention to her differences, and she grew up with a sense of equity that often surprised Tom and me.

Aunt Peg came over to the table. Uncle Burt leaned forward. "A black man showed you how to get to our house?"

"It must have been Mr. Joe from the fruit stand," Aunt Peg said. "Did he have a limp?"

"No, not at all," Hannah said. "Our angel was big and strong. He carried me the whole way."

"He carried you?" Aunt Peg echoed. "I don't recall your saying that he carried you."

"The whole way," Hannah said.

"Oh, my. That couldn't have been Mr. Joe. The poor man barely can carry a watermelon to my car for me. I wonder who it was."

"I do believe," Grand Lady said, drawing out her words and taking the attention off of Hannah, "the Bible makes it clear that we do entertain angels unaware."

No one had a reply.

Aunt Peg turned to go back to the kitchen. "Well, come on now, supper's on, such as it is. You girls dish up what y'all like, and I'll warm it for you in the microwave. Grand Lady, are you hungry? We have plenty of food here."

Grand Lady raised a hand and gave a wave of dismissal such as a queen might give to a court jester who was failing at his craft on an especially dismal day.

"Well then, Abby, you come now. You're our company. And what about you, Miss Hannah? You want me to bring you a plate, Sugar?"

"I can get over there okay." Hannah pushed out the sturdy chair.

I steadied her as she made her way around the edge of the counter, and then I introduced my daughter to her first helping of black-eyed peas. She tried them but whispered that she preferred the macaroni salad and fried pork chops.

While we ate, Grand Lady sipped a glass of cranberry juice as if it were a fine wine, and quietly took in the conversation.

I kept smiling at Grand Lady, and each time I did, she smiled back. She saw me. Even with her aging eyes, she saw me. Her tender gaze made my heart swell.

If I had to define why I was so enamored with my grandmother, it would be for this very reason. Every other reason would fall in under this one.

When I was a blossoming young woman, she looked at me, and she saw me. She saw not only who I was then but also who I could become, and for some reason, she decided to lavish her affection on me. She was the first person in my life that made me feel as if she saw me and loved what she saw.

Taking small bites and chewing slowly, I felt like a debutante, at her charm school graduation banquet. Would I pass? Would the Grand Dame raise her scepter and deem me worthy of promotion to fully vested womanhood? Her opinion of me mattered more than even I had realized previously. I shuddered to think of what would have happened inside me if I hadn't made this trip. If I hadn't had a chance to be with Grand Lady this one more time before she left earth, how would I ever know if I turned out okay?

I had told myself for all these miles that I was taking Hannah to receive the womanly blessing that only Grand Lady could bestow. Now that we were here, I saw that I was the one who was desperate for approval. I was the one who needed the blessing.

Grand Lady said she was growing weary. I rose and kissed her soundly on each cheek. She received the kisses with her neck stretched up and her eyes closed, like a cat stepping out into the fresh air and sunshine after being closed up too long in a musty garage.

Uncle Burt said he would walk Grand Lady back to her place while Hannah and I followed Aunt Peg upstairs to our guest quarters.

The room we were being led to belonged to my cousin, Tammy Jean, when she lived at home. Tammy

Jean was Burt and Peg's "surprise baby," born the summer I graduated from high school. I'd never met Tammy Jean, but every Christmas we received her picture inside a card that usually had snowmen on the front.

I mentioned that fact to Hannah, as we slowly took the stairs together, and Aunt Peg said, "Oh, those snowmen cards. For some reason, Tammy Jean adores snowmen. Her father tells her that snowmen are the only men she can keep around for more than a few days."

"Why does he say that?" Hannah asked.

"It's his little joke, honey. Tammy Jean is a ball of energy. I think she's never stood still long enough to fall in love."

"Where does she live now?" Hannah asked.

"Nashville. She's working for some big music company doing advertising of some sort. She's so busy we never get to see her."

"What about your boys? Do they come to visit often?"

"Not often enough. BJ and his wife and their kids live over at Lake Clayborne. You remember going to the lake, don't you, Abby?"

"Is that the lake we went to for the Fourth of July?" I asked.

"I imagine so. It's the only lake we ever go to. BJ has a house right on the lake."

Aunt Peg opened the bedroom door and flipped on the light. A kaleidoscope of pink greeted us.

"Mom, a canopy bed!"

"Wow."

"And look at all the stuffed animals! What a cool room."

Aunt Peg seemed pleased. I couldn't picture a high school girl keeping her room this cutesy, but then I'd never met Tammy Jean.

"I put fresh towels in the bathroom for you. We'll be up by seven. Uncle Burt is in the church choir, and he usually leaves around eight or so. Service is at 9:30."

"Is tomorrow Sunday?" Hannah asked.

"You poor sweet thing! You don't even know what day it is, do you? Yes, tomorrow is the Sabbath. But if you two aren't up in time for church, or if Hannah is feeling poorly, we certainly will understand if you don't make it to church. You just make yourselves feel at home and help yourselves to whatever you find in the kitchen. We'll be back before lunchtime."

"I'm sure we can make it to church with you." I turned to Hannah, who was quietly perched on the edge of the pink ruffled bed, fingering one of the throw pillows. "What do you think, Hannah? Do you suppose your foot will feel well enough for you to make it to church in the morning?"

She shrugged. "I guess so."

"If we're not up by seven, Aunt Peg, will you wake us?"

"I surely will. You two sleep tight and holler if you

need anything. Anything at all." Aunt Peg exited, closing the door behind her.

"Isn't this a cool room, Mom?"

"Yes, it is." I wasn't sure how well I'd be able to sleep in the double bed the way Hannah scooted around in her sleep.

"Did you sleep in this room when you stayed here?"

I glanced around and tried to picture how this room looked almost thirty years ago. "You know, I think I did sleep here. But it wasn't a girl's room then. It was Grand Lady's sewing room. That was before Uncle Burt and Aunt Peg moved into the house with the boys."

Hannah looked around. "What was this room before it was a sewing room?"

"I don't know."

"Do you think it was Grandma's bedroom?"

"Grand Lady's bedroom? No, she and Grandpa slept in the big room at the end of the hall."

"No, I mean your mom. Grandma Celeste. Do you think she slept in this room?"

"I don't know."

"I wonder if she ever painted in here. Uncle Burt would know, wouldn't he?"

"I imagine he would."

"This is an old house, Mom."

"Yes, it is."

"It smells old. Even with the air-conditioning blowing

all the air around and making it cold. It smells like antique dolls."

I sat next to my perceptive daughter. "Hannah, what does a cloud smell like to you?"

"Clean and fresh. Not sweet or stinky in any way. Just clean and fresh."

"And that's how the man smelled to you?"

"You mean the angel?"

"Do you really think he was an angel?"

Hannah nodded. "Don't you?"

This felt like an important conversation. It seemed that whatever I said to my daughter at this moment would be recorded deep in her memory. One unplanned day in the future she would probably think of this conversation and come to some kind of conclusion as to what kind of mother I had been to her. I had to answer wisely, but I had no idea what to say.

I stretched out on my side, propping up my head with a hand and wedging my elbow between two of the frilly pillows. Hannah followed my stretched-out example and asked again, "Don't you think he was an angel, Mom?"

"I don't know," I finally said.

The look on her face made it clear I hadn't given the answer she had hoped for.

Scrambling to recover lost ground, I said, "I mean, I've never seen an angel before. I don't know what to look for. I know that angels are real, and the Bible does make it clear that there have been times when God sent his angels to deliver messages and sometimes to comfort his people. But I don't know, Hannah. I don't know if he was a real angel."

"Well, I think he was. Why else would he be out walking on the road in the middle of nowhere? He was right there at the right time with a clean handkerchief and everything, and he protected us and helped us. He was my guardian angel."

I wondered if I'd let my daughter watch too many Christmas specials on TV. Or maybe I hadn't watched enough of them with her to help filter her perception of heavenly beings.

"You know what?" I pulled Hannah close. "I'm not sure it really matters if he was an angel or not. What matters is that we got here safely, and I think God did that. We drove thousands of miles, and the only thing bad that happened was that our mirror fell off in Arizona and that we ran over part of the chicken crate."

"Mom?" Hannah pulled back and gave me an apologetic look. "Can I say something, and you won't be mad?"

"Yes, of course. What is it, Hannah?"

"You don't exactly smell like a cloud."

I laughed. "No, I imagine I smell pretty bad."

Hannah pulled back farther and fanned herself. "You smell kind of like chickens."

"Then I think I better take a shower before we go to bed. We both could use a shower."

"But I can't get my foot wet."

"Then we'll wrap it in a plastic bag."

I realized our luggage was still in the car. "I'll be back in a few minutes."

Uncle Burt was coming up the stairs as I was going down. I told him I hadn't brought in our suitcases yet, and he said he would help me. He also supplied me with several plastic trash bags for Hannah's foot and offered me a couple of bedtime molasses cookies from the alligator-shaped cookie jar on the counter.

Our showering procedure took much longer than usual since we had to wrap Hannah's foot and then try to keep it out of the direct spray of the water. I lathered up her long blond hair while she leaned her head toward the open door of the shower stall, trying to keep her balance. I could tell she was uncomfortable having me in the bathroom assisting her since her grooming rituals had been her own private experience for the past few years. She definitely was developing into a young woman, and shy about moving around without her skin being covered.

When my turn to shower came, Hannah wanted to stay in the bathroom rather than return by herself to the bedroom. Now I was the timid one, slipping out of my dirty clothes and stepping into the shower. Hannah patted her hair with a towel since we didn't have a blow-dryer with us. She hummed a little and reported on the dryness of her bandage, but I knew she was watching and taking notes on what her body might have to look forward to in the advanced stages of this womanhood journey on which she had embarked.

I thought about how I'd rarely if ever seen my mother undressed. She was private about everything. There never had been a time when the two of us went camping or even stayed together in a hotel. I didn't know if my mother had stretch marks or not. I doubted it, with her slim figure. I definitely didn't take after her in my frame the way Hannah had. I was much more like Grand Lady through the hips, only I was thinner and taller by at least five inches.

"Mom?" Hannah asked after we had managed to get thoroughly scrubbed-up, freshened, pajamaed, and tucked together under the fluffy dome of pinkness. "Can I ask you something?"

"Sure. Anything."

"What's that white line below your stomach?"

"White line? Oh, the scar. That's from the cesarean section."

"What's that?"

"The cesarean procedure they did when you were born. You weren't turned the right way, and you were having trouble moving down the birth canal. The doctor did a procedure in which they opened me up so they could remove you before the umbilical cord choked you."

Hannah lay in the fresh stillness, smelling of Ivory soap and peppermint toothpaste.

"I never knew that," she said in a low voice.

I tried to think back if I had ever told Hannah about her birth. I certainly had talked about it many times with girlfriends, but the older Hannah got, the less of a topic it was. I had even gone to a baby shower a few years ago and listened to two young mothers give all the details of their birthing experiences, and I didn't feel compelled to jump in and add my story to the batch.

Hannah's birth was only a little traumatic at the time. When she came through it safely, Tom and I were relieved and thrilled to have our little girl. I healed quickly and life went on.

"You know what, Hannah? I don't think I ever told you how you were born."

"Was it awful? Did you scream like in the movies?"

"No, it wasn't awful. It was . . ." I drew her close while trying to find the right word. "It was intense. That's what it's like to have a baby. It's intense. Your body starts doing what it's supposed to do, and it surprises you how strong your muscles are without your telling them to do anything."

"But what about the operation? Didn't it hurt when the doctor cut you open?"

"I'm sure it was uncomfortable at the time, but I was very tired from being in labor with you for many hours and—"

"How many hours?"

"Seven, I think."

"Was that longer than you were in labor with Justin?"

"No, his labor was longer. About fifteen hours. But then he came real fast once I dilated all the way."

"Like when Pua was born," Hannah said.

I had to remind myself that she meant Pua the baby llama and not her friend Pua from school.

"So you were in labor for seven hours, and then the doctor cut you open because he thought I might be in danger?"

"That's right. The doctor lifted you out, and you cried, and everything was just fine."

"Did you bleed a lot and get stitches?"

"I remember the stitches, yes."

"How many did you get, Mom? More than four?"

I realized the concept of stitches was fresh in her mind after having her foot sutured that evening.

"I don't remember. I know it took a while to heal up, but not too long. I had to be careful not to stand up the wrong way, I remember that. But I didn't mind. All that mattered was that I had you in my arms and that you were safe."

Hannah nuzzled her nose against the edge of my jaw.

"Mom, do you think I'll have a scar on my foot, too?"

"You might. Not a very big one."

"Will it turn white like your scar?"

"Probably."

I yawned and felt the fatigue of the day and of the whole trip come over me. The weight of the dense exhaustion seemed to press me deep into the bed, as if the covers were the top of a waffle iron and my totally relaxed body was the lumpy batter.

"Mom?"

I yawned again and answered with an "mmm-hmm?"

"Thank you."

"For what?"

"For having me and protecting me and getting stitches because of me and for being my mom and bringing me here and for talking about all this woman stuff with me."

If my muscles hadn't been so mushified, I would have smiled a huge smile and made my neck turn and my lips pucker so I could kiss my Hannah good night. But all I could manage was a sincere but sloppy, "I-love-you-Hannah."

She snuggled into the curve of my neck where she fit perfectly and whispered, "I love you, too, Mom. Even more than I used to think I did."

Chapter 12

I woke to the sound of Hannah laughing. Not beside me, but downstairs. Her giggles rose with the scent of pancakes and roused me from the pink canopy bed. Slipping into the only skirt I'd brought with me, I found a clean but crumpled collared shirt that matched and tried to shake out the wrinkles. Bare-legged and wearing my only pair of closed-toe shoes, I headed downstairs.

Uncle Burt was leaning against the kitchen counter with a spatula in his hand while Hannah was reading him the Sunday comics. Hannah was dressed in her summer dress with a sock on her injured foot, which she had elevated on a counter stool.

"Now try it again," Uncle Burt said to Hannah. "And do it Southern this time."

Hannah cleared her throat and flashed me a cunning grin. I listened as she read the comic strip to Uncle Burt, employing her best imitation of a Louisiana drawl. She didn't have it quite right, but the effect was charming.

Uncle Burt grinned from ear to ear. "That's right. You almost have it. We'll teach y'all to speak the right way before you leave here."

"It looks like you two are off to a good start this morning," I said.

"I was reading the funnies to him, but he said he couldn't understand me," Hannah explained. "I told him sometimes I couldn't understand him, so he's trying to improve my speech."

Uncle Burt flipped another thick buckwheat pancake on the griddle. "When she starts in with her island slang, I can't tell what she's saying."

I raised my eyebrows at Hannah and smiled. It was my way of telling her I adored her, but I hoped she was behaving. She and Justin could really put on the pidgin accent when they wanted to. They learned it from the other kids at school, who found the shortened sentences a lazy and cool way of talking to each other.

"Truth be told, I don't see how a person can get through an entire conversation without saying 'y'all' at least once," Burt observed.

"We'll probably go home saying 'y'all' when we leave," I said.

"And maybe I'll start saying . . . what was that word, Hannah?"

"*Da' kine.*"

"That's it. Dah-kine. She came in here asking me

what dah-kine breakfast I was making. I never heard such a word in my life."

"It's a common saying where we live," I said. "Whenever a person doesn't know what word to use, they slip in the word *da' kine* and it fits for whatever the missing word is."

"Like we might say whatchamacallit," Uncle Burt said.

I nodded. "Same idea."

"Read me another one, there, Miss Hannah."

Uncle Burt flipped the last few pancakes onto the stacked-up pile on a plate and put the plate on the kitchen table, motioning for me to come eat. He returned to the oven and pulled out a tray of spicy pork sausages, staying warm on the cookie sheet.

"I have to be on my way," Uncle Burt said. "Don't you mind me. Y'all take your time. Peggy should be down any minute, and she'll keep you company."

"Did you get to eat?" I asked.

"I ate while I was cooking." He reached for his navy blue sports jacket that was hung over the back of one of the chairs. I couldn't imagine how uncomfortable it would be to wear such a heavy jacket in this summer heat.

As Uncle Burt slipped out the back door, Aunt Peg came downstairs wearing a dress, nylons, and high-heeled shoes with a sweater over her shoulders.

"And a good Sunday morning to you, Sweet Abby and Miss Hannah."

"Good morning," we said in unison.

"Uncle Burt just left," Hannah added.

Aunt Peg seemed to study our choice of Sunday-go-to-meeting outfits.

"Are we dressed okay for your church?" I asked. "My shirt is a little crumpled."

"No, you're fine, darlin'. Everyone will know you're just visiting. I'm going on over to Grand Lady's to see if she's interested in having some breakfast with us before we leave for church."

"I'll go with you," Hannah said, getting up. "I want to see her cottage."

"Her cottage." Aunt Peg chuckled. "That dear woman calls it her cottage, but I hope you won't be disappointed when you see her little place."

Now I was curious. "I'll go, too."

Aunt Peg led us out the back door and across the cement slab patio that held an umbrella-covered table with four chairs and an old wheelbarrow filled with potting soil. The charming planter was spilling out a cascade of geraniums and pansies.

"There it is," Peg said, "Grand Lady's cottage."

To thc left, on the wide-open grassy space, sat a singlewide mobile home with a small deck and an avocado-green and white awning over the front door.

"That's her cottage?" Hannah asked.

"I said y'all might be surprised. Grand Lady has a way of using her words to make the best out of ordinary situations. When we bought this place for her twenty years ago and had it set up on the property, she took one look and said, 'What a lovely cottage.' Ever since then it's been referred to as her cottage. Whatever you do, don't use the word 'trailer' around her."

"Mom, look at the pool." Hannah quickly redirected her attention and gave me a little pout.

The swimming pool was directly in front of us. On its gleaming blue water floated a single, vacant, yellow air mattress, waiting for someone to come lounge on its billows.

"In a few days," I said softly to Hannah, "you'll be able to go in."

I stood still for a moment, trying to remember how this backyard had looked so long ago.

"Did you have to take out the magnolia tree?" I asked. If my calculations were correct, the diving board was now located where the wonderful magnolia tree had been.

"Oh, yes, that old nuisance. It took Burt and the boys a week to cut that old thing down and pull out the stump."

"I loved that tree."

"I remember you used to do lots of reading under the shade, didn't you?"

"Yes, I did," I said wistfully.

We followed Peg up three steps to Grand Lady's raised porch. The small wooden deck was covered with green indoor-outdoor carpeting. She had one sturdy lawn chair positioned under the shade of the awning in such a way that she had a sweeping, elevated view of the pool, the vegetable garden, the garage on the far side of the yard, and the back patio of the Big House. I could picture Grand Lady sitting there and holding court on a mild spring afternoon.

"We can go on in." Peg pulled open the screen and rapped on the front door with her fist. "She can't always hear us when we knock. Especially if the air-conditioning is running on high."

The inside of the cottage was more of a surprise than the outside. Everything was in avocado green and harvest gold, standard decorating colors for this used mobile home that were just beginning to go out of vogue when Grand Lady moved in here.

"Hello!" I called. The loud whir of the air conditioner camouflaged my voice.

"Yoo-hoo!" Aunt Peg yodeled. "It's me, Grand Lady. And the girls are with me."

"I will be with you all momentarily," came the return call.

"We can have a seat here." Aunt Peg motioned toward the crushed-velvet couch. The three of us lined up like sparrows on a wire.

I glanced around at the swivel rocker, coffee table, and beautiful antique secretary desk. The pieces were familiar but looked so different in this confined space. Above the heavy, console-style television hung a lovely painting of an English cottage surrounded by a well-tended flower garden.

I wonder if Grand Lady views her home as being the equal to that quaint cottage?

"How did y'all sleep?" Peg asked, making small talk.

"Great," Hannah said.

"Fine," I agreed. My apprehensions about Hannah's romping all over the bed turned out to be unfounded last night. We had fallen asleep snuggled together and both slept the night through.

"Your foot seems to be doing better, Miss Hannah."

"It's doing okay."

The bedroom door opened, and Grand Lady made a leisurely entrance, using a cane. I hadn't seen the cane last night since she was sitting the whole time at the kitchen table. I also hadn't seen how stooped over she was or how slowly she moved. Instinctively, I rose to my feet and went to greet her.

She waved me off with her free hand, as if she thought I was coming to assist her, and she wanted to make it clear that she didn't need any help. I wondered how long it had taken her to get fully clad in her bright floral dress, stockings, and sturdy shoes. She had her pink lipstick in place and her hair tucked up neatly in a tighter twist than the gardenia-embellished hairdo from last night.

Watching Grand Lady make her way toward me, I couldn't help but feel that some of the charm of my view of her had dissolved into a more realistic picture of an elderly yet resilient woman. To have lived nearly a century and to be so vibrant and mobile was a wonder in and of itself. I'm sure it was no small accomplishment that she had maintained her independence and still lived by herself.

But I knew, as I watched her hobbling across her uneven linoleum, that she was mortal. Human. She wasn't the fairy-tale figure I had elevated in my imagination.

Nonetheless, I loved her. No, more than that, I adored her.

What followed was a slow procession of the four of us down the steps of her deck and across the lawn to the Big House. With Hannah hobbling a little and Grand Lady using her cane, we moved slower than Uncle Burt driving his Lincoln Continental through town.

Grand Lady promised to give Hannah and me a full tour of her cottage when we returned from church. Breakfast was a more important topic, and Aunt Peg made sure our pancakes were warm before directing us to our choice of clear Karo syrup or homemade apricot jam as topping. She also served us deep black coffee that came from a place in New Orleans called Café du Monde. Aunt Peg said it was a special blend with chicory, and they only drank it on Sunday mornings and birthdays.

Taking precautions for both Grand Lady with her cane and Hannah with her wrapped-up foot, we slowly made our way to Aunt Peg's Oldsmobile and drove three whole blocks to a white clapboard church complete with a steeple and church bell. The bell was ringing as we walked up the front steps, taking them one at a time.

Grand Lady nodded at everyone who greeted her. They all expressed how happy they were to see her. I loved that she was receiving lots of attention.

"Why, Mrs. Sunderland. How lovely to see you up and about," Grand Lady said, taking the hand of a woman who was at least her equal in age. "I heard about your regrettable misadventure. I do hope your fine son is on the mend."

"Indeed he is. We have no complaints around our house."

Hannah and I looked to Aunt Peg, who whispered, "Mrs. Sunderland lives with her son. He got a fishing hook caught in his nose while at the Gentleman's Fish Out last week at Lake Clayborne."

Hannah began to giggle but I gave her a firm look. If Grand Lady could address the incident with dignity, we would follow her example.

Dozens of smiling parishioners introduced themselves

to Hannah and me, welcoming us to Howell and making a splendid fuss over Hannah's poor foot. Some of them already had heard the story of my smashed car window. Apparently Uncle Burt had shared our situation, as a "prayer request," when he arrived early for choir practice.

If anyone ever doubted that such a piece of Americana as a little country church and faithful congregation still existed, I'd be glad to point them to this assembly. Hannah and I were welcomed into the fold and made to feel like honored guests.

We stood to sing from hymnals that were waiting for us in racks on the backs of the pews. To Hannah's and my shared surprise, the first hymn was "Rock of Ages." In my mind's eye I saw the Carlsbad Caverns' awesome formation and tried to memorize the words as we sang them.

Summer morning light illuminated the stained-glass window at the front of the church and sent out fragments of refracted color like illusive butterflies.

"Look, Mom," Hannah whispered to me, as the choir stood in their red robes with gold, pointed collars and turned to face the director, ready to begin their call to worship. "Uncle Burt has a yellow triangle on his collar."

As soon as she spotted the refraction, it flitted away and was replaced by a purple-winged illusion on Uncle Burt's forehead. Hannah leaned forward, enraptured by the skittering stained-glass colors as the rainbows played leapfrog across the two rows of serious-looking choir members.

Their song was powerfully delivered, and I nearly applauded at the end, but caught myself right before my hands came together. Hannah looked at me and covered her mouth gleefully.

Grand Lady sat beside me with slightly hunched posture. I was very aware of her frailty this morning. Last night, positioned so regally behind the kitchen table, she had still seemed a force to be reckoned with. Today she seemed diminished in many ways.

During the sermon I noticed she nodded off for a few moments but caught herself. Smacking her lips and clearing her throat, Grand Lady pulled back her shoulders and focused on the pulpit. The pastor drew his message from John 3. It was a "Ye must be born again" sermon, and just the sort I remembered hearing here in the Bible Belt long ago.

So many thoughts and feelings collided inside me. I was here. I was in Howell, sitting with my Grand Lady in her dear, old church. We were sitting in the same pew where I'd sat beside her nearly three decades ago, the same pew her small frame had been warming since before World War II.

Yet it was as if nothing had changed in the past twenty-eight years except me. I tried to imagine what was going on at home, in my previous reality. How many hours' difference was it? When would Tom and Justin be getting up? I missed them. I wished they were here to experience this.

Reaching to the right, I took Hannah's hand in mine and gave it a gentle squeeze. I then slid my left hand into Grand Lady's and laced my long fingers around hers. She was so small. So frail. With unexpected strength, she squeezed my hand, and I let the miracle of this moment seep into my spirit and fill me up.

I was literally in the middle, holding on to both sides. It was as if I'd entered a rare bubble that opens up in midlife for only a brief moment in time. What did they call this on the outer space shows on TV? Wormholes? Yes, that was it. I was sitting in a wormhole, linked to my deep past while holding on to all my hopes for the future.

I felt essential and indestructible and at the same time as thin and diaphanous as the fleeting prisms of color that darted from the stained-glass window, leaving their mark for only a moment.

I wanted to remember what this felt like. I didn't want to let go of Hannah or Grand Lady, even though they both loosened their grips. Something inside dared me to hold on to both ends as long as I could.

After the service, we stood on the church's front steps, shaded from the rising summer sun by the spire. The bells sounded, making it difficult to hear what people were saying to us. Grand Lady stood firm. She had a kind word for each person who stopped to greet her, and they, in turn, gave her words full of graciousness and admiration.

Uncle Burt joined us, and instead of driving the three blocks back to the Big House, he drove all of us in his car a half-mile the other direction to the cemetery.

"Grand Lady thought Hannah might want to see where her great-grandfather is buried," Uncle Burt explained. "Do you remember when we brought you out here, Abby?"

"I remember riding bikes here with BJ and some of his friends."

"You kids came out here?" Aunt Peg asked. "Whatever for? Those boys didn't try to frighten you, did they?"

"No, they didn't frighten me, Aunt Peg. Your sons were all perfect gentleman." I said it with a hidden grin. My evaluation of her rowdy brood was overly generous.

"I had no idea you kids ever came out here."

I imagined Aunt Peg didn't know a lot about what happened while her sons were tearing up the streets of Howell in their younger years. It was probably for the best that she hadn't been given all the details.

We all maneuvered out of Uncle Burt's car and walked a few feet to a simple grave marker with the names carved in marble. I stood silently beside Hannah.

"This is where your great-granddaddy is buried," Uncle Burt said. "William Ferrington Burroughs. My daddy. He died forty-three years ago this October. Slid through an intersection in Gallaway Parish on a rainy night and ran smack-dab into a tree."

I didn't remember ever hearing how Grand Lady's husband had died. I was trying to imagine what it would be like to live forty-three years after the death of your life partner and to be alone all that time. It was the first time I wondered if my mother hurried into her second marriage after watching her mother's long journey through singleness.

"Who is Charlotte?" Hannah asked, looking at the grave marker.

An awkward pause followed.

"*I* am Charlotte," Grand Lady said.

"But who is that Charlotte?" Hannah pointed to the gravestone. "Charlotte Isabella Burroughs."

"That is I." Grand Lady used her cane to point to the inscription on the marble marker. "Do you see how the date of my birth is recorded but not the date of my departure from this earth? That is because I am still alive. Or perhaps you noticed that fact without my having to tell it to you so plainly."

I grinned at her dry wit.

Hannah looked confused.

"But if you're still alive, then why is your name there?"

"I am one of those who is of the persuasion that one can never be too prepared. As you see, Hannah, all is in readiness. When I draw my final breath, I shall be brought to this cemetery where I shall take up residency here in my final resting place. All that will be needed is for someone to remember the date of my passing and have the numbers etched in the stone." Grand Lady tapped the gravestone with her cane as if marking the conclusion of her speech.

Hannah didn't blink. Her expression made it clear that she was disturbed by the concept of someone preparing such details of what would happen after death. It didn't seem so unusual to me. In fact, if I knew my grandmother at all, I would almost guarantee that she had written out a guest list for her funeral and a suggested menu for her wake.

And she would expect a wake. Not just a memorial service. Oh, no, Grand Lady would be mortified if she thought for one moment that the entire community of Howell would not rally on the day of her departure from this earth and wail loudly into the night. The drama of it all seemed fitting to me, but Hannah was not tracking.

"Are we going home pretty soon, or do we have to go look at some more graves?" Hannah asked.

"You come on with me, Miss Hannah." Aunt Peg took my daughter by the hand and led her away from this huge dose of mortality. "You're best off giving your poor foot a rest. Why don't you and I go wait in the car while your mother pays her final respects?"

I was ready to go as well but gave a last, obliging look at my grandfather's gravestone. A stream of red ants was streaking across the bright green grass and marching across the gray marble marker, scattering in all directions. Grand Lady had apparently awakened the nest of red ants when she tapped her cane on her gravestone. She was now using her cane to combat the little red devils one by one with the rubber stopper on the end.

"Take that, you fire devil, you!" Grand Lady cried out. "And that!" She was entering into the challenge of single-handedly exterminating this intrusive colony of ants with more energy than I had seen her expend since we arrived.

"Burton!" Grand Lady shifted her feet and kept annihilating the creatures with her cane. "Burton, you have sturdy shoes on your feet. Do something, will you?"

My uncle looked as if he were entering a hokey-pokey contest as he stomped out half a dozen red ants in a series of rhythmic smashes.

I tried stepping on one of the ants that was heading my way in the grass. It scampered up to the top of my shoe, and I shook my foot like crazy to get rid of the pest. I remembered vividly the red ant bite I'd gotten on my bare foot when my cousins and I were catching fireflies one night under the old magnolia tree. The burning itch started immediately and the swelling lasted for days. After that, I always wore shoes when I went outside.

I wonder if that's why I became so insistent that our children always wear shoes.

"You are not fast enough, Burton! What is wrong with you?" I'd never heard Grand Lady snap at anyone like that before, and it surprised me. "Get after those brutes as if you mean to end their wicked existence!"

Instead of snapping back at his mother in response to her emotionally charged accusations, my uncle respectfully stomped faster to accommodate his mother's wishes.

"I know how much you hate these creatures," Uncle Burt said firmly. "I'll come back here tomorrow and set out some poison by their anthill."

"Incarnation of the worst sort of devil, they are!" Grand Lady declared. "And to think they have burrowed themselves into a hole right there, of all places!" She stomped her cane one more time in defiance.

"We best be getting to the car." Uncle Burt reached to steady his mother's arm before she summoned up another assemblage of angry fire ants. "I'll come back later to deal with the ants."

I steadied Grand Lady's other side as we hobbled back to the car. She continued to mutter about the audacity of those demon ants.

Uncle Burt cruised home at such a slow pace that I had the eerie feeling the fire ants would be able to keep up with us and follow us all the way home.

My uncle's words at the graveside about how his father had died in a car crash came back to me. I wondered if his unbearably slow driving stemmed from that incident. Was Uncle Burt afraid he'd meet the same fatal outcome as his father if he drove too fast?

We all have our fears, don't we? Stinging ants. Car accidents. Blood. We are all so alike. We are all so . . . human.

Chapter 13

The lazy heat of the Sunday afternoon lured my relatives to their respective couches for a traditional Sabbath snooze after our big meal of ham and scalloped potatoes. Hannah and I made our way outside. She and I were used to the tropics and not used to being in such highly air-cooled buildings.

The temperature was in the low 80s, the humidity bearable, and the pool torturously inviting for Hannah. I spotted the hammock and suggested we move it to a shady spot. Together we pulled the freestanding, green-and-white striped whale over to the side of the Big House next to the huge gardenia bushes that were exploding with sweet fragrance and sweeter memories.

A Sunday afternoon nap in the hammock seemed like a great idea until we climbed aboard and my wiggle-worm daughter said she couldn't find her "happy spot." We tried to position ourselves at opposite ends to gain some sort of balance. Hannah adjusted her legs, precariously tilting the hammock too far to the right.

"Hold on, Mom."

"Hannah, don't rock the boat!"

"I'm not. Just hold still, Mom."

"I'm not moving an eyelash."

"Yes you are. You blinked. I saw you." Hannah giggled. Little Miss Giggle and Wiggle.

"Are you settled?"

"Yes. This is nice." Hannah drew in a deep breath and closed her eyes. "What is that sweet smell?"

"Gardenias." My contented smile matched hers. "Delicious, aren't they?"

"Mmm."

"I love gardenias," I said. "My wedding bouquet was made from gardenias. Did I ever tell you that? Your daddy wore a gardenia boutonniere, and we had gardenias floating in glass bowls on each of the tables at the reception."

"It must have smelled pretty," Hannah said.

"Very pretty." I thought of how the exquisite fragrance had followed me down the church aisle and lingered like a blessing over Tom and me. It was a blessing that had taken its cue from this bush, whose sweet aroma now covered my daughter and me like an invisible comforter.

"I have something to tell you, Hannah."

"You're not leaving me here, are you?"

I opened one eye and lifted my head to look at her face. She was looking at me questioningly.

"Do you mean leave you here in Louisiana?"

Hannah nodded.

"No, of course not. Where did you get that idea?"

"I don't know. I wanted to stay at Grandma Celeste's, but you said no, and then you said I'd like it better here. I thought maybe you were planning to leave me with Grand Lady or something."

"No, Hannah." I cautiously sat up and reached for her hand. "I wouldn't leave you. I wouldn't make a plan like that without first talking to you and seeing what you wanted to do."

"Did your mom ask you before you came here when you were a girl?"

"No. The plans were made before I knew what was going to happen, but the situation was difficult. My dad was dying, and no one wanted me to know."

"Oh." Hannah closed her eyes, and I leaned back slowly so the hammock wouldn't wobble. "That must have been awful."

"In some ways it was, but in some ways it turned out good, because I loved it here."

"Do you still?"

"Yes, in a way. It's not exactly as I remembered. Some parts are the same, like the church. But it's different, or maybe I'm different."

"Not to be mean or anything, Mom, but it's not exactly a fairy-tale place."

"I know, Hannah. It seemed that way to me at a hard time in my life."

A huge horsefly buzzed past us, and I was glad he kept going. I remembered how those monsters could bite.

"What were you going to tell me?" Hannah asked.

"I was going to tell you that you were right. There is a reason for everything. When you cut your foot yesterday, I remembered why I don't do well with blood."

Hannah leaned forward, and the hammock rocked. "Why?"

"When I was a little girl, I cut my hand on a broken drinking glass, and it bled a lot. It frightened me."

"Did you get stitches?"

"A few."

"Let's see your hand." Hannah sat up all the way and made the hammock wobble.

I held out my left hand, palm up. I had to search to find the slightly raised spot where the glass had pierced the skin.

"I can barely see it," Hannah said.

"I know. It healed up, didn't it? Your foot will heal up, too."

We both reclined and silently swayed, listening to some kind of bird repeating a trill with three high notes and a low one. The melody was soothing.

"I like it when you tell me your stories," Hannah said. "I wish I had good stories to tell you."

"I don't care if they're good or bad or about blood even. I just like to hear your stories. Like how you had gardenias at your wedding, and what you told me last night about how I was born. I like knowing stuff like that."

I breathed the sweet air and wondered if I really had any stories left to tell Hannah. Louisiana and my summer with Grand Lady was my best story. Apparently that's why I'd told it often and elevated it to fairy-tale status. Hannah now could see the truth behind those stories. Grand Lady didn't live in a cottage with pink roses. She lived in a singlewide mobile home with avocado green trim. In some ways I liked it better when Hannah didn't see life the way it really was. For so many years I had sheltered and protected her from life's less-than-charming aspects. Now she was facing a string of irrefutable realities, and I felt sad about that.

The beastly horsefly came back and brought a pal with him. The two dove at Hannah and me, determined to snatch a couple of afternoon snacks from our perspiring flesh.

"Get outta here!" Hannah squealed, swatting at the pest and flailing around on the hammock.

"Hannah, don't rock like that!"

She rolled to her side, arms swishing through the air

above her head, and yet she managed somehow to gracefully spin herself off the hammock and land on her good foot.

I didn't fare as well. Hannah's departure tilted my weighted side of the hammock, and I spilled out on the lush grass like a gunnysack full of sweet potatoes.

All our commotion must have discouraged the horseflies, because they weren't bothering us now.

Hannah giggled at me as I tried to get up off the grass.

"You knew that was going to happen," I said with a tease in my voice.

"No, I didn't. Are you okay?"

"Yes. No broken bones." I brushed myself off.

"I think I'm ready for some of Aunt Peg's lemon meringue pie," Hannah said.

"Good idea." I followed her to the kitchen where we sat on the counter stools, licking our lips after each deliciously sour spoonful of Aunt Peg's pie.

Earlier in the day, as Hannah had cleared the Sunday dinner dishes from the table, I had watched Peg smooth her pie meringue with the rounded side of a frozen drinking glass.

"Glass is so much better to work with than a wobbly rubber spatula, don't you think, Sweet Abby?"

I'd never tried it and was thrilled with the cooking tips Aunt Peg already had passed on to me in the short time we had watched her prepare meals. Then she had offered her recipe box to me.

"What should we do now?" Hannah asked after the generous pieces of pie were contentedly settled in our tummies.

"I was thinking of copying some of Aunt Peg's recipes. Would you like to help me?"

"Not really."

"You could go over to Grand Lady's. She said we could visit her after she rested a little. Remember? She said she had a treat she wanted to make for you."

"What is it?"

"I don't know. You'll have to go find out."

"Are you going to come with me?"

"In a while. You can go on over, if you want."

Hannah examined the salt and pepper shakers. She read all of Aunt Peg's handwritten notes on her message board and watched me copy a recipe for fried okra and chili beans before she said, "I guess I'll go over there now."

"Have fun."

"I'll try." Hannah hobbled out the back door.

My recipe project became addictive. Aunt Peg's recipe box was a treasure chest full of clever food combinations like turkey and cranberry dumplings. She had more than fifty recipe cards dedicated to cakes alone and at least another fifty cards for cookies.

As eager as I was to spend time with Grand Lady, all of Peg's tried-and-true, down-home recipes made my mouth water, and I wanted to copy them all. For the past week I'd eaten nondescript fast food in every state, which delighted Hannah, but now I realized how much of the regional specialties we had missed out on.

The lemon meringue pie had put me on a sugar high, and I was writing as fast as I could. When I looked up at the clock, I realized I'd been at this for an hour.

Hannah walked in through the back door with an exasperated expression. "Why didn't you come over?"

"I'm sorry, Hannah. I got caught up in these recipes." I put down the pen and asked, "Did you have a nice visit?"

"You know that special treat Grand Lady wanted to make for me?"

"Yes."

"It was a drink. She called it a 'Purple Cow.' It was milk and grape juice mixed with ice in the blender." Hannah gave a shiver. "Please don't ask her for the recipe, Mom."

"Grape juice and milk. Sounds interesting."

"It's not."

"What else did you and Grand Lady do?"

"Nothing, really. She showed me a bunch of her things, like some pictures, her thimble collection, and her stack of old calendars. She's kept calendars from every year since I don't know when. She said sometimes she sits and reads them to remember what she did sixty years ago."

"That must have been interesting."

"Interesting?"

"Okay, different."

"Try boring."

"You didn't tell her it was boring, did you?"

"Of course not. I was nice and polite. I also tried to say everything slow and loud so she could understand me."

"Good. Did she say anything special to you?"

"Special like what?"

"Special. You know, something you'll remember for a long time. A blessing kind of special."

"No, not really. Where's everyone else?"

"I thought they were in the backyard."

"I didn't see them."

"Aunt Peg went out there awhile ago. She said she was going to poke around in the garden. I don't know where Uncle Burt is."

"What are we going to do for the next few days?" Hannah asked. "Aunt Peg said at breakfast that you all were going to talk about it this afternoon, but nobody said anything at lunch."

I stopped filing the recipe cards and looked at Hannah. "Did you just say, 'you all'?"

Hannah flapped her hand over her mouth. "No. I didn't say 'you all.'"

"I think you did, honey."

"It must be contagious then. Everybody around here says it."

"I know."

"You wait, Mom. It'll pop out of your mouth any minute now."

I smiled and finished returning the cards. "As far as what we'll do the next few days, I'd say we'll take it easy and find things to do around here."

"Like what?"

"Like get to know your relatives and just relax."

My daughter's expression was screaming the word *boring!* so loudly that she didn't need to say anything.

"Hannah, we only have a few days here, and I'm really hoping that you and Grand Lady will make a special connection. That's what we're doing the next few days. Getting to know our relatives. Especially Grand Lady."

"I'm trying, Mom."

"I know you are. I appreciate it."

Uncle Burt came into the kitchen wearing a pair of plaid swim trunks and a sleeveless white undershirt. His appearance was a startling change from his Sunday best that he had worn earlier that day.

"There you are. Wondered where y'all were hiding. Peg and I are going for a swim. I came in to get us a pitcher of sweet tea. Do y'all want to come out and keep us company?"

"I'll dangle my one leg in the water," Hannah said.

"Uncle Burt," I said before he popped out the back door again. "I was thinking that if Aunt Peg wouldn't mind, I'd be happy to make dinner tonight."

Uncle Burt laughed. "Not in my wife's kitchen, I can tell y'all that right now. This is her domain. Y'all are company. Peg wouldn't hear of you putting yourself to work in her kitchen. Besides, you have to cook all the time at home. This is your vacation. You're supposed to relax and take it easy."

"I wouldn't mind," I said.

Uncle Burt put up his hand. "End of discussion. Y'all come on out and sit by the pool with us."

Hannah and I obliged. We found Peg in her bathing suit, sitting with her legs stretched out in the water. She had a bucket of freshly picked green beans beside her and a round bowl in her lap. On her head was a wide-brimmed straw hat.

"What are you doing?" Hannah sidled up to Peg and lowered her unbandaged foot into the pool.

"Snapping beans. Would you like to help?"

"Sure."

I took a seat on the padded lounge chair a few feet away and watched Hannah snap the ends off of handfuls of green beans. I hoped she could see that this was what we came for. These simple, easy-living moments were what I knew she would remember for a long time.

Uncle Burt swam his laps, and I settled into the unhurried cadence of a Southern summer's eve. A low hum of conspiring insects rode on the sluggish air, punctuated by the occasional *zzup* of a dragonfly. Even with my eyes closed, I knew where I was.

After we ate a light supper that evening, we lingered by the pool in the flicker of four large citronella candles. The air around us seemed padded with cricket music and moist dragon's breath. A lone firefly performed a double-axel loopy-do in front of my nose, and I was impressed.

Hannah, however, was impressed with Uncle Burt's stories. Grand Lady had retired for the evening when Hannah asked Uncle Burt about my mother.

"Did you and your sister, Celeste, get along when you were growing up?"

"Sometimes. Most of the time, I suppose."

"Do you have any favorite stories about her?"

Uncle Burt told Hannah about the time my mother tried to make oatmeal molasses cookies. "They turned out so hard we couldn't eat 'em. My dad used them for sinkers on his fishing line until they got too soggy, and then he used 'em as fish bait. That is, till the fish in Lake Clayborne spit 'em up."

"Not really." Hannah grinned.

"That's what my daddy said. He said the biggest fish in Lake Clayborne came up to his boat that day and made a special request that, from then on, my daddy only use fresh worms or horseflies and no more of my sister's oatmeal molasses cookies."

Hannah smiled.

That night I thought of my mother as I lay in bed. Had her cookie disaster and the evident teasing that followed put her off cooking at an early age? Could a relatively small incident like that affect a person for the rest of her life?

The answer seemed evident.

I lay still, listening to the low hum of the air conditioner, accompanied by the steady breathing of my sleeping daughter. Years ago it had been the hum of crickets outside the open window that sang me nighttime lullabies. Since the installation of air-conditioning, this house had taken on a different feel. We didn't sit out on the porch swing to cool off in the evening. During my first visit here, we occupied the porch swing every evening.

I remembered the summer evening routine distinctly. My job was to open all the windows of the Big House and start the three metal fans in the upstairs bedrooms. Grand Lady and I would wait on the porch swing while the fans forced all the hot air out of the bedrooms. Sometime after ten, we would venture upstairs and fall asleep to the sound of the oscillating fans turned on low, like a metronome for the steady concert of the crickets outside the open window.

I rolled over on my side and studied my daughter's

profile in the amber light from the hallway. *Why are you so intrigued with my mother, and yet you're not connecting in a significant way with Grand Lady like I thought you would?*

The low humming answer in the back of my mind was that every girl wants to love her grandmother and know that her grandmother loves her back. Hannah was instinctively doing the same thing I had done at her age. She was idolizing her grandmother.

I brushed the thought away as if it were an annoying horsefly and closed my eyes, ready for a deep sleep.

The next morning, while the rest of the Big House occupants slept, I rose and tiptoed downstairs in my bathing suit. Pausing just outside the back door, I drew in a deep breath and surveyed the surroundings.

Oh, the sweetness of a bright Louisiana summer morning when the air is at its freshest!

Across the yard the grass stood up straight like uniformed troops of green soldiers ready for inspection. I knew that by noon the entire company of emerald sentinels would be at ease, snoozing their way through till suppertime. However, at the start of this new day, all the straight-backed soldiers were charged with vitality.

Reviewing the grassy troops with a nod of approval, I strode across the rallying blades and lowered myself into the pool. The water, like the air, was alive with buoyant implications.

I floated on my back, taking in the pastel shades of the morning sky. The wide, celestial canvas resembled the background of one of Monet's water lily paintings. With a careful eye, I studied all the staccato streaks of color smudged together, circling this globe, and thought of how Hannah would like this. She would want to take a picture.

The front door to Grand Lady's cottage opened. I flipped around on my stomach just in time to watch her step out on her deck in her pink housecoat, wearing pink terry cloth slippers that were just like the ones she sent me every year for Christmas.

I waved, but she didn't notice me. With her eyesight so weak, I guessed I would look like little more than a colorful floating raft in the slightly ruffled water of the pool.

Drawing in a deep breath, Grand Lady lifted her arms to her sides and slowly raised them. She repeated this exercise five times and then twisted from right to left five times.

Her morning workout. Good for her.

I remembered how she had gotten me to do sit-ups and deep knee bends with her when she was in her late sixties. She certainly had taken good care of herself. An elegant dignity clothed her, even in her morning robe and slippers.

Grand Lady reached over and touched her knees three times, then returned to her cottage.

Getting out of the pool, I dried off and wrapped the towel around my waist. I squeezed the chlorinated water from my hair, shook my head like a wet dog, and sauntered around the house to the gardenia bush. Bending to sniff the largest gardenia, I felt as if I could swallow the sweetness.

After selecting a handful of the finest flowers on the bush, I carried them to Grand Lady's cottage, sniffing them and smiling with each step. I pulled open the screen door and knocked on the doorframe, calling out the way Aunt Peg had done the day before. Stepping inside, I called out again.

"Just a moment," came the wavering voice from down the hall.

"It's me, Grand Lady. It's Abby."

The bathroom door opened, and she came out blinking in my direction and looking flustered. "Yes?"

Up close, she was a sight to see. A polka-dot shower cap covered her hair. Her glasses were off, and her left eye wandered without the strong lenses to help it focus. Her face was covered with white cold cream, and she was wearing only her underwear and a slip. The most startling sight was her teeth. Or, I should say, the absence of her teeth. Without her dentures, her pale lips curved into a mouth that seemed to be sinking into her face.

"Good morning," I greeted her.

"A person should always be at their best," she prattled, sounding like a page from a book on etiquette.

"This is how one should receive their guests. It takes the slightest effort."

It seemed she was mumbling to herself rather than directing her comments to me. She waddled down the hall, and I stood there with outstretched arms, holding out my fragrant offering before my childhood icon, who had fallen to earth this morning in a polka-dot shower bonnet and a great deal of sagging, jiggling flesh.

Chapter 14

Grand Lady closed the bedroom door behind her. I didn't know if she was fully aware of my presence or not. It seemed the best thing to do was to wait for her to reappear and offer her the morning gardenias once again.

Searching through her kitchen cupboards, I found the pottery bowl I'd used decades ago and set the gardenias to float in it. Placing the bowl on her cluttered kitchen table, I noticed the place mats. They were ruffled and depicted two red cardinals exchanging bird news with each other on the edge of a wooden feeder. I could see why the bright colors and large size appealed to Grand Lady. She could see these cardinals more easily than the real ones outside her window that visited the feeder on the corner of her deck.

Sitting down at the table, I drew in a deep breath and thought about getting old. In the same way that Hannah had been confronted on this trip with so many of the facts of life, I was being confronted with many facts about death. And I didn't like what I was seeing. Not a bit.

If I was going to be granted a long life, I wanted to live peacefully and well, like Grand Lady. But I didn't want to become blind, saggy, and toothless. I didn't want to be relegated to a trailer, no matter how much I tried to imagine it being as charming as a cottage.

Yet, at the same time, I would rather be given the chance to live independently, like Grand Lady, than to be closed up in some sort of care facility.

The raw truth was that I didn't want to get old.

I stood up and pulled a hand towel from the stove handle and used it to pinch the remaining pool water from the ends of my dripping hair. With quick fingers I loosely braided my hair so I'd look more presentable.

It takes the slightest effort.

A small book on the kitchen table caught my eye. It looked familiar. The fabric cover was of bright red strawberries. I picked up the book and found Grand Lady's lovely handwriting with the following title meticulously printed:

"Gems Collected Along My Path in Life"
By Charlotte Isabella Burroughs

Oh, Grand Lady, you never told me! You wrote a little book, didn't you?

I carefully turned to the next page and read her collected "gems," starting with the first entry, made on her seventy-third birthday:

"If it's going to be, it's up to me."

"In a small town people know when you are ill, and care when you die." —Dan Rather, CBS evening news, 1982.

"Grandchildren are God's compensation for growing older."

"A sweater is something I wore whenever my mother was cold."

That one made me smile. Hannah probably would grow up saying that shoes were what she wore whenever her mother thought of red fire ants.

"So take a new grip with your tired hands, stand firm on your shaky legs and mark out a straight, smooth path for your feet." —Hebrews 12:12-13, Phillips Modern Translation.

"There's never been a fragrance as wonderful as a sun-dried pillowcase against my cheek."

"On my 81st birthday, I am prone to declare that I have loved life after eighty. I have become aware of little happenings such as the cardinals at the feeder, the frozen moisture on the windows, looking like stars, the warmth of a streetlight. Before eighty I never had time to notice such small wonders."

The bedroom door opened. I snapped the book closed. Grand Lady came out with her cane and made her way to the bathroom. She still wore the shower cap and had the cold cream on her face. Over her arm she carried a carefully smoothed dress. She didn't seem to notice that I was at the kitchen table, so I opened the book again and skimmed the pages, collecting more "gems" along the way.

"Dad grew vegetables for our stomachs; Mom grew flowers for our souls."

"The important thing to remember about the future is that it arrives one day at a time. Thank you, Lord, for holding my hand each day."

"When we try to live in the past, we miss God's plan for the present."

"Each day is a messenger from God."—Russian Proverb

"Though much is taken, much abides."—Alfred, Lord Tennyson

"One should tell it like it is. Roses are red and violets are really violet.

"The lark's on the wing, the snail's on the thorn, God's in His heaven, All's right with the world."—Robert Browning

"I will sing of the mercies of the Lord for ever." Psalm 89:1, King James

"Keep your temper. Nobody else wants it."

"Resolutions on my 88th birthday: Be kind, be loving, be compassionate, give of myself, accept graciously."

"There are 365 'fear nots' in the Bible. One for every day of the year. Today I will fear not."

"Zippidy do dah. That's how you spell it."

"At 90 years old, I find that insomnia is a lot like being sick, except it does not hurt anywhere specific."

"Stop and consider the wondrous work of God." Job 37:14, Phillips

"God is present in the endings as well as the beginnings."

I noticed how all the pages had some little bit of hand-sketched art. One page had trailing vines up the side, another was sprinkled with tiny daisies across the top, and one page had a simple sketch of what I recognized as the old magnolia tree.

I never knew Grand Lady had a flair for drawing. Is that where my mother gets it? Or did every child raised in the shadow of the Victorian era receive training in the skill of beautiful penmanship and sketching?

Grand Lady exited the bathroom, looking like a different woman from the gnomelike creature who had toddled in fifteen minutes earlier. Her hair was arranged in a smooth twist; she had her dentures in place. Adjusting her glasses, she seemed to scan the room to see if she only had imagined she had morning visitors.

"Good morning," I said shyly. "I brought in some gardenias. For breakfast." I wondered if she remembered.

"Why, Abby, you are here. What are you doing up so early, Honeygirl?"

"I went swimming. I also picked some gardenias."

She stopped her hobbled approach and breathed in deeply. "Why, yes, you did. They are quite fragrant this morning. Would you like some hot chocolate, Honeygirl?"

It seemed she hadn't yet connected all the pieces. Did she know that I was no longer a child, waiting for her to give me something sweet and yummy to eat?

"I have an idea, Grand Lady. Why don't you sit down and let me make you breakfast?"

Grand Lady tilted her head, looking at me. "Why, yes, I would like that. Thank you."

I rose and pulled out a chair for her, as she continued to study me carefully. Once she was seated she asked, "Is that a towel you are wearing around your waist, or is that a skirt?"

"It's a towel. As I said a few minutes ago, I went swimming this morning. Remember?"

"You are most certainly welcome to borrow my robe. It will be much more comfortable for you."

I hesitated but then realized this was her home, and if it was unsettling for her to have someone walking around in her kitchen wearing only a bathing suit and wet beach towel, then I should honor her request.

Slipping into the bathroom, I pulled her robe off the back of the door and put it on. The seersucker fabric carried the long-ingrained scent of Noxema and witch hazel. I fastened the pink buttons and wondered if it was crazy to ask Aunt Peg to send me this robe, unwashed, after Grand Lady had exchanged it for the pure white one waiting for her in the courts of heaven.

"So, what would you like for breakfast?" I asked Grand Lady. She was sitting patiently, with her hands folded on the red cardinal place mat.

"I would like a cup of coffee, one slice of toast with marmalade, one soft-boiled egg, and a small bowl of my special raisins."

I couldn't tell if she simply knew what she wanted, or if she viewed me as a waitress, standing there in a pink seersucker uniform, taking her order.

"Coming right up."

I found the bread and eggs easily enough in her sparsely occupied refrigerator. Reaching for the jar of marmalade, I asked, "Do you have a coffeemaker?"

"No, I prefer instant coffee with water heated in the teakettle."

When I delivered the marmalade to the table with a plate, knife, and spoon, Grand Lady looked up and said, "Are you going to join me?"

It gave me comfort to know that she at least knew I wasn't a waitress. I set a place for myself and eased another egg into the pan of boiling water. "Do you like sugar in your coffee?"

"No, thank you. However, I do like my coffee served in a china cup with a saucer."

I found two china cups and saucers in the cupboard and placed all the requested breakfast food before her. She looked up with a pleasant expression. "This is most kind of you. I do not remember the last time I had breakfast prepared for me while I waited."

"I love doing this for you."

"I do so appreciate it. Now, the raisins, if you please."

I found the raisin jar, but the contents looked like a batch of swollen fish eggs floating in formaldehyde. "Are you sure these are edible?"

"Indeed, they are. Those white raisins are cured in whiskey. A mere half a cup a day at breakfast, and a person can experience a remarkable improvement in her health, particularly as it relates to troubles with arthritis."

The raisins looked "cured" all right. I doubted anything would bother those little plumped-up babies in their fully emaciated state.

"I have also found that on difficult days," Grand Lady continued, "another half a cup at two in the afternoon helps me to nap and takes away the stiffness."

"I imagine it would." I kept a straight face and took my seat beside her at the table.

"Would you return thanks for us, Abby?"

I bowed my head and was about to pray a freestyle prayer, when I remembered the morning prayer she had taught me so many years ago. I knew it would please her if I offered the familiar prayer. "For these Thy gifts, which we are about to receive, may we be truly grateful. Let the words of my mouth and the meditation of my heart be acceptable in Thy sight this day, O God, my rock and my redeemer. Amen."

Grand Lady smiled at me when I looked up. She saw me. I knew she saw me. Despite her formal approach to everything and the aloofness that she seemed to treasure, I knew that when she looked at me, I wasn't a waitress her imagination had superimposed over reality. I was Abby. Her Honeygirl.

"Would you like to try the raisins?" she asked.

"No, that's okay. Thanks anyway."

"You might find that you enjoy them. They are quite tasty."

"I'm sure they are, but I'll stick with the egg and toast this morning."

She ate slowly and didn't speak.

I looked around at the stacks of miscellany on her table. To my right was a bundle of Christmas cards tied with twine. Next to the cards was a plastic bag with a variety of tapered candles, all of which appeared to be brighter on one side than the other. I wondered if it was due to sun damage or to age.

Across from me lay a large photo album and the small, strawberry-covered journal of gems I had just thumbed through. To Grand Lady's left side was a tidy stack of magazines. I noticed that everything had its place, the same way rows of beans, tomatoes, and carrots are all separated and marked in a garden.

"This is my table garden," Grand Lady said as if she'd read my thoughts. "I am afraid that this table is about all my hands can manage to tend to these days."

"Well, it's a very beautiful garden, and it looks like you have a bountiful harvest."

"My bountiful harvest is my family," she said. "My grandchildren and great-grandchildren. You are my harvest."

With perfect timing, my little "harvest" appeared at the front door. Hannah tapped on the screen door and then peered inside Grand Lady's home. "Are you over here, Mom?"

"Yes, I'm here. Come in, Hannah."

"I didn't know where you went."

"Good morning, Hannah," Grand Lady greeted her graciously.

"Hi."

I stretched out my arm, and Hannah came to my side, resting her arm on my shoulder. She smoothed her hand over the seersucker fabric of the robe. "Where did you get this?"

"It's Grand Lady's. I went swimming, and she let me borrow it."

"What smells so good in here?"

"The gardenias," I said.

"That's what I thought. What are those?" Hannah pointed to the jar of pickled white raisins.

"It's the cure for arthritis," I said.

"It looks nasty. Remind me never to get arthritis."

Grand Lady chuckled. "How are you today, Miss Hannah?"

"Pretty good. My foot's a lot better. I wish I could go swimming, though."

"Have you eaten yet?" I asked.

"I had some cereal. What are we going to do today?"

"Perhaps," Grand Lady said with her slow drawl, "today would be a good day to go shopping."

Hannah smiled. I knew that to her almost every day was a good day to go shopping.

"I have to take the car over to Chester to get the window fixed," I said. "I think Uncle Burt said the repair shop was next to Wal-Mart."

Grand Lady seemed to brighten at the prospect. "Well, now, that would be lovely. I had thought all along we would go to Sylvia's, but Wal-Mart is a fine idea."

Hannah eagerly started formulating a plan for the day. By nine o' clock we were ready to leave. We had to use a stepping block to get Grand Lady into the front seat of the SUV. She chuckled and took it in stride. I made sure we took the step with us so we could get her out without causing a scene at Wal-Mart.

Aunt Peg climbed in the backseat, and Hannah pointed out to her all the custom features: the refrigerator, the TV, and the selection of DVDs. Aunt Peg was astonished at all the "contraptions," but she regained her composure when I asked her which way to turn at the end of the driveway.

"Go right, Sweet Abby. You want to take the same road that brought you into Howell from Minton."

I drove to the first stop sign and waited while a rusted sedan came rolling to a stop on my right.

"Why is that car stopping?" I asked. "He doesn't have a stop sign."

Aunt Peg glanced out her window at the rusty old jalopy. "He's waiting for you to go."

"Why?"

"You have the right of way."

"Actually, I don't. He does."

"Not here, Sweet Abby. You have the right of way. Go ahead."

"But that car has the right of way."

"Just go, Mom," said Hannah.

I rolled through the intersection and glanced back at the sedan as it crawled forward. "I don't get it. I had the stop sign; he didn't. How does that give me the right of way?"

"Let's just say the traffic rules are a little different down here in Louisiana."

"How would they be different in this state? A stop sign is a stop sign."

"Yes, but you have the right of way," Aunt Peg stated emphatically.

"Why?"

"Because, Sweet Abby, you're the white woman at the intersection. All right? You have the right of way."

I turned and glanced at my aunt incredulously. Grand Lady was looking straight ahead, as if none of this conversation had touched her ears. I realized the driver of the sedan must have been African American. I hadn't noticed that while waiting at the stop sign.

"That's not right," I stated firmly, feeling my neck muscles tense.

Aunt Peg's calming hand patted my shoulder. "Right or not right, that's the way things are around here."

"Then things need to change."

Aunt Peg took a slow moment before saying, "Yes, I suppose things do need to change. And perhaps they will one day."

In an attempt to cool off in more ways than one, I turned the air-conditioning to high. My broken window was letting in all the warm air, and my angered mind was letting in all kinds of heated thoughts about hypocrisy and prejudice. It was easy for me to judge them. Very easy. Perhaps as easy for me to judge my aunt as it was for her to fall into an automatic judgment of the black people in her small town.

I thought of how twenty-eight years ago I had bounded over this same road with my cousins in the flatbed of a truck on a jaunt to Minton. I remembered eating watermelon that BJ cut open with his pocket-knife and squinting most of the way from the sun and the wind blowing my hair in my face. Not once did I notice who had the right of way.

So many of the deeper layers of this place were unseen by me when I was young. What other life truths have I been oblivious to?

I wasn't sure I wanted to know.

When we arrived at Wal-Mart, I pulled up to the front of the store to let Grand Lady out.

"Look, Grand Lady." Hannah pointed to a motorized shopping cart that had a triangle-shaped blue flag on the top of a tall pole. "You can use one of those. Then you won't have to walk."

Grand Lady bristled as Aunt Peg helped her out of the car. "I am able to walk just fine, thank you. I prefer to use a regular cart like everyone else."

"I think Hannah wanted to be the one to ride in the motorized cart," I said hoping to soothe Grand Lady's ruffled feathers.

Aunt Peg peered at mc over the top of her glasses.

"Are you sure you'll be okay taking the car over by yourself?"

"Yes, I'll be fine. I'll meet you in the snack area in a few minutes."

The window repair shop was, as Uncle Burt had said, right next to Wal-Mart. My uncle also had called ahead and made arrangements for me so all I had to do was drop off the vehicle and walk through the parking lot back to Wal-Mart.

Instead of meeting the others at the snack bar, as previously arranged, I found they had only gotten a few feet inside the store. Grand Lady was busy greeting the Wal-Mart greeter.

"Does she know him?" I quietly asked Aunt Peg.

"No," she whispered behind the back of her hand. "It's like this wherever we go. You'll see. Grand Lady enjoys checking in on her subjects even if they don't know who she is."

I thought it was kind of cute. We waited patiently while Grand Lady introduced all of us to "Mr. Otis," the Wal-Mart greeter. She carried off the moment as if this were the social event of the season. And then I realized that, for her, it might very well be.

Otis kept nodding and grinning. He was interested to hear from Grand Lady that Hannah and I lived in Hawaii and said he always had wanted to take a trip there. Maybe he would someday, now that his dear wife had passed away.

Grand Lady expressed her condolences.

"Well, that's mighty kind of you," Otis said. "Louise has been gone for seven years now, and I do miss her somethin' awful some days. I even went out and got myself a cat."

"Is that right?" Grand Lady said.

"She weights eighteen pounds," Otis said.

Our eyes widened.

"Lulubelle is a big girl, but she's also the most curious cat you've ever seen. She climbs up on everything. If I had her with me right now, she'd be climbing up on your shoulders. She'd perch herself right there on your head just so she'd be able to have a look around the place."

Hannah let out a giggle, and I gave her a nudge. I knew she was picturing my dear Grand Lady standing in Wal-Mart wearing Lulubelle, the eighteen-pound cat on her head. I knew that, because the same image was now stuck in my mind. I also wanted to let loose with a laugh, but dear Otis seemed to be earnest with his cat stories, and if there's one thing the women in Louisiana knew how to do, it was to put on congenial manners when it counted.

I followed Aunt Peg's lead and forced a straight face.

"Grand Lady, do you suppose we should get to our shopping now?" Aunt Peg asked diplomatically.

"Yes, indeed we should. It has been a pleasure visiting with you, Mr. Otis. I hope you have a lovely day, and do greet your charming Lulubelle for us."

"I will, indeed. Y'all have a nice day, now!"

Our entourage had progressed about ten feet away from Otis, when my little pixie turned to Grand Lady. "He's not your type, Grand Lady."

"I beg your pardon?"

"Mr. Otis," Hannah said with charming irreverence. "I know you were flirting with him back there."

Grand Lady blinked several times, as if processing Hannah's teasing and trying to decide if she approved or not. Reaching into one of her many pockets of resiliency, Grand Lady pulled out a response equal to Hannah's mischief. "He was rather handsome. Would you not agree? Although I believe it would be challenging to compete with Miss Lulubelle for Mr. Otis's full attention."

Hannah burst into laughter. I laughed along with them, smiling to see the two dearest women in my life finding each other at last.

Chapter 15

Now, Hannah," Grand Lady said after we had made our way to the clothing section for junior girls. "I would like to buy something special for you. Do you know what you would like?"

Hannah shrugged. Looking at me out of the corner of her eye, she hesitantly said, "Some makeup or something, maybe?"

I was still getting used to shopping in the junior girls section and not in children's. Hannah's asking for makeup left me speechless.

"Perhaps a new dress would be nice for you," Grand Lady said softly.

"I don't really need a new dress, but I do need another pair of shorts and some more socks."

Hannah had three women immediately reaching for a variety of shorts. I knew she didn't enjoy taking the time to try on clothes, so her selection of a pair of denim shorts took about five minutes. She held them up, declared they would fit, and off we went to the sock section. Hannah selected four pairs of socks. One of the pairs was orange with blue and yellow polka dots.

"The dotted anklets are certainly notable," Grand Lady said.

A playful twinkle appeared in Hannah's eye. "I think all of us should get a pair. Even you, Grand Lady. And you know what? I'll buy your pair with my own money. What do you think of that? We'll be twins."

Grand Lady stood a moment, leaning on the shopping cart handle, gazing at Hannah. "How kind of you," she said at last. "I would be honored to receive a pair of anklets from you."

This seemed like a memorable moment, and I recalled I had my camera in my shoulder bag. Without pausing or posing my subjects, I pulled out the camera and set off the flash, capturing my grandmother holding up her new pair of "notable" socks, comparing them to Hannah's.

"What was that?" Hannah asked, as I quickly slipped the camera back into my bag. "Did you just take a picture, Mom?"

Playing innocent, I looked up at the overhead lighting. "Maybe."

"Mother, people don't go around taking pictures inside the underwear department at Wal-Mart!"

Peg and I laughed.

"I'm serious, Mom!" Hannah's voice turned to a low growl. "I can't believe you did that! As if it's not embarrassing enough to be here like this! Mother, do you see anyone else taking pictures in the underwear department?"

"May I say to you, Miss Hannah," Grand Lady cut in with an air of admonishment. "You would do well to mind the manner in which you speak to your mother in public."

Hannah didn't seem to know what to make of Grand Lady's honey-coated rebuke. A moment ago they had been teasing each other about Mr. Otis.

As if scrambling to build her case, Hannah said to Grand Lady, "My mother does the strangest things in public. One time we were standing at an art awards ceremony, and I turned and looked at her and there she was, with a piece of dental floss hanging out of her mouth while she was clapping!"

"I had a piece of chicken caught between my teeth." I pointed to the teeth in question as if I, too, were ready to defend my side of the story before our white-haired judge.

Without looking directly at either of us, Grand Lady lifted her chin. "Mothers. Indeed. We all certainly have them, do we not?" Gripping the cart handle, she shuffled into the aisle.

"What was that supposed to mean?" Hannah looked

at me, as if I could interpret Grand Lady's strange comment.

I had no answer for Hannah because a sharp memory assaulted me. I no longer was tuned in to my grandmother's words in the underwear department of Wal-Mart. I was caught up in the remembrance of standing beside my mother in the underwear department of a Sears department store when I was thirteen years old.

My mother was still a newlywed, all wrapped up in her elation over Stan, and I still was trying to decide where I fit in our reconstructed family. Added to that I had a really bad head cold and a volcanic burst of hormones, and my mother was standing next to me holding up a pair of red Valentine boxers she wanted to buy for Stan. She turned to me and said, "Did you know you have a pimple right there?"

And then she touched it. In public. As if I didn't know the status of every throbbing pore on my rebellious face and hadn't been watching that particular quadrant for the past two days.

I fled.

All I could think about was getting out of there and never going back. Never having to see my mother again. Never holding another image in my mind of my stepfather wearing those ridiculous boxers.

I ran through the store, out the door, across the parking lot, and into the music store across the street. Hiding just to the side of the big window, I blinked back the agonizing flow of tears and pretended to read the back of a Blood, Sweat and Tears album. I could see my mother as she calmly stood in the parking lot next to the car, looking right and left.

I wanted her to come find me. I needed her to come to me.

But she didn't come. She stood her ground, waiting for more than twenty minutes. Maybe it was half an hour. Maybe it was only five minutes. All I know is that the fire drained from my belly, and I stopped crying and remembered I had homework I had to finish before I could watch my favorite TV show that night at eight o'clock.

I don't remember what the show was, but I will never forget what it felt like taking that first step out of the music store and placing one belligerent foot in front of the other until I stood before her. My heart held enough volatile kegs of severe shame and smoldering fury to demolish our relationship for all time. But to my credit, I held back.

It was my mother who lit the fuse. She looked at me, mascara smeared in the corner of both my eyes, and said with no emotion, "You are just like your father. Now get in the car."

"Sweet Abby? You okay, honey?"

I blinked and realized I was standing in Wal-Mart.

Not the Sears parking lot. I was the mother. Not the daughter.

"Yes, I'm fine, Aunt Peg." I cleared my throat.

I turned to see that Hannah had not run off to the music department to hide from me. Instead she had fallen in line behind Grand Lady and was following her down the book aisle.

Peg and I joined them as Grand Lady said, "I would like to buy you a Bible, Miss Hannah."

"I already have . . ." Hannah swallowed the rest of her intended sentence and finished with "that would be nice of you. Thanks."

"To my way of thinking, every young woman should have a Bible that she knows is her very own to read every day and to carry with her to church on Sunday."

My eye went to a colorfully illustrated children's Bible. I lifted it and said, "Did you see this one, Hannah?"

She looked mortified and growled in a low voice, "Mom, I don't think that's very funny."

I didn't understand why she was so upset until I saw her reaching for the one with the splashy cover labeled, "Teen Bible."

"I like this one," my twelve-year-old said.

Crayons to lipstick. I'm not ready for this.

The rest of our shopping trip I did my best to guard my actions and my words. I slowly was beginning to understand. I remembered what it felt like to be embarrassed by my mother in public. Humiliating Hannah was the last thing I intended to do. I would give anything not to alienate my daughter.

Does every mother feel that way, or am I overly sensitive because of the lingering hurts of my childhood?

Leaving Aunt Peg and Grand Lady to complete the shopping with Hannah, I walked back to the auto shop next door and paid for the window repair. The SUV was ready, and when I pulled up in front of Wal-Mart, Aunt Peg, Hannah, and Grand Lady were all set to go with their multiple shopping bags.

As I drove, I kept glancing at Hannah in the rearview mirror. She had pulled a tube of lip gloss from her shopping bag and was smoothing on the shiny, almost clear color and pressing her lips together.

"Thanks for the lipstick, Aunt Peg," Hannah said. "It tastes like cotton candy."

"You are so welcome, Miss Hannah. I remember the first tube of lip gloss I bought for my Tammy Jean. She went through the entire tube in a week and a half."

"I hope mine lasts longer than that," Hannah said.

"It will, if you don't apply it every ten minutes, the way my daughter did."

Hannah pulled out the new teen Bible and flipped through the pages. "Aunt Peg, do you know where that part is about the woman who was bleeding for a long time, and then Jesus healed her?"

Now I was the one who felt embarrassed. Of all the passages in the Bible, why in the world did Hannah ask about that one? Was it because the woman had a flow of blood? I tried to remember if the pastor had made reference on Sunday to the woman who reached out and touched the hem of Jesus' robe. No memory of such a comment came to me.

Aunt Peg thumbed through the Bible for a good while before announcing, "Here it is. The eighth chapter of the book of Luke. Luke was a doctor, you know. I took a guess that he would write about Jesus healing someone."

"What does it say?" Hannah asked.

I still couldn't imagine why Hannah was curious about this Bible passage. Aunt Peg read the first few verses aloud and said, "My, that is a modern version, isn't it? Certainly makes the Bible easier to understand. Here, Hannah. You read this last part, starting at verse 47."

I didn't expect Hannah to read aloud, but she did. Whether she was trying to impress her great aunt or simply was engaged in the passage, she read.

"When the woman realized that she couldn't remain hidden, she knelt trembling before him. In front of all the people, she blurted out her story—why she touched him and how at that same moment she was healed.

"Jesus said, 'Daughter, you took a risk trusting me, and now you're healed and whole. Live well, live blessed!'"

"Is that the part you were looking for?" Aunt Peg asked.

"I think so."

I glanced in the mirror, and Hannah was looking up at me. Our eyes connected, and her expression startled me. Was she trying to tell me something about her period? What was going on with this emerging young woman in the backseat? I barely knew who she was.

We were almost to Howell when Hannah begged me to pull over where we had our mishap with the chicken crate. Slowing down, I put on the blinker and asked Hannah if she was okay.

"Yeah, I just wanted to see if we can take that chair up there beside the road. Unless it belongs to somebody who lives out in the woods here."

"That's unlikely," Aunt Peg said. "It's been there quite some time. I'd imagine it was tossed out as rubbish since the seat is broken through."

"I have an idea what to do with it," Hannah said. "Can we put it in the back? Please, Mom? I want to paint it."

"I don't think so, Hannah."

"Why not?"

I glanced out the windshield at the dilapidated chair and knew I didn't want to load the ugly thing into the back of my brother's SUV.

"It's not a good idea." I tried to sound authoritative.

I noticed that Grand Lady had fallen asleep against the window and didn't appear to hear our mother-daughter power struggle.

Swinging wide to avoid the chair, I eased the vehicle back onto the road, assuming the mattered was settled.

"I don't see why I can't take it." Hannah's voice rose from the backseat. "Aunt Peg said it's been there a long time. I want to fix it up. Why don't you want me to have it, Mom?"

My eyes connected with Hannah's in the rearview mirror for only a second, and I knew by her expression that she didn't intend to let this go. What was I to do? Give in? Stand firm? Scold her for being disrespectful? Why was she pushing me like this?

Aunt Peg interjected a saving solution as we came within view of the Big House. "I would imagine, Miss Hannah, that you are looking for things to keep you busy until your foot heals up, and you can go swimming."

I watched Hannah nod her head.

"You tell me how you feel about this, Abby, but if Hannah wants to paint that old chair, why, I wouldn't mind going back and getting it for her in my car. I'm sure we have some paint in the basement. It might be an interesting project to keep her occupied."

"Could I, Mom?"

How could I say no? Especially after Aunt Peg had taken all the mess and effort out of the equation?

"Are you sure you don't mind, Aunt Peg?" I asked cautiously, still not ready to give a final answer.

"Course not. I don't mind a bit. If we need any art supplies, Hannah and I can drive ourselves on over to the Piggly Wiggly, can't we, Miss Hannah?"

As soon as Aunt Peg said "Piggly Wiggly," Hannah was all smiles.

"All right," I said with a hint of irritation. Then, just to sound as if I still had some position of authority in this relationship, I added, "Make sure you clean up after yourself, Hannah. And lay down newspapers before you start painting."

"I know. I will, Mom."

Hannah sprang from the car as soon as I pulled into the driveway, ready to go back and nab the chair with her new pal, Aunt Peg.

I woke Grand Lady in the front seat of our parked car and walked her back to her cottage. She insisted that I pour two glasses of sweet tea while she changed from her shopping clothes into a housedress.

A few minutes later her twittering voice called from behind the closed bedroom door, "You may come in now."

"Would you like me to bring the iced tea with me?"

As a girl I remembered only being allowed to have food in the kitchen. I wasn't even allowed to take a glass of water upstairs to the bedroom in the Big House. Apparently the house rules had changed for the cottage.

Grand Lady welcomed both the sweet tea and me into her inner sanctum.

Opening the bedroom door, I felt as if I'd stepped back in time. Everything was as I had remembered it in her bedroom in the Big House. The double bed had the same chenille spread with the little white pom-poms. I recognized the two pillows that were placed just so.

"You still have these." I went to the pillows and ran my hand over the orange terrycloth trimmed with yellow crocheted lace.

"None the worse for the wear," Grand Lady said.

I got all choked up. "I made these pillows for you in a sewing class at the teen community center. I must have been fifteen. Maybe sixteen. I can't believe you still have them."

"I rarely have parted with any of my true treasures." She lifted her swollen feet out of her good shoes and calmly put on her pink slippers. "However, I believe the time has come for me to make an adjustment to my way of thinking. I have set aside several meaningful items I wish for you to have."

Shuffling a few feet to her dresser, Grand Lady opened the top drawer and pulled out a stack of cards and letters tied with a ribbon.

"I have read these a hundred times and savored every one. I do believe I have your clever words memorized." She handed me the stack. It was at least three inches thick.

"My words?"

"These are all the letters I received from you over the years."

"I had no idea I'd written so many."

She allowed a silken grin to ease across her thin lips. "Each one was truly a treasure to me."

Reaching in the dresser drawer, she withdrew a narrow box. "I have labeled some of my belongings so that after I am gone they will be sent to you directly."

She lifted a strand of pearls from the box and held them up with a look of tender admiration. "These pearls will be yours one day. Your grandfather gave them to me on our wedding day. They belonged to his mother."

Rising and going to her side, I touched the delicate strand of creamy pearls. "These are beautiful. Thank you, Grand Lady. Thank you so much. I would love to have your pearls. They will mean a lot to me."

"I was in hopes that you would feel that way." She returned the pearls to their box, and I noticed that my name was written on the lid.

Mustering a tiny smile on her pale pink lips, she said, "I have one more gift for you, Honeygirl. I must admit, I am not certain I am ready to give it to you at this moment."

"That's okay. I'm sure you're getting tired. Why don't you take a rest? You can give it to me later."

Grand Lady lowered herself to the foot of her bed

and took a sip of tea from the glass I held out to her. She drew in a fortifying breath, and I wondered if she was considering another serving of those arthritis-fighting raisins before her nap. Apparently the sweet tea was all she needed to give her a boost of energy. With a gentle tilt of her head, Grand Lady said, "Honeygirl, I have waited a long time to give this one last gift to you."

I sat beside her and nested her hand in mine. "You already have given me so much, Grand Lady. You don't need to give me anything else."

"Oh, but I do, Honeygirl. Before it is too late, I must give you my story."

"Your story?" My heart beat faster. *Hannah should be here for this.*

She nodded and asked if I would go to the kitchen table and bring back the small, strawberry-covered journal I'd secretly perused earlier that morning. I handed it to her, and she said, "This little book is the beginning of the end of my story."

I thought it would be best to start this conversation with honesty, so I said, "I have a confession for you, Grand Lady. I saw your book this morning, and I peeked at it."

"Did you? Well, then perhaps you realized this book is for you."

"For me? Are you sure?"

"Yes, this book has always been for you. I have been writing down these thoughts so that you would have them one day."

I leaned over to kiss her on the cheek. "Thank you."

"Did you read the final page?" Grand Lady asked.

"No, I didn't get that far."

She raised her right hand, motioning that I was to proceed.

I expected to find some sort of benediction. However, what I found were two sentences:

"I forgive my mother. I pray my daughter will forgive me."

"What does this mean? You forgive your mother for what?"

Grand Lady didn't respond.

I wondered if I had gone too far, asking her such a blunt question. Grand Lady held her privacy in highest regard; yet she was the one who had given me the book and had pointed out the last page. How did she expect me to respond?

Grand Lady adjusted her posture. "Perhaps I should first ask you a question. How is your relationship with your mother?"

"It's fine," I said. The words sounded the same as they had when I had given them to Su Ling after she asked if I was looking forward to visiting my mother.

"Is it fine?"

"Yes. Hannah and I were just there last week, you know. It was fine."

I was feeling prickly under the skin now. I wanted to change the subject and talk about something else. Unfortunately, I was the one who had invited this conversation.

"I will tell you what happened with my mother." Grand Lady leaned forward. "And I will tell you what happened with my daughter. It is my aspiration that you will listen carefully, Honeygirl, and that you will learn from my experiences before you become an old woman, like myself."

I nodded, urging her to continue.

"My mother," Grand Lady began, taking her customary breath and lowering her tone. "Your great-grandmother, was a strong and determined woman. She selected husbands for my two older sisters, and they willingly abided by our mother's preference. However, the man on whom my mother set her eye as a match for me was not the man with whom I fell in love. And it was love. Truly. William and I knew we were right for each other when we were only fifteen years old. Due to the circumstances, you can see why we were forced to keep our love a secret from my parents."

I had never heard any of this before. I knew Grand Lady had married when she was young, but I had no idea she and Grandpa William shared a Romeo and Juliet sort of love story.

"My mother was determined for me to marry Roland Conners."

She paused, as if waiting for me to recognize the name. I didn't, so she continued.

"When I was sixteen, I told my mother I did not want to marry Roland. She said I had no choice. She said when I grew up I would understand.

"I went to my father and told him that William and I were privately engaged. Keep in mind that young ladies did not speak to their fathers in this manner. As you might imagine, my father was furious. After one week of consideration, he agreed to our marriage and offered his blessing.

"My mother was honor-bound to comply with my father's decision. However," she took a sip of her iced tea before continuing, "my mother kept her temper on a long fuse. She would burn it slowly and silently for days."

"I know how that is," I said sympathetically.

"Yes," Grand Lady said knowingly. "I imagine you do."

"So what happened?"

"I finished high school. William and I moved ahead with our plans, knowing we had my father's blessing. We hoped we would also have my mother's blessing when the time came.

"However, on the day of our wedding, my mother did not come to the church. She was not ill. She was not injured. She simply did not come."

Grand Lady stared straight ahead, speaking softly. "Until the day she died, my mother did not offer an apology to William or to me. She lived her life without any further involvement in mine from my wedding day on."

"That's awful," I murmured.

"I only heard from my mother over the years when she would send to me articles from the newspaper."

"Articles?"

A thin wrinkle started at the corner of Grand Lady's mouth and carved a path to her temple. "Have you ever heard of Roland's Tires?"

"Of course. Tom always buys Roland's because of their great warranty."

"That is, you see, Roland. As in Roland Conners, the man my mother wanted me to marry. Roland Conners became a very wealthy man."

"And your mother never accepted that you married Grandpa for love and not money?"

"Unfortunately, she did not."

"I'm so sorry you had to live with that." I reached over and gave her cool hands a tender pat.

"But, you see, the truth of the matter is that I no longer have to live with that. I have forgiven my mother. It has taken me far too long. I carried the wound for many years, and I am sad to say that I taught my own daughter how to carry a grudge."

"You can't blame yourself for that," I said.

"Oh, but I do blame myself. You see, your mother, Celeste, took in every one of the helpings of the poison words I spoke about my mother. I believe Celeste swallowed them, and they slowly poisoned her."

"I still don't think it's the kind of situation in which you can put the blame on yourself," I said.

Grand Lady shook her head. "I know my own heart, Honeygirl. I have had many, many years to think about this. I suppose I could make the excuse that I wanted to know my daughter was on my side when it came to my bitterness toward my mother. But in the end, you see, Celeste did not grow up to be angry with her grandmother, the way I was. She grew up angry at me for keeping her from her grandmother."

The sharp truth of comparison sliced the air. Now I was the mother slowly working to turn my daughter against her grandmother. Without much effort I could easily turn Hannah against me instead. I sat numb and silent.

"Your mother did a fine thing when she let you come here that summer so long ago," Grand Lady said with evenly paced words.

"The only reason I came was because my father was dying. She didn't want me to be in the way."

"Yes, but Honeygirl, she sent you here. Despite hard

times, your mother found the money to buy your airplane ticket. Do you see? She trusted me to take care of you. That was no small effort on her part."

"But, Grand Lady, I still don't understand why you wrote that you hope your daughter will forgive you someday. You didn't do anything to alienate my mother. She's the one who doesn't pursue others. She doesn't try to spend time with me, and she doesn't try to spend time with you. That's not our fault."

"Oh, but you see, I am at fault in this as well. I am ashamed to say that I have not always acted as a Christian woman toward my daughter. When Celeste set her heart on marrying your father, I did everything in my power to dissuade her from that decision. As you most likely know, she eloped. I was not invited to have any part in their wedding."

"No, I didn't know that."

"I believe it was I who taught your mother how to hold on to bitterness for a miserable long time. I taught her how to act in an unseemly fashion toward her own mother. We all certainly do reap what we sow."

I didn't want to hear this. It was unpleasant enough to feel as if I were taking my dear grandmother's final confession. But the painful reality was that I was part of this. I was using the same techniques that had been employed for generations by stronger women on my family tree than I. Maybe it was a good thing Hannah hadn't heard all this.

Still siding with Grand Lady, I asked, "Didn't my mother ever see that you were right about my dad? He *was* unstable. He made her life miserable for a long time. He was cruel to Jon and me. You were right about him all along. She should have listened to you. Nothing good ever came of their marriage."

"Ah," Grand Lady held up her finger and pointed at me. "On the contrary. Don't you see? Something very good came from their marriage."

"What?"

"*You,* Honeygirl. You came from their marriage."

Chapter 16

I leaned back on Grand Lady's bed. The room seemed to wobble. My grandmother saw me as the "good thing" that came from my parent's difficult marriage. I was the blessing.

Through this whole conversation, Grand Lady hadn't said a negative word about my mother. I realized, also, that I never had heard a negative word about my father come from Grand Lady's lips. Even the day he died, she didn't say to me any of the words she must have been thinking.

Grand Lady reached over and gave me a comforting pat on the leg. "Now you have heard my story. I lived far too many years before I realized that forgiveness is the only way for the heart to be truly free. And I do pray that Celeste will one day forgive me. Now, I do believe I am in need of a short nap."

She made herself comfortable while I tucked a yellow,

crocheted blanket around her slight frame. Leaving Grand Lady resting contentedly, I headed for the Big House, still feeling the impact of her story. I looked for a quiet corner to reflect on all my grandmother had just told me, but Uncle Burt stopped me on the patio.

"What do you think, Sweet Abby?" He was examining the top coat of navy blue already drying on Hannah's beat-up old chair.

"How did Hannah manage to paint that so quickly?"

"She had a little help from her aunt and uncle," Burt said as he squared his shoulders.

I glanced at my watch and realized I'd been with Grand Lady much longer than I had thought. The afternoon was nearly spent. It was clear that this project wasn't going to keep Hannah busy for long. I wondered if Aunt Peg or Grand Lady had anything else they needed painted.

"I'd say this chair is a mite improved, wouldn't you, Sweet Abby? I sanded it down while Hannah and Peg pulled the paint out of the basement. Once this dries, Hannah has plans for the next layer."

"Thanks for helping her with this."

Uncle Burt swatted at a mosquito. "Don't think twice about thanking us. That girl of yours is a natural artist, you know. She's just like your mother."

I winced and managed to nod. The similarities between

my mother and Hannah were evident even to Uncle Burt. I couldn't ignore the bond between the two of them. It was a blood bond.

Having just been handed Grand Lady's story, I refused to live a lifetime disconnected from my daughter the way Grand Lady had been from hers. No wonder Grand Lady connected with me. She had no other women of her own blood that she was free to love.

What was it Su Ling said? Something about how we chose whom we want to love and how love never gives up.

I knew that I would never give up on loving Hannah, no matter what.

"Did Peg and Hannah go to the store?" I asked.

Burt nodded. "First they were going to drop off some green beans at Mr. Joe's fruit stand, and then they were heading for the Piggly Wiggly. Were you planning to go with them?"

"Not exactly."

"If you decide to go, they just left a minute or so ago. I'm sure you'd be able to catch up with them. I'd be happy to drive you down to Mr. Joe's, if you like."

My first thought was that the way my uncle drove, I could walk there faster than he could drive me. "Where is Mr. Joe's?"

"Down at the old Southern Belle Gas Station," he said.

"I know where that is. I think I'll walk."

"You sure? It's awful hot to be walking a couple of blocks like that."

"It's not far. I don't mind the walk at all."

"Well, you should be able to catch up with 'em if you cut through the Cooper's side yard."

"Thanks, Uncle Burt. I remember that shortcut. I'll see you in a while." I took off with long-legged strides through the neighbor's side yard and came out at the corner of Beaumont and Plantation. The old Southern Belle Gas Station was less than two blocks away and not far enough for me to have time to sort out my thoughts on all that Grand Lady had told me.

Mr. Joe's fruit stand consisted of several folding tables set up under the shade of the battered covering where the old-fashioned gas pumps once had protruded from the ground. Various fruits and vegetables were arranged on the tables. A customer could drive right up to the tables and have a look at what was available that day.

I vividly remembered when this place was a gas station and my cousins and I rode bikes over here to buy sodas in bottles from the machine.

"Hello!" I called out, as Hannah and Peg lifted two grocery bags full of green beans from the backseat of Peg's car.

Hannah looked surprised. Her expression changed to annoyance as she said, "What are you doing, Mom?"

"I walked over," I said brightly. "Thought I'd join you two. Need some help?"

"It's only these two bags," Aunt Peg said. Then adding a "Yoo-hoo!" she called out, "I brought some beans, Mr. Joe. Do you need any today?"

Mr. Joe sat on a couch located in front of the broken windows of what used to be the gas station's office.

"Why, yes indeed, Mrs. Burroughs. Do you know, I was just thinking to myself how nice it would be to have some of your green beans here for sale today."

He rose from the couch and walked toward us with a limp, smiling and holding up his right hand as if taking an oath. "I truly was. Not more than five minutes ago. And look at you, standing here in the bright light of day, holding out a bag of beans for me."

"Mr. Joe, this is my niece, Abby, and her daughter, Hannah. They're visiting us for a few days."

"Is that right?" He folded his arms and squinted at us in the sunlight. His hair was white and grizzled, covering his small head like dish suds. He reminded me of some of the old men who used to spend their afternoons on the outdoor benches by the Ace Hardware store in Lahaina. That was before the plaza area was cleared to make room for a new Foodland with an adjoining Starbucks. The benches were gone now, and so were the old men. I missed them and their leathery, spotted hands resting on their canes, their squinting eyes observing every passerby and offering a congenial nod.

"I have some real fresh peaches over here from Miss Blanchard's," Mr. Joe said to Aunt Peg. "And some early corn, if you don't mind shucking the ears yourself."

"Corn? Already?" Aunt Peg asked.

"Like I said, you have to shuck a few ears before you find some that's worth more than pig feed. You're welcome to have yourself a look."

"I know I'll want some of those peaches," Peg said. "What else did you get in today?"

"Just the peaches. Might be getting some more melons by the end of the week. Say, that reminds me, did y'all hear the good news about Miss Josephine's daughter?"

"Miss Josephine? From the library?" I asked.

"You know Miss Josephine?" Mr. Joe looked surprised.

"Yes, I met her years ago."

"She's not the Howell librarian anymore, you know. She moved to Virginia when her daughter got the job."

"Her daughter?"

"That's right. Her daughter, Evangeline. If you ever met Evangeline, you'd remember her."

A wispy, tender feeling came over me as I remembered Miss Josephine, the librarian who sat straight as a pin at her low desk right by the front door of the Howell Public

Library. Like a customs officer, she would look at me over the top of her jeweled glasses and ask me a few questions whenever I brought my stack of new books to her desk. While I stood before her, she carefully would turn back the front covers of the musty-smelling books. Her hand would come down with the date stamp on the inside page of each book and *fwapp!* my "passport" was stamped. I was cleared to take off through those blessed library doors, off on another journey through my imagination.

Someone once told me that novels were dangerous because they were full of lies about real life. I've thought about that a lot over the years in relation to the hundreds of stories I read. I came to the conclusion that those stories didn't lie to me; they gave me hope. More accurately, God gave me hope, but he used all those stories to do it. He is, after all, the author and finisher of every true story.

"What's the good news?" Aunt Peg asked Mr. Joe.

"Miss Evangeline graduated from law school and got herself a job in Washington, D.C.," Mr. Joe said proudly.

"Well, mercy sakes!" Aunt Peg exclaimed. "I had no idea that girl did such a thing."

"Not a surprise to some of us folks around here," Mr. Joe said. "That child always had her nose in a book. She made her mama proud, and I don't mind saying the rest of us feel mighty proud as well."

"That's wonderful," I smiled at Mr. Joe. It seemed Evangeline had done something her mother wanted to do; she got out of Howell. She broke the mold. I remembered the day Miss Josephine stamped one of my books and turned to the last page to show me how slaves were brought from Africa to America, chained in the hulls of ships like the one in the drawing. Miss Josephine then looked at me over the top of her glasses and said that her ancestors came to America on such a ship. I knew that Evangeline's breakthrough brought esteem to her mother and all the women in her lineage.

"If you hear from Miss Josephine, you tell her Mr. Burt and Miss Peggy are real happy for her." Aunt Peg nodded to add emphasis to her greeting.

"I'll do that." Mr. Joe took the bag of beans from Hannah, who had been standing there patiently waiting and listening.

Evidently Aunt Peg was working off a bartering system in which a bag of her fresh beans would equal so many peaches and so much early corn. I wondered how Mr. Joe made any money.

Hannah and I followed Aunt Peg to the table that held the bushel of corn.

"What do you think, Hannah?" Aunt Peg asked. "Would you like to shuck a few ears to see if we can find five or six good ones?"

Hannah hesitantly reached in the bushel and pulled out one of the small ears. "What do I do?" she asked.

"Shuck it."

"What does that mean?"

Aunt Peg chuckled. "You pull back the green husk, like this, and pull off this stringy yellow silk. Then you can see if the corn is ready to eat."

"Is that one ready?" Hannah asked, looking at the ear Aunt Peg was stripping.

"No. See how far down these rows of kernels begin? It's too early for corn. I wonder who brought these in?"

Aunt Peg wandered over to the other table and pressed her thumb along the sides of the plump peaches. I followed her and shooed the flies away from an overly ripe muskmelon.

"These are nice." Peg reached for another peach.

I ambled past the tables and walked around the old gas station, remembering how it felt to guzzle that ice-cold soda after pedaling like the wind on the tail of my cousins.

Turning back toward the tables, I saw that Hannah had gone to work, shucking ear after ear in search of golden kernels. She was dropping all the greenery on the ground and making a mess.

"Hannah," I called to her with a laugh in my voice. "What are you doing? You can stop digging for gold now."

She shot me an offended glare.

"Honey," I walked toward her, swatting at a tiny bee. "You don't have to shuck any more ears. We're probably not going to get any corn. It's not ripe yet."

The tears started to fall. "First you guys tell me to do something, and I don't even know what you're talking about, and then I try to do it, and you tell me I shouldn't be doing it, as if I was supposed to already know that. Why did you have to make fun of me?"

"I wasn't making fun of you, Hannah."

I wanted to put my arms around her. I understood her feelings. I really did. But I didn't hug her, just in case that would cause her even more public humiliation.

Hannah briskly gathered up the green mess, and I stood there paralyzed because I didn't know what to do that she would interpret accurately.

"So, where am I supposed to put this stuff?" she snapped.

I looked around for a trash can and didn't see one. "I don't know. Just a minute." I walked toward the office.

"Mom," Hannah growled through clenched teeth. "Don't ask him."

I turned around, and with a firm tempo I spoke so that only Hannah could hear me. "I don't see a trash can around here, Hannah. I'm going to ask for one. Please don't tell me what I may and may not do."

Her expression made it clear that she got the message.

I stalked away clenching my teeth. *Is this hormone induced or is Hannah simply trying to see how snippy she can be without getting into trouble?*

Returning with a garbage can, in silence I helped Hannah to clean up the mess.

Aunt Peg had loaded her bag of peaches in the car and was waiting for us to bring the other bag of her trade—all the ears Hannah had shucked.

"Sorry, Aunt Peg," Hannah said as soon as she got in the car.

"Don't you worry one little speck about it, Hannah. You didn't know what I was asking of you. I'm the one to be making an apology."

"It's okay," Hannah said.

"I must say, the way you two work out your differences as a mother and daughter is a beautiful thing to watch."

I wanted to laugh aloud. To me, there was nothing beautiful about this new "twitch and pout" dance that had us both tripping over our feet. We hadn't worked out anything. I'd merely established once again that I was the boss.

"Tammy Jean and I had a terrible time of it when she was your age, Hannah. It's a lopsided thing when two women with the same blood try to occupy the same space."

I thought of how lopsided it had been when Hannah and I tried to share the same hammock. The moment my daughter was ready to spring forward and exercise her freedom, I tumbled out the other side.

This may be normal, but it's not the way I want it to be. How can we both keep our balance?

We shopped calmly together at the Piggly Wiggly. Hannah didn't giggle at the name when we pulled into the parking lot. She told Aunt Peg it reminded her of the old Foodland market at home and used her own money in the checkout line to buy a Cow's Tail candy roll-up.

As soon as we arrived at the Big House, Hannah quietly went to work on what she was now calling her "gypsy chair." Uncle Burt helped her rig an old plastic salad bowl in the seat of the chair with holes poked in the bottom for water drainage.

I busied myself in the kitchen with Aunt Peg by cutting up the fresh peaches for a cobbler. She had chicken frying on the stove and cornbread baking in the oven.

"Y'all will have to tell me what you think of my honey butter," she said. "I add nutmeg. Burt isn't particularly crazy about it, but I like it."

I thought the nutmeg was a nice touch and made sure to mention it at dinner so Aunt Peg would know how much I appreciated her cooking for us. Grand Lady still was weary after our big shopping trip and had told Uncle Burt she would be "keeping her own company" that evening for supper. Hannah finished eating quickly and went back to work on her gypsy chair on the patio.

Around eight o'clock I went outside to check on her.

"Hi. How's it going?"

"I think I'm finished," she said. "What do you think?"

She had painted colorful yellow, green, and orange dots over the navy-blue base, creating a charming, vibrant, spotted planter.

"Aunt Peg says it looks like the socks we all bought at Wal-Mart because of the polka dots. Uncle Burt helped me fix the bucket in the rotted-out seat. All I need are some flowers, and Aunt Peg said tomorrow we could dig up some of her patsies."

I smiled. "You mean her pansies."

"Yeah. The blue ones she has in the wheelbarrow. She says they don't mind the sun, and they come back every year."

"They're perennials," I said.

Hannah gave me a perturbed look at being corrected again. "I don't know about that, but I like them. I think they're friendly flowers. I might have them at my wedding, the way you had gardenias."

I didn't dare tell Hannah that pansies were not practical for a wedding bouquet. It hardly mattered that "perennial" meant they came back every year. I was the one feeling like a "patsie" for correcting her. Some things in life she would figure out soon enough on her own.

"Come here." I wrapped my arms around her and gave her a big hug. "I love you. You know that, don't you?"

Hannah pulled away and looked at me as if I were ruining her moment. "Yeah, I know that."

"Good." I tried to keep my expression cheerful. "Just so you know that and don't ever forget it."

"Okay." Hannah headed for the back door. "Make sure you don't touch the chair. It isn't dry yet."

I lingered in the subtle scent of the drying acrylic paint and watched as a friendly firefly came by and blinked a consoling hello. I was trying to be a good mom. Really, I was. The undertaking was more challenging than I had ever imagined it would be.

I thought of how my instincts had reared up in me all those months ago when I began to dream of bringing Hannah here. Even before Grand Lady had revealed so many details to me today, I knew in my spirit that with all the painful disconnect between so many generations of women in our family, the time had come for healing.

It seemed clear to me that Hannah needed to receive the touching affirmation from Grand Lady so she could pass it on to the next generation. If Hannah knew she was unconditionally loved and accepted by the grand matriarch of our family, wouldn't that fill her with confidence and empower her to be so much stronger than the rest of us? The women in our family were desperately in need of a blessing after such a long-standing curse.

I watched two fireflies who were joined by a third

and then a fourth. They dipped and blinked and managed to loop back and forth without injuring each other or interrupting the other's unique flight pattern.

"How do you do that?" I asked the silent quartet.

Chapter 17

Our final day in Howell started out as the best day of our visit. Hannah was up and dressed before me, and when I finally went downstairs, I found Uncle Burt sitting alone at the kitchen table, reading the paper.

"You ready for some breakfast?" he asked.

"No, not yet. Where's Hannah?"

"Peg has her up in the attic over the garage lookin' for our Christmas lights."

"Christmas lights?"

"Guess you didn't hear all the hoopla this morning. BJ and his family are coming for supper. Miss Hannah said we should make it a pool party, and of course, that was all my wife needed to send her into a party spin."

"That sounds like my daughter's influence. You really don't have to go to any trouble."

"Are you kiddin'? This is the most excitement we've had around here in a coon's age. I'm gonna string the lights as soon as they bring 'em down, and then I'll cook us up a barbecue that you won't likely forget for a good long time."

"Thanks, Uncle Burt. That's really kind of you. What can I do to help?"

"You can check on the ladies, if you want. They've only been out there a short time, but they might need some help. Our attic is a frightful mess."

"Is that why you're sitting here?" I asked with a tease in my voice.

Uncle Burt grinned. "You won't tell on me, now, will ya?"

"Never." I gave his shoulders a hug. "Do you know if Grand Lady is up yet?"

"No, she's sleeping in this morning. Peg called over there first thing, and it seems my mother is all tuckered out from your big shopping trip yesterday."

I went out the back door and walked around to the side stairs that led to the storage room above the garage. "Hannah? Aunt Peg?"

"We're up here, Sweet Abby. Come on up."

Entering the moldy, neglected room, I ducked to avoid a cobweb the size of a giant's hand hanging from the supporting beam by the door.

"I don't think I've ever been up here before." I looked around at the crowded space stacked with a variety of boxes and bins.

"I haven't been up here in a day and an age myself,"

Aunt Peg said. "This attic is atrocious. I have no idea where Burt stored all those old lights."

Hannah was sitting on one of the dusty steamer trunks. "We're going to have a party, Mom. Did you hear?"

"Yes, that's why I'm here. I'm ready to help any way I can."

Peg nodded at the trunk where Hannah was seated. "Why don't we have a look in there?"

Together Hannah and I pushed open the trunk's creaky lid. We were overwhelmed with the odor of mothballs.

"Well, I'll be." Peg looked over my shoulder. "So that's where those ended up."

"What are they?" Hannah touched the top of one of the worn-out cardboard boxes.

"These are my old formal gowns."

"Can we see them?" Hannah asked.

"Sure, if you want. They're bound to just about be disintegrated."

"I love old dresses." Hannah helped Aunt Peg lift the boxes from the trunk.

One by one, Aunt Peg extracted what Hannah viewed as a treasure trove of vintage formals fit for a princess. I stood back, watching as Hannah and Peg held up the faded beauties to their bodies and pulled the yards of taffeta and netting out to the sides.

"I was quite a socialite in my day." A rosy blush shaded Aunt Peg's creamy complexion. "This one was for the winter cotillion I went to with Bobbie Viceroy. He was four years older than I, and my daddy almost didn't let me go. I remember the theme that year was 'Catch a Falling Star.'"

"How old were you?" Hannah asked.

The blush continued to creep up Aunt Peg's neck. "Fourteen," she said shyly.

"Your parents let you go to a formal dance when you were fourteen?"

"I told you they almost didn't let me go. But times were different then, Hannah. Least they were in Baton Rouge. I wasn't the only young girl at the cotillion. Lizzy Engerman came with a boy from the high school, and she was only thirteen. She told the boy she was fifteen, and he believed her because she looked it."

Aunt Peg shook her head. "Funny that I remember her name like that. I haven't thought of Lizzy in the longest time."

Aunt Peg held up the yellowing dress with one hand at her shoulder and the other across her waist. Caught up in her private memory, she began to sway on the dusty wooden floor.

Grand Lady's advice from long ago came back to me in that dusty attic. She had told me to listen to other people's stories, and my story would come and find me. I had been listening. I'd listened for years to all kinds of stories. But yesterday and today these stories were coming from the hearts of my blood relatives, and they were going deep into the wounded places of my heart.

"Did you go to any more dances with Bobbie what's-his-name?" Hannah asked as she held up a pink dress that had a wide satin sash around the middle.

"No." Aunt Peg quietly let the faded dress double over in her arms. "Bobbie Viceroy was shipped out three days after the dance. He died in his first call to duty. In France. Out in a snowy pasture. It was the saddest thing ever."

Hannah looked confused. All she knew of World War II was what she had learned when her class took their big field trip to Pearl Harbor on our neighboring island.

As Aunt Peg neatly folded up her winter cotillion formal, my unabashed daughter leaned close to Aunt Peg and asked, "Did he kiss you?"

At first Aunt Peg looked startled. Then she lowered her chin and leaned toward Hannah as if they were both fourteen and the only two girls in the room.

"Twice," she whispered with her finger to her lips. "But I never told a living soul. Not until this very minute." Aunt Peg giggled. "And I'll tell you what, Miss Hannah, I was the first, the last, and the only girl that boy ever kissed. And I'll tell you what else. I'd do it all again if I had the chance. I'd do it all exactly the same."

Hannah smiled.

Aunt Peg chuckled to herself and went back to straightening her long-forgotten dresses.

"What are you going to do with all these?" Hannah asked.

"Put them back in the trunk, I suppose. Unless you want them."

Hannah looked as if her fairy godmother had appeared and was about to grant her dearest wish. "Are you serious? I would love to have your dresses, Aunt Peg. Would you give them to me? Really?"

"Sure. If you like. They're falling apart, you know."

"No, they're not!" Hannah pressed the pink gown to her chest. "They're beautiful! And they're full of stories. I want them. All of them. Really bad. If you don't mind."

"I don't mind." Peg gave a flustered laugh. "I don't mind a bit. As a matter of fact, you honor me by asking such a thing, Miss Hannah."

"These are so cool!" Hannah extracted a blue chiffon gown from a weevil-eaten box. "Tell me the story that goes with this one."

As the heat of the Louisiana day seeped through the cracks at the roof's edge in that grungy attic, my amazing daughter urged Aunt Peg to do what the Hawaiians called "talk story."

I sat on the "Plumbing Parts" bin, flicking away anything that vaguely resembled any sort of insect and thinking how, whether she knew it or not, Hannah was being entrusted with a part of her great aunt that would continue long after Peg was gone. Whenever Hannah pulled out these formals and found someone who would listen, the story of Great Aunt Peg who kissed a soldier—twice—would live on.

Christmas twinkle lights long forgotten, the three of us exited the storage attic with our arms full of the fluffy, dusty dresses.

As we tromped across the yard with the gowns, I noticed that the shades still were closed at Grand Lady's cottage. It seemed like a good idea for her to sleep as long as she could since tonight promised to be a late one. Hannah trotted ahead of us and disappeared upstairs with the dresses.

Expressing charmingly bogus disappointment that we couldn't find the Christmas lights, Uncle Burt promised Peg that he would go up and have a look later. We all knew he wouldn't make good on that promise.

Hannah came scampering down the stairs and made a merry entrance to the kitchen. Her foot obviously was improved.

"Mom, can you come upstairs for a minute?"

I followed Hannah up to our room where the dresses were laid out in a tidy row on top of the bed.

"I think I can go swimming now," Hannah said.

"Oh, good! This is the perfect day to spend in the pool. When your second cousins arrive later this afternoon, you'll all have a really good time."

"Did you say 'y'all,' Mom?"

"No. I think I said *you'll all.* That's not quite the same thing."

Evidently Hannah's cheerful disposition had returned. I decided to ask her something I'd hesitated to ask the day before. "By the way, Hannah, why were you asking yesterday about the Bible passage in which the woman was healed?"

"I heard the story before in Sunday school, but I didn't know where it was in the Bible."

"Yes, but what was it that made you curious about the story? Was it because the woman had been bleeding for twelve years?"

Hannah nodded.

"Do you have any other questions for me about your body or what's happening with your period?"

Hannah looked surprised. "No. I wasn't thinking about me. I was thinking about you."

"Me?"

"Yeah. You told me how you cut yourself on the glass a long time ago, and that made you afraid of blood."

"But Hannah, I haven't been bleeding since then."

"I know, Mom." She gave me one of her "no duh" looks. "But you aren't healed yet."

Hannah examined the torn hem on Aunt Peg's pale blue gown, and without looking at me she said, "I just knew that Jesus healed the woman when she asked him even though she had the same problem for a long time. Twelve years is, like, my whole life."

I paused a moment to let Hannah's wisdom sink in.

"Do you think Aunt Peg would mind if I tried on this dress? The hem already is ripped, so I don't think I'm going to make it worse."

"I'm sure it's fine if you wear it." I tried to collect my thoughts. "Didn't you want to go swimming?"

"Not yet. I have something to do first." She shimmied out of her shorts as I left the bedroom, closing the door behind me. I tried to leave Hannah's piercing insights in the bedroom with her.

Returning to the kitchen, I asked Aunt Peg what I could do to help her get ready for the barbecue that night.

"Not a thing, Sweet Abby. By the way, did you and Hannah ever eat any breakfast? We just had toast and cereal this morning."

"I'm fine. You've been feeding us very well all week. I don't think I've thanked you enough."

"I'll leave the coffee and cereal here on the counter, if you change your mind and decide to have a little bite."

"You know what I could go for? Some more of your peach cobbler. That was so good."

"I'm afraid your uncle beat you to it late last night. I could make another one, if you like."

"How about if you let me make the cobbler? I'll run over to Mr. Joe's to see if he has any more peaches."

"Why, that would be very kind of you," Aunt Peg said. "I don't have any more green beans to send over today. Let me fetch my pocketbook, and I'll give you some spendin' money for the peaches."

"No, Aunt Peg. I'd like to buy the peaches. Please? You've been doing everything for us all week. The least I can do is to buy some peaches from Mr. Joe. Is there anything else you need? I could stop at the Piggly Wiggly."

"No, just some peaches would be fine."

Hannah swished past us and flitted out the back door with the crinkly blue formal sweeping the floor. She looked like a miniature fairy godmother late for Cinderella's pre-ball makeover.

"I hope it's okay if she wears that one now," I said, catching the lit-up expression on Aunt Peg's face. "She said the hem already was coming out."

"Of course it's okay! Did you see her? The little princess!"

"Yes, a little princess on a mission. She wouldn't tell me what she was doing."

"I think I know. She asked me earlier if she could string some leis. I gave her my sewing basket and told her to use the gardenias from the bush on the side of the house. That thing is overrun with blooms this year."

I smiled. My little princess was going to grace our Southern barbecue with Hawaiian leis made from gardenias, no less. This would be a great final day. Once Grand Lady entered the festivities, I was sure I would at last feel that the reasons for coming here had been fulfilled. The nagging oppression that kept coming to me would be lifted. We'd drive out early tomorrow morning feeling fully blessed.

It seemed a good idea to eat at least a little something before shopping for food, even if the food was only peaches at Mr. Joe's. So I poured a small bowl of cereal, covered the flakes with milk, and leaned against the counter while I ate.

A few minutes later I rinsed out my cereal bowl and went upstairs to retrieve my purse so I could buy the peaches. From the upstairs hallway I could hear the sound of the porch swing creaking with an even rhythm. I could picture my little princess contentedly stringing gardenia leis on the front porch swing. Even though she might be mortified, I tiptoed toward the front door with my camera ready to snap a picture that would mean more to me than any complaint she might offer.

Opening the front door slowly, I popped out my head and snapped a picture of Hannah on the porch swing, crying her eyes out.

"Hannah, what's wrong?" I flew to her side and put my arm around her. "What happened?"

She kept crying.

"What is it? What happened?" My eyes scanned her for blood or bruises.

Gathering enough voice to spew her emotions, Hannah wailed, "Your grandmother is a mean old lady, and I don't ever want to see her again!"

"Grand Lady? Why?"

Hannah drew in a wobbly breath. "I tried to give her the gypsy chair, and she . . . she cussed at me and told me to go away!"

My hand flew to my mouth. "Oh, Hannah! What happened?"

"I carried my gypsy chair all the way over to her trailer, and I put it on her porch and knocked on the door. She came out and, Mom, she didn't have any teeth in her face!" Hannah started to cry again.

"Oh, honey, I'm sorry I didn't tell you. Grand Lady wears dentures. She doesn't have any of her own teeth anymore."

Hannah looked at me with painful skepticism, as if I were making up stories as I went along.

"It's true. Her teeth were all pulled years ago. She always wears her dentures when she's around people."

"She frightened me! And then she reached over and

touched my face, and she said, 'What do you want?' in a really mean voice."

"Oh, Hannah!" I drew her close, knowing how startling it could be to see Grand Lady without her grooming aids in place. Especially if she had just woken up, which was probably the case. Still, I couldn't imagine why Grand Lady would be so mean.

"All I was trying to do was give her the gypsy chair as a surprise. I said, 'Grand Lady, I made this for you,' and then I pointed to the chair, and she cussed at me."

I smoothed the tears from Hannah's cheeks as she released another round.

"Oh, Hannah, Hannah. It's okay. Shhh. It's okay."

"But it's not okay, Mom. She stared at me with that one eye, like, looking at something over my shoulder. And she said, 'What am I supposed to do with such a . . .'" Hannah hesitated. "I don't know if I should say the word."

"It's okay. You can tell me."

Hannah drew in a breath and lowered her voice. "Grand Lady said to me, 'What am I supposed to do with such a peculiar apparatus?'"

I waited for the rest of the story, but that was it.

"A 'peculiar apparatus!'" Hannah reiterated. "That's what she called my chair, Mom."

Hannah let the tears flow. I drew her close. "Oh,

Hannah. You worked so hard on that chair. I didn't know you were going to give it to Grand Lady."

"I wanted it to be a surprise. This whole trip I know all you wanted was for me to love your grandmother, but I don't think she likes me the way she likes you. So I thought if I could make something for her, then maybe she'd like me and you'd be happy about that."

For the first time I realized how much subliminal pressure I'd put on my daughter to be like me and to choose to love the one relative on whom I had set my affections. I had pushed Hannah into this corner.

"I'm so sorry, Hannah."

"It's not your fault, Mom. It's Grand Lady. She was the one who was mean to me. If she doesn't like my gypsy chair, that's her choice, but why did she have to cuss at me?"

"What did she say?"

"I already told you. She said . . . that word."

"What word, honey?"

"*Apparatus,* Mom. That's what she said. That's a cuss word, isn't it?"

"No, *apparatus* isn't a cuss word, Hannah. *Apparatus* is another word for a thing, a device. It could be used to describe something when you don't know what to call it."

She steadied her breathing. "You mean like the way we say, *da' kine*?"

"Exactly."

"Oh."

"What did you think it meant, Hannah?"

Her voice was low and contrite. "I thought it meant a donkey's behind."

"No." I shook my head and pulled her close.

"Well, maybe she didn't cuss at me, but she still was mean and told me to go away."

"Hannah, you did a wonderful thing. You designed and crafted something beautiful and creative, and then you offered it as a gift. A surprise. That was a lovely thing to do." I stroked her long hair and smoothed back the silken strands that clung to her forehead and cheeks.

"I was only trying to do something nice."

"I know you were, honey. You did something very, very nice. I'm so proud of you for thinking up the gift and making it yourself in such a creative way. I'm sorry Grand Lady didn't receive your gift the way she should have."

Pausing and sniffing, Hannah said, "Maybe she couldn't see it since she didn't have on her glasses."

"That's a very strong possibility."

"Maybe she didn't even know it was me."

I nodded, smiling and encouraging my adolescent to continue to work her logic muscles.

Hannah let out a long sigh. "It was still awful."

"Yes, it was." I kissed her on the top of her head.

"You know what else? If Grand Lady doesn't want

the gypsy chair, I'll give it to Aunt Peg. She liked it a lot. So did Uncle Burt. He said I reminded him of his sister, when she used to make art projects."

"Yes, I know."

Hannah looked up at my face, trying to read my expression. "Did he tell you that?"

"Yes." I tried to give her my most comforting smile.

"Mom?" Hannah asked in a small voice. "Is it okay if I kind of remind you sometimes of your mother?"

"Yes, of course. Oh, Hannah, I have made such a mess of things. I want a blessing for you, not a curse. I don't want to pass all my problems with my mother on to you."

Hannah leaned her head against my shoulder and sniffed loudly. "Twelve years is a long time."

I didn't know if she was making reference to the woman Jesus healed or that she had gone twelve years without the opportunity to get close to her own grandmother. Either way, something had to give.

I had to get some air, find some perspective. I wanted to start by marching over to Grand Lady's cottage and yelling at her for yelling at my daughter.

"Do you think we should go over to Grand Lady's right now and talk to her about this?" I asked.

"No! Please don't say anything, Mom. That would only make things worse."

"Okay." I tried to think what I should do next. "Hannah, I told Aunt Peg I'd buy some more peaches at

Mr. Joe's. Do you want to drive over with me to the fruit stand?"

Hannah gave me another pained expression, and I realized her time at Mr. Joe's wasn't a happy memory either.

"Can I just stay here?" she asked.

"Sure. I'll be back in a little bit. We'll figure this out, Hannah. You and me. We're a team."

"Figure out what?" Hannah asked.

"Figure out, you know, how to work through all these communication problems with the women in our family."

"How?"

"I don't know. We'll figure it out. We'll make things change."

I thought of the very first entry I'd read in Grand Lady's journal: "If it's going to be, it's up to me."

That's it right there. It's up to me to fix this. I don't know how exactly, but I'll do this. I'll make things right with Grand Lady, and I'll make sure Hannah and I always will stay as close as we are at this moment.

Hannah quietly slid off the seat. The porch swing continued to sway. I watched her shuffle inside the house with her shoulders slumped. The thought that encompassed me was a strange one. It was the same thought that came to me after I pulled the glass from Hannah's foot. *I don't have what I need to heal my daughter's wound.*

Chapter 18

I drove the few short blocks to Mr. Joe's but then couldn't force myself out of the car. My mind spun with the tangled complications of all the relationships I was determined to fix. Time was running out.

Kicking myself out of the driver's seat, I painted a smile on my face and called to Mr. Joe on his dilapidated couch, "Good morning! I've come back for some more peaches."

"Why, yes, indeed, Miss Abby." He pulled his stiff leg to the side so he could stand up. "We still have those nice peaches from Miss Blanchard. She does grow the sweetest peaches around."

"I'll take all you have left," I said, holding out a twenty-dollar bill.

"Well, now, I'm not quite sure I have change for you, Miss Abby."

"That's okay. You can give it to my aunt the next

time she comes by. Or better yet, why don't you just keep it as my way of saying thank you for the kind way you treat my Aunt Peg."

Mr. Joe gave his head a bow. "That is mighty kind of you, Miss Abby. Your aunt and uncle have always been kind to me and mighty generous, too. I can see the apple doesn't fall far from the tree with you and yours."

With all the disengaged layers of women in our family, Mr. Joe was more right than he knew. More right than I wanted him to be.

Leaving with half a sack of peaches, I started to walk down the street, as if I'd come to Mr. Joe's on foot, the way I had the day before. I was nearly a block away, caught up in my thoughts, before I remembered I'd driven my brother's SUV, which was parked in front of Mr. Joe's.

The faint scent of something fresh caught my attention. I stopped and drew in a deep breath. I was standing in front of the Mt. Zion Fully Redeemed Tabernacle. A man, whom I took to be the janitor, was standing on the newly mowed grass in front of the church sign. He held a boxful of the alphabet and was placing the final word on the message board. He stepped back. I paused to read what he had posted.

PSALM 6:2

O LORD, HEAL ME

The world around me seemed to grow very still. *I do not have what I need to heal my daughter's wound.*

Hannah was right. I, too, was a woman who had been bleeding for a long time. The old wounds had never healed, no matter how often I'd tried to bandage them or how much I told myself the wounds were small or of no significance. At last I knew why they weren't healed.

Only Jesus could heal. The sign invited me to come to Him.

O LORD, HEAL ME.

I had never asked him to do that for me.

All these years I had wished endlessly that my mother would come to me, that she would be the one to speak the words that would heal and restore. But the truth was that no one—no human—could heal my wounds. Only the one who had made my heart and had allowed the pain to come into my life had the power to heal me.

He was waiting for me, just like the woman in the Bible, to ask.

I dropped my sack of peaches and dissolved into a puddle of tears right there in front of the Mt. Zion Fully Redeemed Tabernacle. Stumbling over to a big boulder in the middle of the grass, with great hope, I lowered myself and whispered, "O, Lord, heal me."

A calm settled over my spirit. I felt light. Unencumbered. I looked up and was startled to see the janitor standing there, the box of letters still in his hands. He had the power to make so many words, but today the words he had made on that sign had set me free.

"You all right?" he asked.

I nodded and whispered, "Yes, I'm fine now."

He turned to go. "Yes, I do believe it is so."

Where did I hear those words before?

I looked up and remembered. *The front porch at the Big House! Hannah's angel!*

Once again, he was gone. I sprang to my feet and hurried in the direction he had walked, around the side of the church building. He wasn't there. I hurried to the other side of the church and back to the front. No sign of him anywhere.

I closed my eyes, drew in a deep breath, and smiled. On the air was the scent of a cloud.

Gathering my bag of peaches, I hurried back to the SUV at Mr. Joe's and drove to the Big House, trying to piece together what had just happened. I pulled into the driveway and stopped the car.

I noticed that Hannah had positioned herself on the porch swing, still wearing the blue princess gown. She was stringing together her leis and already had created a long, elegant garland of gardenias. I was about to go to her when the front door opened, and Grand Lady exited the Big House onto the porch, the metal legs of her walker clunking as she took each precarious step. It seemed like a good idea to hang back behind the foliage and watch what was about to happen between Hannah and Grand Lady.

Obviously, Grand Lady was still stiff from our outing to Wal-Mart since this was the first time I'd seen her use the walker. She had come a long way from her cottage, across the lawn and through the Big House, to meet Hannah on the front porch. I hoped Hannah recognized the effort, regardless of what Grand Lady had to say. My grandmother had come to her.

"Miss Hannah." She steadied herself on the porch. "I do believe I have an apology to make to you."

I pressed my lips together and tried to blink back the tears.

"I am in great debt to you for the flower apparatus you made for me. I am afraid I had difficulty understanding what transpired on my front deck earlier this morning. Without my glasses I was of the opinion you were a child from the neighborhood trying to make a sale at my front door."

Hannah giggled. "The *keiki* in your neighborhood must really dress up when they do their fund raisers, if you thought I was one of them."

Grand Lady looked at Hannah, as if she didn't understand a word my daughter had said.

Hannah quickly said, "Oh, I meant kids. I said *keiki.* Sorry."

Ever the picture of grace, Grand Lady smiled. "Perhaps you can see why I had difficulty understanding you earlier today."

Hannah nodded.

Instead of harboring what could have been a hurt to her young heart, Hannah rose from the swing and brought with her the fragrant garland of gardenias. She draped the elegant lei over Grand Lady's neck.

It was Lei Day for the second time this year, and my daughter was ascribing honor in the way that was most familiar to her. King Kamehameha the Great had united the islands in his lifetime. Grand Lady had come from her cottage to the front porch to be united with my daughter, and I knew this was the blessing I had hoped for all along.

"I made the gypsy chair for you," Hannah said.

"I am most grateful."

"I hoped you would like it."

"I like it very much indeed. It will be a delight to water the pansies each day and remember you and your kindness toward me with a little prayer."

"I'll pray for you every day, too."

Grand Lady looked so regal in her string of gardenias. She reached to touch my Hannah's face. "I hope you know in the deepest corner of your heart that you are a wonderfully talented artist. Just like your grandmother, Celeste."

All I could do was hide in the bushes and weep. Forgiveness and blessing were spilling out on the porch while I watched.

The remainder of the day and far into the evening, the fine Southern air canopied us like a benediction. Each splendid moment felt like a fairy-tale farewell to the journey of a thousand miles that had ended well.

At nearly midnight, I stole away from the party to settle on the porch swing and punch in a few strategic numbers on my cell phone. One final firefly in our female quartet was not yet flickering with Hannah, Grand Lady, and me. While a chorus of night critters cheered me on with their soothing chitter-buzz, I risked writing a scene for the next page of my life. When I hung up, I knew my story was about to come find me.

"Are we almost there?" Hannah asked, stretching and peering out the window of the SUV. The lush Alabama countryside was coming into focus with the first light of day.

"No, we have a long way to go to the Atlanta airport. How did you sleep?"

"Pretty good. I had nice dreams."

"Is that right?" I gave her a girlfriend grin. "Did you dream about anything or anyone in particular?"

"Maybe." Hannah tried to wink, which was altogether irresistible. She turned away, her cheeks glowing a tender shade of pink. Reaching for the gardenia leis that hung from the rearview mirror, she tickled the browning flowers.

Hannah glanced at me and saw that I was still grinning. "What?" she asked.

"You and your cousin Blake seemed to have fun yesterday in the pool and running around the yard with the sparklers. I thought maybe you had a few dreams that went along those lines."

"Mom, it's not like we're kissin' cousins or whatever it was that Uncle Burt called us. Aunt Peg said we were second cousins."

"Kissing cousins, huh? Did I miss something?"

"No!" Hannah turned to look out the window. "I mean, it's not like Blake is someone like Bobbie Viceroy who is about to go off to get killed in France in the snow or anything. Blake is only twelve!"

"Thirteen," I corrected her.

"He is?" Hannah paused before asking, "Mom, do you think I could get my own e-mail address?"

"We'll see."

"I felt like such a baby when I didn't have my own

e-mail address to give him—I mean, to give any of our relatives."

"You have a street address. Blake could write you at your street address."

"Mom, it's not the same. Don't you remember when you were my age?"

"We didn't have e-mail when I was your age, Hannah. Or home computers for that matter."

"You didn't have cell phones, either, did you?"

"No."

"That is so weird. Did you know that Blake told me Grand Lady never had a driver's license? Her whole life she never has driven a car. Not even once. You know what? I'm really glad I got to meet her."

"So am I, Hannah."

"I don't think I'll ever meet another person like her. Did you see the way she was writing her name in the sky with sparklers last night? It was like she was a little kid, playing with the rest of us, all happy and silly."

"She is a Grand Lady, that's for sure."

"I think I understand why you like her so much."

I glanced at Hannah. "May I tell you a story?"

She sat up and turned to me with her full attention. "Definitely! You know I like it when you tell me your stories."

I started with when I was twelve, sitting on the porch swing with Grand Lady. I told Hannah I had been waiting for my story to come and find me. Without bitterness or blame, I told her the truth about my father and how disconnected my mother and I became, especially after he died.

Hannah repressed a giggle when I told her about the way my mother touched my pimple in public. I told her how I ran away to the record store and how often my mother and I argued after that. I confessed that I hadn't done a good job of pursuing a relationship with my mother.

"Maybe it's like at Carlsbad Caverns," Hannah said.

"What do you mean?"

"Remember how, when we were leaving Carlsbad, I said God put a secret vault of all that art down there?"

"Yes."

"Well, it might feel dark and unknown from the outside, but maybe your mom really is full of a lot of beauty deep inside, and nobody has ever gone in far enough to discover it."

"Hannah, you amaze me."

Her eyes lit up as I went on to tell her how I saw her angel again in front of the Mt. Zion Fully Redeemed Tabernacle and how the Lord had healed me.

"Wow," Hannah said. "Just like the woman in the Bible."

I nodded, still not sure if I could explain fully what had happened to me the day before. All I knew was that the pain that had enclosed my heart and kept me from reaching out in the past was now gone. I'd heard it said before that "hurt people hurt people." I wondered if "healed people heal people." Is that how the cycle is broken? Is that how the blessing comes when all that was there before was a curse?

Hannah was quiet a moment before saying, "You know what? I don't think he was my angel after all."

"You don't?" I was surprised to hear her say that after I had become convinced he smelled like a cloud and everything.

"No, I think he must have been *your* guardian angel, Mom."

Until that moment I'd never entertained the thought of having a guardian angel.

"I mean, think about it," Hannah said. "I wasn't there at the church when he was putting the words on the sign. Those words were meant for you to see, not for me. If he had been my guardian angel, wouldn't he have been with me at the Big House instead of with you?"

Hannah had a point. We rode together in silent contemplation for many miles. Then we arrived in the vicinity of the Atlanta airport, and I had to turn all my attention to finding the right exit for the international terminal. I glanced at the clock and knew we had cut it far too close.

Pulling into an airport parking space, I hustled Hannah

along. We had to tidy up the inside of the car and take all our belongings with us. By the time we made it to the right place to find Jon, he and his aggravated, exhausted family were already there, waiting impatiently for us. I did little more than explain about the repaired rearview mirror and driver's window, hand Jon the keys, and tell him where we parked the car.

"Looks like that's all we need," Jon said. "Thanks. Call me sometime and tell me about your trip."

"Okay. And you, too, Jon. I'd like to hear about your trip."

We waved and started off in separate directions, but something tugged at my spirit. I turned to Hannah and said, "Wait here. I'll be right back."

I took off, bustling through the crowds, desperate to find my brother. "Jon!"

He turned around and waited while Patty and the girls kept going toward the parking lot. "Did you forget something?" he asked.

"Yes, I forgot this." I wrapped my arms around my brother's neck and hugged him. "Thank you, thank you, thank you. This trip was the best gift you could have given me. I will never forget this, and neither will Hannah."

"Well, good." He pulled back before I was through hugging him. "Glad it worked out. Thanks for taking care of the car."

He turned, but I grabbed his arm again, trying to

make eye contact, which was always an elusive thing with Jon. His brain seemed to be skipping around so fast that not even his eyes could stay focused on one arena more than a few seconds.

"Jon, one more thing. I want you to know that I love you."

"Okay." He nodded, his eyes still in sync with mine. "Thanks. Okay. Well, I'll see you later."

I hurried back to Hannah, worried that she would be standing there with a look of abandonment on her face. Instead, she was leaning on the handle of the luggage cart, carefully tracing her lips with the tube of shimmering lip gloss Aunt Peg had bought her at Wal-Mart.

"Are you okay?" I asked her. "I'm sorry I ran off like that. I shouldn't have left you."

"Mom, you don't have to stay with me every second. I can do things by myself, you know."

We made it to our gate with time to spare and even managed to grab some breakfast. Hannah and I boarded, and I immediately fell asleep to the lulling roar of the turbo engines.

Somewhere over Texas I woke and leaned across Hannah to see out the window. She was sleeping soundly. I wanted to wake her and ask if she recognized any of the terrain. Were we over the Guadalupe Mountains she had traced with her finger on the map as she had directed me to Carlsbad Caverns? Or were we closer to Dallas, where the sky had opened up and pelted us with giant-sized teardrops?

It was mind-boggling to think about how we were traversing in a few hours the same distance it had taken days to cross in the car. All those states were connected in my memory now, like that clever U.S. of Lei that had awakened such a deep longing within me on May Day.

I watched Hannah sleeping with the wilting gardenia lei cradled in her lap. She had had such a fun time the night before when my cousin BJ had delighted everyone by pulling out a box of fireworks. He presented his gift just as the uninvited dusk arrived at our pool party with a sultry pout. None of us wanted our time to end. Not even the evening sky, it seemed.

Hannah, in her gardenia halo, had approached Grand Lady with a slow-burning firework punk. Grand Lady stood, holding out her unlit sparkler and—*kazing!*—the air was alive with exploding glitter.

All the kids joined in, and Grand Lady became one of them, waving her sparkler with all the triumph of a regal matriarch on parade. I thought she was grand. Grand in every way.

We landed at the Los Angeles Airport on time. Hannah woke with a smile on her face. I turned on my cell phone and made a few necessary calls. The day before I had changed our flight home, hoping the adjustment was going to be worth the extra money.

I also hoped I was doing the right thing. Tom said I was. Hannah was thrilled out of her skin. She jabbered the first hour out of Los Angeles about how she would spend the week painting every day with Grandma Celeste.

"And now I can go with Grandpa Stan to pick out a new dog."

"We'll see what happens," I said for the tenth time. It was only because I didn't know what would happen. On the phone, my mother had sounded cordial and open to the arrangement. She didn't seem to mind that I would be flying home the next day and that she and Stan would have to drive Hannah back to the airport at the end of her week's visit.

The winding road to Lake Arrowhead felt familiar and strange at the same time, as our small rental car took the turns in the dark. It was already after ten PM. Hannah and I would have to enter through the unlocked back door and tiptoe our way to the guest room in the dark. All of that was fine as long as I could convince myself that my mother really did want Hannah to be there. She didn't have to want me. I wasn't asking for miracles. I only wanted to make sure I wasn't setting up my daughter for a broken heart.

Parking the car and pulling out our luggage as quietly as possible, Hannah and I picked our way to the back door and slid inside. A nightlight glowed in the hallway, and Hannah went ahead to the guest room while I made sure to wipe my feet and locked the door behind us.

I was about to tiptoe down the hallway to the guestroom when I heard footsteps coming my way. The hall light snapped on, and there stood my mother in a flowing robe.

"Sorry if we woke you." I offered barely a whisper down the hallway.

"You didn't wake me." Her voice was as gentle as a teardrop. "I've been waiting for you."

Then my mother came to me.

Epilogue

My Dearest Honeygirl,

May I begin this overdue letter by saying I hope you can forgive my long delay in writing to tell you how deeply I appreciated your visit to my cottage this past summer. It was, indeed, the high point of my year. I trust all is well with you and yours.

After you left, I found myself contemplating several significant topics of conversation that I failed to discuss with you when you were at hand. I wanted you to know that I am delighted with the way you have grown into a fine woman and an exceptional mother. I found great hope for the future of the women in our lineage because of the way you and your Hannah have forged an abiding friendship at such an early stage.

I am sure that, by now, you have heard from your mother that she and I have come to a new and tender place of understanding in our relationship. I am assuming it was your spontaneous visit to her home that prompted this glad change of circumstances. When Celeste and I reconciled, I knew the final page of my story had been written.

Yet, I linger in this earthly realm another day, another month, perhaps another year. I am indeed ready for the angels of our Lord to pay me a long-anticipated visit and carry me from this life to the next. However, the angels seem to be busy attending to other matters at the moment. Perhaps somewhere more chickens are trying to cross the road or more barefooted twelve-year-old girls need to be carried someplace other than where I am eager to be carried.

Mind you, I am not trying to be morose or hasten the Father's time. However, when that day comes, and you hear the news there on your tropical island, I have one request. Do not send some expensive bouquet of flowers. The flowers will no doubt be taken to the grave site, and you know how I cannot abide the thought of those devil fire ants turning your beautiful gift into a feast for their wicked bellies.

Rather, I would ask that you go to your florist shop and buy for yourself one grand gardenia to wear in your hair all that day. I like to think of you mourning my passage wearing that single white flower and spreading its sweet fragrance wherever you go.

Do sleep with the flower under your pillow that night, my dear, Sweet Abby. Then when you waken in the morning, I hope you will think of me one last time, for I shall be in heaven, no doubt feasting on gardenias for breakfast.

Forever and for always,
Your Grand Lady
Charlotte Isabella Burroughs

Jesus said, "Daughter, you took a risk trusting me, and now you're healed and whole. Live well, live blessed!"

—LUKE 8:48

Gardenias for Breakfast Discussion Questions

Name two women who have brought beauty into your life. Try to sum up what that beauty is (e.g., the beauty of touch, the beauty of words, the beauty of forgiveness).

What memories, like Abby's gardenias, make your childhood seem like a pleasant dream? Be specific and try to recall one of each of the following: a sight, a sound, a fragrance, a type of weather.

What do you think enables a woman to "age gracefully" like Grand Lady? How do you feel about growing older?

How did Abby's remembrance of Louisiana and of her family square with what she found there? What does that show us about our memories? About how life changes us?

Who do you think the man with the chickens was? Why?

What changes did Abby need to make to reconcile with her mother? What does that tell us about reconciliation?

Tom's wife, Su Ling, told Abby, "I think love is a choice, and it's funny whom we end up choosing to love and who ends up choosing to love us. It's rarely the people we think it should be." Tell about a time in your life when you found that statement to be true.

What did Grand Lady mean when she told twelve-year-old Abby they would have gardenias for breakfast? Why was that the most memorable Louisiana breakfast for Abby?

What do you think was changing in Abby that enabled her to veer from the carefully planned drive to Louisiana and to visit Carlsbad Caverns?

In what ways did Abby bestow motherly blessings on Hannah? Which of these would you like to consciously bestow on your children, grandchildren, nieces, or nephews?

In what ways did Hannah bestow blessings on Abby? Abby uses words to paint pictures; Hannah sees colors as art. How do you express your artistic side?

What moments in Abby's past had become baggage in her present? Why do you think she had trouble letting them go?

Abby never thought to tell Hannah about giving birth to her. Why would that be a meaningful story? Choose a special moment to tell your children about their births. Or ask your mother about yours.

Abby was afraid of blood; Grand Lady of fire ants; and Uncle Burt of car accidents. What is one of your greatest fears? What might it be keeping you from?

Who, like Grand Lady to Hannah, has spoken words that crushed you rather than blessed you? How did Hannah and Grand Lady make amends?

What do you think the phrase "your story will come find you" means?

In what ways has your story found you? If it hasn't, what do you think would need to happen for it to find you?

For this and other WestBow Press Reading Group Guides, please visit www.westbowpress.com.

Also Available from WOMEN OF FAITH™ *fiction*

THE DEBT

When Emma first met Abel Howard, she was a woman with a past, a woman who had not always made the right choices. But after twenty-five years of marriage to Able and with his world renowned ministy career at its peak, she doesn't often have a reason to dwell on things of the past.

Until Christopher Lewis—the son she gave up for adoption years before—arrives at her doorstep.

This young man's entry into her life rock Emma to the very core of her being, Challenging everything she's ever believed about God and His Purposes for her.

The Debt is a tender, bittersweet story of redemption and forgiveness.

COVENANT CHILD

When Amanda's husband dies unexpectedly and her two step-daughters are given over to their grandparents, Amanda desperately tries to keep ties with them through support money and letters. Now she struggles to understand the wounds of two girls she longs to know—trying to overcome their doubt—and prove her love is genuine.

THE NOTE

When PanWorld flight 848 crashes into Tampa Bay killing all 261 people on board, journalist Peyton MacGruder is assigned to the story. Her discovery of a remnant of the tragedy—a simple note: "T - I love you. All is forgiven. Dad."—changes her world forever. A powerful story of love and forgiveness.

Also Available from WOMEN OF FAITH *fiction*

A TIME TO DANCE

The decision has been made. After 23 years of marriage, John and Abby are getting a divorce. But before they can tell their famly, their daughter announces that she is getting married so they postpone their own announcement until after the wedding. But as the big day approaches, they wonder if the decision they've made is irreversible or if they can find once again what they've been missing for so many years. The time for love, the time...to dance.

A TIME TO EMBRACE

Like newlyweds, the reunited John and Abby Reynolds laugh, love, and dream of a long future together. But in an instant, a car accident changes the Reynolds and their entire community. The driver of the car fully responsible for the accident is Jake Daniels, the high school football star who knows John Reynolds as Coach, mentor, and friend. In the wake of this near death accident, can tragedy be overcome by the possibility of a transforming miracle?

SANDPEBBLES

Recently-widowed March Longfellow efficiently commandeers the lives of her son, and the staff members of the small-town newspaper she owns, all the while grappling with grief and issues unresolved before her husband's fatal boating accident. When a new pastor comes to town and his family's lives become intertwined with her own, March finds her life thrust into a new direction—one she cannot control. As March begins to release the things of the past, God rekindles her faith and offers her renewed hope for love.

ROBIN JONES GUNN

SISTERCHICK n.: a friend who shares the deepest wonders of your heart, loves you like a sister, and provides a reality check when you're being a brat.

Say "Ole!" the Sisterchick way...

SISTERCHICKS IN SOMBREROS

Two Canadian sisters embark on a journey to claim their inheritance—beachfront property in Mexico—not expecting so many bizarre, wacky problems! But they're nothing a little coconut cake can't cure...

How Low Can You Go?

COMING APRIL 2005!

SISTERCHICKS DOWN UNDER

Deb meets Kelli at the Chocolate Fish Café in New Zealand and they instantly forge a friendship. Now Robin Jones Gunn reveals their crazy adventures in classic Sisterchick style!

Sisterchicks™

The complete SISTERCHICK™ Series

SISTERCHICKS on the Loose! ISBN 1-59052-198-6
SISTERCHICKS do the Hula! ISBN 1-59052-226-5
SISTERCHICKS in Sombreros! ISBN 1-59052-229-X
SISTERCHICKS Down Under! ISBN 1-59052-411-X

FOR MORE INFORMATION ABOUT
ROBIN JONES GUNN
AND HER WRITING
PLEASE VISIT HER WEB SITES:

www.robingunn.com

www.sisterchicks.com

www.finechinaplate.com

A Letter to Our Readers

Dear Reader:
In order that we might better contribute to your reading enjoyment, we would appreciate your taking a few minutes to respond to the following questions. When completed, please return to the following:

Andrea Doering, Editor-in-Chief
Crossings Book Club
401 Franklin Avenue, Garden City, NY 11530

You can post your review online! Go to www.crossings.com and rate this book.

Title ____________________ **Author** ____________________

1 Did you enjoy reading this book?

- ❑ Very much. I would like to see more books by this author!
- ❑ I really liked____________________
- ❑ Moderately. I would have enjoyed it more if____________________

2 What influenced your decision to purchase this book? Check all that apply.

- ❑ Cover
- ❑ Title
- ❑ Publicity
- ❑ Catalog description
- ❑ Friends
- ❑ Enjoyed other books by this author
- ❑ Other ____________________

3 Please check your age range:

- ❑ Under 18
- ❑ 18-24
- ❑ 25-34
- ❑ 35-45
- ❑ 46-55
- ❑ Over 55

4 How many hours per week do you read? ____________________

5 How would you rate this book, on a scale from 1 (poor) to 5 (superior)?

____

Name____________________

Occupation____________________

Address____________________

City____________________ State__________ Zip__________